I0732678

THE FLESH AND THE SPIRIT

VESELA PATTON

WORKBOOK PRESS LLC
187 E Warm Springs Rd,
Suite B285, Las Vegas, NV 89119, USA

Website: https://workbookpress.com/
Hotline: 1-888-818-4856
Email: admin@workbookpress.com

Ordering Information:
Quantity sales. Special discounts are available on quantity purchases by corporations, associations, and others.
For details, contact the publisher at the address above.

ISBN-13:   978-1-955459-05-1 (Paperback Version)
                978-1-955459-06-8 (Digital Version)

REV. DATE: 20/04/2021

THE FLESH AND THE SPIRIT

Vesela Patton

Part I

Lucy

Her present – Searching for the key

CHAPTER 1
1954

My beginning is behind the door they keep locked, thought Lucy.

She had never heard the grandparents mention her mother's name, but the girl had often asked about her parents through the years. Grandma Annie said that her mother, Rose (their daughter), had died in childbirth, and not long after, her father in an accident at work. They had always succeeded in avoiding more questions. Neither of them ever mentioned Rose to anyone, as if she never existed, each trying perhaps to exorcise his or her phantoms.

The young girl escaped the war unharmed with Mark and Annie. Their house, reduced to a pile of rubble, caused them to move into a slightly more modern terraced building nearby. From the very start, Annie's attitude towards Lucy had been one of deep resentment. The task of raising a child inclined to misbehave from an early age proved to be a difficult one. Now sixteen, Lucy disliked anyone who told her what to do. Today, grandma was again on the warpath.

'Lucy, you're too young to plaster your face with all that junk. It isn't right,' said Annie while watching her applying a flaming red lipstick and a face powder.

'I like it. What's wrong with it?'

'And that perfume! It's so strong. It's not good for you!'

'Says who? I like wearing it! I'm not going to give this one up just because you're so old-fashioned! I love perfumes.'

'You can't go out just now! I need you around the house.'

'I can't. I'm going out.

She is always impossible to please. I'm sure she hates me. But Granddad's so good to me! She thought while marching up to him.

'Grandma said I must help with the ironing and the cleaning, but I'm going out. It's warm and sunny, and I can't stay inside for the stupid housework. She wants me to be a nun,' she ranted.

'Well...go. I'll talk to your gran.' He always yielded to her will.

'She hates me and tells me nothing I want to know.'

'She doesn't hate you but dislikes it when you speak of the past, as you remind her too much of your mother,' her Granddad explained.

'Any time I ask about mum, she clams up and refuses to talk, saying it upsets her. I want to find out. I have the right to know. Tell me now, please! Do I look like her? What was she like as a teenager?'

'You look like your mother. The same face – almost. Same eyes, nose, but she had brown hair, not red like yours.' A pregnant pause followed. She saw the far-away expression on Mark's face as he regressed in time.

'You loved Mum a lot, didn't you?' His skin flushed.

'A great deal. Too much, in fact. I wish I could turn back the clock.'

'And my father? What was he like?' Another silence followed.

'What's wrong? 'She went to place her hand on his shoulder. He stroked and kissed it fondly, then stopped as a tear of self-pity surfaced from his past: no more succumbing to temptation. It was clear to Lucy that some memories could still hurt deeply no matter how far back.

'Are you not well?' she asked.

Remorse advanced to the forefront now. Mark had tried to

The Flesh and the Spirit

dismiss it, live with it, and to make amends for what he was, for what he had done. Now the truth hit him with violence, rendering him incapable of adding more.

'I... don't want to speak of it. John, your father, was a fine man. Your mother was his world, but the past is too painful.' He hoped these answers would satisfy her for now.

Lucy wanted to know more about her parents. She had searched every room, hoping to find clues, but no trace of them existed in the house. No photographs, nothing at all. To ask Annie was useless, and the girl resented her silence. Why the secrecy about her mother's life as a child, growing up and getting married? Something did not add up, but Lucy wanted to know. Should she insist? Yes, of course, it was her right to find out. After all, Rose was also their daughter. Perhaps one day, she might succeed in making her grandparents unlock the past. *Little by little. One question, one push at a time.* She thought.

To restrain the girl was a challenging task. Lucy's unyielding character was a continuous source of frustration for Annie. To ask for any minor thing seemed too much for this teenager, whose uncaring replies made her blood boil. She asked again, though.

'Lucy! Help me fold these sheets!' Annie's voice reached her from the kitchen when she was about to go out.

'Cannot do. I'm on my way just now.' She glanced at her new white sandals with a matching handbag and smiled at the thought of generous Tommy.

Annie walked into the room,

'Behave yourself, or you'll end up in trouble, you'll see, just like... and ruin your life.'

'Like who?'

'Someone we knew.'

'What kind of trouble?' She turned to face her grandmother with a mischievous smile. Annie's cheeks had started to redden.

'Never mind, girl!'

'I know what you mean, and believe me, I've got the "rhythm" right,' she answered, giggling.

Her grandmother's face changed to a deep crimson.

'Shame on you! Don't you care about what other folks say? You're a disgrace.'

'I'm not bothered. All I want is a good time.'

'Let her be Annie,' her husband intervened.

'You! You think she's the bees' knees!' She sounded agitated.

'Let it go, Annie,' he said sharply.

Lucy sailed to the door on her stilettos with a triumphant smile and the scented wind of youth inflating her ego. She slammed it, and the sound echoed throughout the house.

'It's the way she looks that attracts men like moths to the light. Not her fault,' he said when his wife complained. 'Maybe you should tell her a little about her mum and dad, Annie.'

His wife's gaze froze him.

'Really? And how can I tell her that her unmarried parents were sinners in God's eyes? Can I tell her that her mother rejected this fruit of her crime, choosing a fancy-free life with her lover?'

Mark's eyebrows knitted together. He became thoughtful, and Annie carried on.

'Are these good examples to set in front of the girl? Her mother, Rose, ruined my life. Her freedom meant my prison. When I could study and improve myself, at last, I had to start all over again, raising another child.' From her list of miseries, she

The Flesh and the Spirit

avoided adding that it had also caused her husband's loss. He had tried to compensate for his wife's behaviour by lavishing affection on his granddaughter alone.

'You've always found excuses for her. She's given us nothing but heartache from day one, and you still do it,' she retorted in a tone of vituperation to which, by now, he had grown accustomed. It would have been foolish to contradict her.

'She has no heart, that girl. No morals. The only thing I succeeded in doing is to make her come with us every Sunday. At least she can hope for the Lord's mercy,' she said, crossing herself.

Annie and Mark thought Lucy's intelligence and common sense less than average. Her notorious gullibility pleased the opposite sex, who queued to go out with her. *"Please, beautiful. I'll treat you to a Queen's dinner!"* or *"I'll buy you that bracelet.'* or *'I'll get you a new dress.'* She trusted them all, only to find herself - most of the times - exchanging the promised luxury meal for a hot dog in a cafe, or a bottle of cheap scent for kisses and often more.

As soon as she turned sixteen, not profiting from the academic world, she had left school for any kind of work. After the war, employment was not easy to gain, but she found a job as a sales assistant in a hardware shop. The place presented itself as a long passage with goods stacked on shelves up to the ceiling. The cantankerous owner, too old for fetching the items, needed young blood to climb the ladder and bring them up or down. Lucy disliked the authoritative man and his silent, stuffy shop. She pined for a place full of noise, people, exciting things, and stylish clothes and planned a change as soon as possible.

When she realized the gender of the majority of the shop's clients, her work became much more appealing, and she stayed.

All the males loved her. The young ones often came to purchase some nails, a couple of screws, just to peek down her blouse. She undid a few buttons when the old man was not looking, enjoying the customers' attention her bust received. *'Let me touch them, Lucy...You drive me nuts. You're so beautiful. Please, go out with me.'* She heard the same tune every time, and in their eyes, she made out lust for her body. She loved it.

Despite her age, she had already learned first-hand at school from the busy body Elspeth, all she needed to know about boys and what they expected from a girl.

'Men, Lucy! Do you know the disgusting things they want from a girl? Wendy said something yesterday about her boyfriend. Let me tell you…' She proceeded to give Lucy a detailed account ending with, 'I'll never do that! And you?'

'Well… did she enjoy it? If you don't try, you'll never know. I will find out!' She said with a mischievous smile.

When she found out about the other sex and told her friends, the girls shunned her due to her promiscuity. She did not spend much time at home when not working or too busy going out with different men in the evenings. Her favourite conquests would give her the best deal - eating in restaurants, clothes, dancing, presents, all the things that represented her only real interests. She knew some were married but never refused what they offered.

Lucy did not understand Annie's conduct, and it made her miserable. Fed up with their war, she decided on a peace offering. Every week the girl saved a little money from her wages in a jar under her bed. When it was full, she resisted buying herself a new scent, purchased a silk scarf, and handed grandma the packet, smiling.

'I think you'll like it, gran.'

Annie let go of the tea towel and opened it. The slippery yellow material unfolded quickly, and the peacock's fan widened. Her expression hardened. She stared at Lucy and thrust it in her hands.

'I don't want it. Keep it. The man who gave it to you will want you wearing it.'

''But I got it with my money.' She defended.

'Another lie. You earn peanuts and spend all your wages. Out of my sight, sinner,' and she hurried out of the kitchen.

Lucy went outside and threw the scarf in the rubbish bin, banging the lid.

'The witch!'

An elderly woman lived alone in the house next to theirs. One afternoon coming back from work, Lucy saw her sitting outside on a chair at the bottom of her steps, enjoying the tepid sun. When she stood up, feeling the way with her stick, Lucy understood. She thought it must be difficult for an old blind woman to be in the house by herself.

It can't be much fun. No one to talk to, only silence. I'd die!' Her mind cried.

The following day Lucy saw her outside again and spoke to her.

'Hello! I'm Lucy next door. What's your name?'

'Jean, my dear. I recognise the sound of your heels hurrying to your door every day. Are you back from work?'

'Yes, I am.'

'Your voice is young, how old are you?'

'I am sixteen.'

'Ahhh… youth! I hardly remember mine.' The woman

chuckled.

Something stirred in Lucy's heart.

'Can I come and visit you now and then? We can chat.' Lucy offered.

'I would love it! You can tell me about your charming self.'

'Nothing much to say, but I bet you've loads!'

'You will yawn listening to my life's story. Eighty years ago… another world from yours.'

'A real-life fairy tale? I'll love it.'

'No fairy tales, just life.'

That is how it began. Once a week, instead of going out with a boyfriend, she went to her house. During the cold autumn days, the eighty-year-old woman from a distant era and the carefree young girl from a changed world sat close to the two-bar electric fire. Jean spoke of her childhood and her work as a dressmaker. She carried on about her marriage at the age of nineteen to the twenty-one-year-old blacksmith. One year later, she had given birth to the first son, then to another two boys, one after another. Her firstborn had died of tuberculosis at the age of five. She had joined the suffragettes and campaigned for women's rights, suffering jail and hunger strikes. In 1915, her other two boys had been casualties of the war aged twenty-nine and thirty-one. In 1938, the couple had run a small grocery shop. When WW2 began, a bomb destroyed the building and the shop with them iside. Her husband died under the rubble, and she lost her eyesight at the same time. Jean's widowed and childless sister, now dead, had taken her to stay in her house, where she had lived ever since learning to cope with her blindness.

Lucy listened spellbound, admiring her extraordinary strength of character. She wondered how a person could survive

                                      The Flesh and the Spirit

the kind of pain life had inflicted on her. Something beyond friendship was taking shape between them, and she liked the feeling of it. Then one day, Jean asked to touch Lucy's hair to guess the colour. She found it amusing and knelt in front of her chair while Jean's hands moved down to the tip of her hair. A toothless smile radiated her face with an aura of such bliss that Lucy embraced her and kissed her cheek.

'My dear, I feel I have a daughter with beautiful red hair,' she said, moved.

'How do you know, "mother?"' asked Lucy jokingly.

'Love has its ways. You don't need eyes.'

Throughout the autumn and the winter months, their friendship developed into something special. Neglect and musty air had deposited a grey film on the old pieces of furniture around. On top of a sideboard, Lucy saw many framed photographs, yellowed by time, and asked Jean.

'They are my family. My sister put them there when I came to stay. They are all in order. I can take one knowing who it is, and then I put it back in the same place. I spend days remembering. I live with my memories.'

'Will you tell me about them?'

'If you wish.'

Jean began her tale from her young days, which kept Lucy enthralled. She was happy and at ease with Jean. Interested in the past, she listened to the old-fashioned ways of life, to the differences in people's thinking. Those had also been the times of her parents' world, and it made her feel a little closer to them. For the first time, she saw Rose and John, her parents, as real people, not ghosts, and she opened her heart to receive them inside it. Jean understood.

'I wish my grandparents told me when I ask, but they refuse

to talk. It upsets me. They say it hurts too much.'

'I think they are still mourning their death. Your mum and dad must have been truly wonderful people. Be happy, my dear, as they would be to have a daughter like you. Their love will always follow you.'

That girl was a hidden treasure. Feeling the love in Lucy's heart, she thought of it as the beacon guiding her towards the remainder of her time on this earth. Lucy, however, never talked about her private business, fearing Jean would not understand her world. They had not finished yet going through all the photographs, but the few left would be today's stories, and she looked forward to it.

When Lucy came back from work and found the door locked, she asked a neighbour.

'Poor woman, she died of a heart attack, it seems. I found her when I brought in the milk this morning, as I always did. She was sitting on the armchair with a smile on her lips. I thought she was asleep.'

Lucy ran away to hide her tears with an exploding heart. No one knew of their relationship, but Lucy went to her funeral, the only one present along with the neighbour. They buried Jean's ashes, but she lived inside Lucy forever.

Lucy grudged Sunday mornings with all her might, trotting to the stupid church with her grandparents.

They can't force me to come here any longer. I could go for a drive with Ritchie. Perhaps for a boat trip on the lake, or even go to the movies.

She smiled at herself, thinking about what might happen in the man's comfortable car. He was handsome, and she liked him a lot. This wondering did not stop her inspecting around in search of familiar male faces or from finding time to invoke the Lord with the same words each time:

'I want a man to take me away. I can't stand living at home.'

That Sunday morning, while waiting to go to confession, she saw him entering the confessional.

A handsome man! Lucky me!

Her turn came, and she sat on the small stool inside the cubicle. Shameless and happy, she poured her heart out to this priest, sparing him no particulars of her erotic escapades.

'His hands crawled under my skirt slowly, then he knelt and uncovered my...'

'That's enough! No need to go further!' he said.

'But I want to confess, I want to tell everything. If you don't know what I did, how can you cleanse my soul?'

He had to let her then. Her young voice came across to him as very disturbing, and her words, even more. It left the young priest breathless. The divider prevented him from seeing her - a piece of thick, perforated wood between the two of them that had to remain closed.

When it was over and asked God to forgive her, he also implored Him to absolve the impure notions flooding his mind. Still, he emerged from the cubicle inspecting the pews, searching to link a face to a voice. Lucy glanced at him and smiled. His face reddened, and he disappeared, going to ask for penance.

When Samuel walked into his room that night, he inspected his surroundings as if noticing them for the first time. All of a sudden, he found the air and dark décor stifling. On the solid oak table, a pen rested beside a half-written sermon waiting for a conclusion. He took it in his hand and stared at the paper, incapable of any thoughts, disturbed by intense, uneasy - mental and physical - sensations he never experienced before.

Go to sleep, Sam. Tomorrow all will be back to normal. Rest.

He undressed, placed his cassock on the wooden coat hanger, and sat on the bed while reaching for his pyjamas. Yet, for the first time, he did not wear it. He slipped instead naked under the covers with a pleasurable sensation, but disturbing, unfamiliar images prevented sleep. In the morning, he knew what he had done was wrong. He had to make amends, but a confession was out of the question. Therefore he bared his soul to the Lord with fervour, promising Him it would never happen again.

The week that followed saw Father Samuel in a state of constant agitation. His worries concerned a girl who would soon enter the little world of his confessional again to turn it upside down. She would add more unrest to his already unsettling musings and once peaceful existence. He dreaded that moment, but did he? Was he honest with himself?

As far as Lucy was concerned, all seemed to have changed. What stirred inside her overshadowed the contentment she had enjoyed, as she surprised herself to think persistently about one man alone - something unusual indeed. He wore a long black robe, a white-collar, had short blond hair and deep blue eyes. His face hounded her.

She fantasised about what it would be like to be in his arms, body against body, with his hands touching her.

But priests are not like other men, or are they?

A wicked smile accompanied that question. Lucy aimed at finding out. She looked forward to Sunday, waiting to reveal to him her innermost and naughty secrets. To tell him how he made her feel and the way he affected her life. Was she in love?

I have never felt like this. I want to be his shadow, be with him every minute of day and night. I want to hear his voice and give him all of me forever. We'll be so happy!

In her uncomplicated world, humiliation did not exist. Barriers never made her question anything nor lessened her determination to achieve her objectives. She overlooked complications and never altered plans already made. Lucy thought herself ready and more than willing to elope with her prince somewhere far from home.

Sunday came, and she made herself up carefully. Her face received a light sprinkle of powder - no rouge on her high cheekbones naturally rosy - then a hint of pink lipstick to her full lips. To finish, she dabbed the most expensive fragrance on her wrists. Leaving her bosom half-exposed, she tucked the white lace blouse under her coat on either side of the bra. She needed him to touch her, longing for his hand on her breasts.

Everything will work out. I'll make him happy!

When her turn came, Lucy's heart raced. Once in the booth, she sat there with a single purpose.

'I can't breathe trapped in this space, slide this piece of wood just a little? I need His forgiveness, I can't go away, Father ...'

He recognized the voice.

'The rules don't allow you to open it,' said another voice inside his brain.

'Please, Father!'

Her plea came across as tainted by painful intonations.

Only this once.

He unlocked the partition with a shaking hand, sliding it just a couple of inches, which allowed him to see part of her face.

'Thank you, Sam. Here it is, the whole truth: I fancy you like crazy. I'm hooked on you. I only dream of you. I want to be with you. I didn't go out with a man since last Sunday, and you are to blame. What prize do I get? Will you meet me somewhere? I don't need forgiveness this time, true? I never did what, according to you, I shouldn't do. I want to do it all with you. I want your body against mine, kiss you all over, your lips on my boobs, on my...'

'Stop! Don't say another word. It's wrong, don't you see? I'm a man of the cloth.'

'Does that mean you're not a man?'

'Not in the way you think.'

Lock the partition Samuel. Now! But that voice weakened considerably.

'I don't believe you. Give me your hand,' she said in a sexy voice.

He needed to run away from the spell that made him pine for this girl with such intensity. He failed to stand up because his legs did not obey him, and he aimed at locking the divider, but Lucy foresaw his move and pulled it open instead.

Samuel stared at her, taking in every detail of her beautiful face: the deep brown eyes, small perfect nose, and full mouth. A mass of wavy and shining red hair fell to her back, framing a silky white skin.

She had caught him in the net. When his fingers met Lucy's, she placed them on her breasts, pleased with their shy exploration. He kept his eyes shut, trying to control the tremor of his hand, and she became sure he was dreaming her very same dreams. It lasted a few minutes, then - with an abrupt movement - he withdrew his hand and secured the panel.

'I'm sorry I couldn't control myself. It's better if you confess

The Flesh and the Spirit

to someone else. Come earlier perhaps, or later. I must go now.'

'Didn't you enjoy it? I loved it so much, Sam!'

'Don't call me Sam, and forget what happened, do you understand?', he said firmly while the voice inside him shouted: *liar!*

'I can't give up on you. I love you.'

'Don't speak untrue words. You'll get over this infatuation. Ask God to help you.'

'No need to ask Him! I am in love with you! Don't be mean. I can tell that what's in your heart is the same as what's in mine. Easy, isn't it? We're in love. Don't deny it!'

'I cannot be in love in the same way as you. I took my vows, and I must abide by them!'

'Forever?'

'Yes… Forever.'

'But you can make an exception!'

'There are no exceptions.'

'But I love you. Does that not matter to Him? I thought He was all for love.'

'In my case, it is about the love of the spirit, not of the body. Now go and pray,' he said, disappearing in a hurry, going to lock himself somewhere safe where he could implore God for strength.

Pacing up and down in his room, when his eyes fixed on the cross, on Christ's crown of thorns, he touched the small scars on his forehead, and the remorse choked him. Impure images sneaked in his innocence and crept inside his mind allowing him no rest. Unknown to him, the repressed instincts of his adolescent years started to assert. Nights acquired a different meaning. His enduring nakedness when in bed transported him to an alien echelon of pleasure that tempted him to perform acts he had learned to dismiss from his life. He determined to tell that girl again to find someone else or to come later or earlier. Yes, he would do so. Nevertheless, a presence either than his God lured him.

Lucy did not intend to surrender. No man ever rejected her, and the conquest of Samuel became a challenge she could not overlook.

All he needs is a little push.

The memory of his hand on her breasts haunted her. She recalled his regular features: the deep blue eyes framed by long lashes and the rebellious strands of hair unable to disguise the thin scars on his forehead.

I'm sure he loves me, too, but it hasn't dawned on him yet. I'll make him. I'll lick his full lips, taste his mouth, and...

Lucy's imagination ran wild. She dreamt of a glorious future with this man, and deciding to have him at any cost, she took a day off and followed him unseen. Samuel paid a visit to an old lady. She waited hidden among trees. On his way back, he stopped into an empty chapel. The heavy door remained half-closed, and on tiptoes, Lucy slipped inside and found a hiding place behind the confessional. She watched him engrossed in prayer for a while, then removed her shoes and tiptoed beside him on the pew. She wore her best and most revealing dress, which left very little to the imagination. Her perfume betrayed her.

'Hi Sam,' she whispered in his ear. He jolted.

'What are you doing here?' He asked without looking at her. The sound of his voice lacked normality.

'I had to see you. I can't go on without you.' She pouted. 'Why can't you love me the way I love you?' With these words,

   The Flesh and the Spirit

she took hold of his head, made him face her, and kissed him on the lips with a long, passionate kiss. Her tongue flickered in his ears, blood rushed to his face, and his veins throbbed. Still, when his eyes paused on the cross, the tabernacle, the altar, he pulled away without a single gesture of encouragement.

'No, I can't. Please go.'

Lucy dismissed his words and, sensing an obstacle, drew closer, ignoring the tears shining in his eyes.

'Oh, Sam! I want you. All of you' she murmured with a voice to wake the dead in the crypt below their feet. He was still praying for strength, but the Creator seemed too far to reply. Or perhaps he was too far away to hear His voice, therefore incapable of resisting her.

He touched her hair, and the shiny mass ensnared his hands briefly. His mouth searched for hers. He exchanged her kisses, moving tentatively to play with her neck. Her skin made him heady, and the pressure of her naked chest on his quickened his pulse. Lucy's breath on his face became the wind that blew his sails and took him to a mysterious kingdom until then hidden to him. He left behind the man he was, all that he had been. Sam felt the curves beneath the flimsy material and searched under her dress, caressed her soft and silky body. She shivered under his touch.

He needed and yearned for her, thirsty for all she was offering. Her smouldering lips joined with his, brushed his neck, her hands explored, wanted him bare. She lifted his vestment - and father Samuel found himself on the way to eternal damnation. Holding her beautiful half-naked body, he transformed from man of the spirit to a man of the flesh. She welcomed his virginity, his lack of experience, and his incredible thirst for her with joy.

'I love you, Lucy,' he revealed, more to himself than to her.

'And I love you. I've never experienced anything like this!'

Satisfied, she turned passionately to him, craving more, insatiable and happy.

Where could he hide now? Was he looking for absolution, or was he striving for a man's understanding from God?

How can I pardon anyone's sins if I can't forgive my own?

Was he so sure it would not happen again? That he might willingly go back to a life without her?

I must. I cannot mock all that is sacred.

On the other hand, Sam ignored that Lucy had no hesitations, confident he loved her and that their lovemaking solved everything. The butterfly, now caught, was a prisoner of the inextinguishable fire inside her. Samuel became her obsession, and she could think of nothing else. Two days after the events in the church, he found her in the vestry.

'Lucy, please understand what I am saying.' He did not exchange her kiss, keeping her at arm's length instead.

'I must atone for what I did. We have to stop, never to meet again.'

Lucy's eyes opened wide. Her jaw dropped, and disbelief crept in her voice.

'But we love each other! What happened was so wonderful. I want it to last forever. Don't you?' Shocked by his reaction, she waited in silence with her head leaning on one side, staring at his face.

'Lucy, if we don't stop, I'll have to abandon my vocation.' His uncompromising honesty had dictated these words, pronounced with great effort.

'Well then, why don't you leave? Think of the life we can

have!' She explored him, her hands burning through his garment, but he closed his eyes and pushed her gently away. Lucy brushed his neck with her lips, pressed her mouth on his, and played with his ear. Sam lost himself again between the sanctity of his body and the uncontrollable hunger for hers. Their physical attraction surged and abated, swept them to crests of new dizzy heights. Oblivious to time and place, their passion overcame them on the floor of the vestry.

The end of the day meant peace, at last, to connect disconnected thoughts revolving around Lucy. Stretched on the bed, he intended to read a few passages from the Bible. Yet his mind retreated to a way of life he had loved and cherished - the only one he had ever known - and to a lifetime spent in his religious cocoon. From a very young age, his mother had taken him to church every morning before school. There he stood in front of the crucifix gazing at Christ's crown of thorns, at His painted bleeding wounds, imagining His pain. He remembered the day he had set foot in the seminary for the first time as a teenager, the happiest of his life.

Within its restful, silent walls, they trained him to avoid transgressions and live a simple life. The church and the understanding of the religious guidance of his parishioners had to come before his own. At the end of his training, he had made chastity and celibacy vows to entail him to a higher inner state.

"You must repress any sexual appetite,' Father Joseph had said, 'You must repress it through ascetic means and deny this dark force."

He had grown up to believe that, as a Catholic, outside his world, there was a foreign land of religious barbarians with flawed beliefs and practices. Then there was him, the blessed one, who had the core truth and the straight path to Him.

Once a priest, always a priest, Samuel; but can you now reject the changes in your mind and body? Can you?

Samuel ached with guilt as his body was destroying his power of resistance. After tasting the forbidden fruit, he had become insatiable. His aspiration to be an exemplary man of the cloth survived intact, but his willpower lacked conviction.

I only yearn to have Lucy beside me forever.

With his cravings for her fully awake, he fell into a restless slumber.

Sam's tranquillity changed into constant unrest, and each meeting with Lucy in the vestry ignited his battle between the love of God and the love of Lucy.

Forgive me, Lord, for my wrongdoings. I would walk on my knees for You, fast until death, or accept a whipping until my end. Anything! Free me, if You can, from my body's weakness. I can't do it on my own. Help me with this torture and give me a sign of Your will.

In his state of confusion, the conflict persisted with a severe condemnation of the self. Still, his flesh retained the pleasure of those moments with her, and he implored the Lord all day. Yet, at night, his prayers lived alongside other images.

She would not understand my turmoil.

Sam fought his battle alone, unable to exorcise her from his life.

Father Samuel looked around: how different it all seemed! His sense of belonging had vanished.

My soul should be as empty as my church is this afternoon, filled with His Divine presence alone.

   The Flesh and the Spirit

Here was an ordinary man dressed in a priest's attire that could no longer comfort or absolve. His cravings for godliness were being stripped a little at the time, replaced by passions either than religion. He needed the advice and peace only the Almighty could grant. A severe look on his face now substituted the innocent child-like traits. His lifeless eyes mirrored the gloom in his mind, and a nervous aura took over his once relaxed manner.

'Father Samuel, please! I need your help,' a man called. He gazed at this person as if seeing a spectre.

He needs help. How can I help this man if I can't help myself? He is watching me. Can I lie to Him and tell Him that I'm cured of the sickness that has taken over my body? Am I one of God's favourites? I cannot be.

'Father, I need help!' the man called

'So do I...so do I...' he whispered to himself.

The enormous detachment of Sam's entire self from his surroundings was so evident that the man just stared at him shaking his head, and walked away.

Every night Samuel shifted from one thought to another, one emotion to another, one craving to another. He compared himself to Adam, beloved of God, cast out of Paradise because of his inability to say no to a woman. When he awoke, images centred on the lost lamb waiting for rescue.

Am I going insane?

It became essential for him to seek the help that others needed. He realized the high risk he would incur with his work, reputation, parishioners' esteem, of other men of the cloth, of his Bishop, family, and friends. The spiritual condemnation of his superiors towered above all these consequences.

He resolved to call for help on Father Joseph, the old teacher who had befriended him in the training college and who always seemed to have the correct answer for everything. He wrote to him.

'Dear Joseph,

I am in a distressing dilemma and cannot find a solution. You are the only real friend I have, and I need your wise counsel urgently. Please inform me when it is convenient for me to come by. The sooner, the better.
Samuel

He received a reply to his letter right away, and three days later, Sam called on him. The person that teetered into Father Joseph's study was not the one the priest remembered. This young man seemed bent under excessive weight. His forehead wrinkled in a tight frown, and his sunken eyes betrayed anguish. A stranger had ousted the happy, serene chap he recollected.

'Are you well, Samuel? Your letter was desperate,' he said, patting his arm in a gesture of familiarity.

Father Joseph sat behind the massive mahogany desk and Sam in front of him. He noticed the young man's hands clasped together, knuckles turning white, and the way he perched on the chair as if on a cushion of nails. In an attempt to gather the courage to face him, Sam launched a scattered gaze on the shelves of dusty books around him, and then his eyes became glued to his muddy black shoes.

'Samuel, I'm here to help you, my dear boy. Tell me the cause of your torment.' Sam lifted his head.

'Yes, Joseph, I need to tell you what's happening to me. There's no serenity in my mind any longer—only sadness and mortification for my weakness. I love God, but also a woman, perhaps just as much. Is it possible? I need both of them, my friend, yet I must choose. I'm betraying Him and Lucy. I'm going crazy!' Pauses interrupted his sorrowful speech. With a lifetime of experience in these matters, the wise man seized the situation right away, showing no sign of amazement.

'I understand. From what you tell me, I think that perhaps you came to the ministry not quite ready. It is a test for every man of the cloth, and a few find that they have to leave us because they discover the physical element stronger than the religious one.'

He stood up, and plodding on, went to lay his trembling and arthritic hands on Sam's shoulders.

'Do not be conscience-stricken at the truth. Hold on to your integrity and reach the solution that you esteem to be right, Samuel, and you will survive. Who knows, perhaps your life is meant to change direction. Everything happens for a purpose, remember?'

'So you don't condemn me?'

'If you submit to your humanity? No! And those who will are wrong. Nobody is justified in passing judgement on anyone else. Morality is in the individual's conscience. As you know, I think you could solve this differently, without denying your vocation for good. You have chosen the most honest and difficult solution. If you're certain about this course of action, I will inform the Bishop and ask if they could shorten the process's time. You will meet with him soon. It usually takes months to resolve similar cases.'

Sam nodded.

'Thank you, Joseph. I decided on this option because I'm no longer chaste and therefore imperfect and unworthy to serve

Him. I hope my soul will be at peace when deciding now.'

'Go, my friend, and remember, whatever route you may choose, our invisible God is always right in front of you, leaving His footprints. Follow them.'

Because of this conversation, Sam wrote to his superior, attempting to explain how he felt about the uncertainties that did not let him go. That same evening, after a long deliberation with the Deity, he made up his mind to tell Lucy he was leaving the priesthood. She arrived at the vestry light as a gazelle, a smile on her lips and the usual joy de Vivre all over her face. He gathered from her excitement there was something new in the air. Her kiss was intense, then she announced casually,

'I'm pregnant, Sammy! What do you say? Happy?'

Her words astounded him. He collapsed on a chair, head between his hands, trying to absorb the news. She remained standing, arms crossed and head reclined to one side as she always did when waiting impatiently for something. He thought for a while and then asked,

'Is it mine, Lucy?'

'Of course, silly! You know fine well there hasn't been anyone else since the day I met you! It'll be hell when I tell them at home. What shall we do about it?'

He believed her. Lucy's confessions were sinful, but lying was not one of her faults. The truth was the norm for Lucy. It never occurred to her for an instant that her conduct could be shameful.

'We can only do one thing. We'll get married as soon as I'm not a clergyman any longer.'

What else could he say? Under the circumstances, it was the right thing to do.

'Oh, Sam. I hoped you'd be happy!'

Licking her lips and moving seductively, she undressed. He locked the door peeking at her beautiful slim body with lust. In a way, he was relieved, as fate had taken over, freeing him from a final resolution. Perhaps He was smiling now. Maybe He had let go of Samuel, the priest, to give him a new role in life, as a husband and father.

CHAPTER 2

1955

'Do not say another word, Lucy. I thought you would end up in trouble the way you were carrying on. Now folk will talk forever, just like when-…

'Like when?' she interrupted.

'Never you mind, and with a priest? A priest! Jesus, forgive us!' she said, signing herself with the cross.

'Grandad said it'll be okay. He's happy for me and didn't make a fuss.'

'He wouldn't! He's spoiled you rotten, and this is the result! He never said no to you and let you do whatever you pleased. Now, this. Sweet Jesus! Forgive her for stealing one of your servants, and help us to climb this mountain.'

'What mountain? Why are you so upset? We're marrying!'

'And for you, all is resolved. Well, good luck! Just don't come and knock at my door!'

'Grandpa told me to come any time I need him.'

'Did he now? We shall see about that!' her face reddened. She swallowed hard, but Annie suspected it was a lost battle.

'Why are you always so nasty to me, gran? What have I done to you?

It took Annie by surprise. It was time to be truthful.

'You took away the life I wanted and planned.'

'How did I do that?'

'I wanted to escape my family's poverty by trying to improve my opportunities. When I met Mark, I was sixteen. He forced himself on me. I was expecting, and we got married. I did all sorts of odd jobs waiting for Rose to grow up and for the moment when she would go to work. I was ready to start a life of learning. My greatest wish was to be a nurse, but she left you with us.'

So! My mother's fault and mine, she thought.

'But you could still do it, gran! Why don't you?'

'I already made my plans. Don't count on me for anything. I'll have no time to spare between working and studying. Do you understand?'

'Yes, fine. Granddad will help if I need it.'

Annie's face hardened. She threw the dishtowel on the floor and strode out of the kitchen.

Lucy and Samuel saw each other whenever possible, their physical attraction overriding any consideration. Even though for different reasons, they were not prepared for the experience ahead.

A few months later, Father Samuel's irrevocable day came. From now on, in this new life, the consequences for choices would be open-ended. He turned up early for his appointment in the big and old sandstone building and gave his name to the sombre man at the reception desk.

'Sit down, please. Someone will be here in a while. You have five minutes to wait.'

Sam accommodated himself on the edge of a black armchair. He wanted to run far away from that place, but he fought that impulse. Soon, the Pearly Gates would regurgitate him, and while deep in thoughts, a priest appeared.

'Samuel?'

'Yes.'

'Follow me.'

Saying no more, he showed him to a vast room with small

leaded windows above the dark wooden panelling and pointed where he should sit. He made his way to the chair, and his resounding steps on the floorboards disturbed the silence. With each slow-passing minute, the sick sensation in his stomach and the whirlwind of uncertainties escalated. Breathing became tricky in the oppressive atmosphere. He examined the room, searching for a little familiar sign, something that would lessen the stiffening of his whole body upon recognition. He found nothing reassuring in the lack of furniture or the severe interior. Twelve heavily carved chairs were lined with precision on one side of a long table in the room's centre. Their deep red cushions appeared out of place in the surrounding sternness. It occurred to him that his chair's position, placed middle way facing the row of seats, might have a ritual significance.

The exact number he thought, *the thirteenth chair, Judas' seat, the judgement seat.* Time stood still in that place, and it seemed to have opened a door into another dimension. Samuel thought of his interviews with the Bishop and the relentless way he wanted him to amend his resolve.

His mind then raced back to a different room - the room of a young man who found comfort, love, and safety in his God. He saw glimpses of a shy and withdrawn boy who spent hours reading the Holy Scriptures, his only friend apart from Father Joseph. He relived the day of his appointment, the joy of that moment. He sprang up towards the door with sweat dripping down his neck, needing to fly out of that place, to go and inhale breathable air and stretch his limbs in the warm sunlight. It was too late.

The heavy door opened on its creaky hinges, killing his past and bringing him back to the present with a start. He rushed to sit down. One by one, his superiors entered in all their clerical dignity and black capes. Intimidated by that sight, his body weakened, his head became dizzy. *What would they say?*

The group sat down, with eyes fixed on him. He endeavoured to interpret their pensive expressions where he read a verdict of "guilty" straight away. His ordeal unfolded with never-ending questions about his time as a priest and the "corrupted" man he had become. There followed detailed long sermons on the consequences that a wrong resolve on his part would entail. After what seemed to be a never-ending time, the audience ended with the Bishop's words:

'We are sorry you're leaving us, Samuel. We cannot condemn you or blame you. If you feel mortified by your actions, it is entirely up to you how you will deal with them. Go now, son. May He help you on your chosen path.'

An air of philosophical acceptance of this inevitable outcome pervaded the room. They had pronounced the sentence. For the clerical body, Sam had just died and gone to Limbo. Once they left, the sound of the door closing behind them shook his soul. Officially cast out of Eden, they had sent Adam to Earth to procreate and live his mortal life with Eve.

He hung his priestly outfit on a peg in the vestry of what was once his church. His dog collar. *Could I?* A voice inside him said *no*. The clothes he still wore did not belong to him. The rule forced him to leave behind anything that reminded him of his treason. The exception became a small, worn-out book he owned since the age of nine. He placed it in his navy trousers' pocket. Venturing outside with a white shirt and no cassock gave him the impression of nakedness. Once home, he made sure to hide the bible out of sight in his rented one-room accommodation. The small book with its shabby black cover and worn gold letters needed to remain hidden. He was not God's servant any longer. He had been disloyal to Him and His Word. He had eaten the forbidden apple, and he should retain nothing to remind him of the man he was.

When he started searching for work, Samuel discovered how difficult it was for a man without any form of working experience to earn a wage. After practising on his front door, he succeeded in securing small sums by painting those of others, delivering newspapers with a cart, and lighting gas lamps. He worried about the responsibility of providing for a wife and a child. Tomorrow frightened him. They had to marry, but where would they live? His meagre income hardly paid for his room.

Unaffected by morning sickness, Lucy went on living at home and working in the hardware shop. She spent any free time with Sam, but she hated his often-absent expression when she sensed him in a place beyond her reach. In any other way, he was attentive to her. Lucy never told him about the furtive and disgusted glances her grandmother launched at her or of her grandfather's frequent and sad sighs.

When Sam received the lawyer's letter about his Uncle Eamon's passing, his father's brother, and the news of the inheritance, sadness mixed to relief. There was enough money to buy a small flat, leaving a minimal amount.

Lucy was elated at the news. They would marry and be happy forever. Their search ended with a two-roomed flat very close to Annie and Mark, as Lucy suspected it would come in handy. She made it liveable with inexpensive and straightforward second hand furniture,and the ivy plant on the windowsill etc.

added a colourful and welcoming note. Sam learned to do the housework while Lucy worked, and he continued the odd jobs for people.

Her pregnancy did not show much, and at work, the men were in hot pursuit.

'Come on, Lucy, let me take you out to that new place! Dancing, baby! Dinner! Want something new to go?'

'No Andy. Someone's waiting for me. Someone special.'

'And who might he be? This lucky fellow.'

'Not telling,' she said with a twinkle in her eyes. Her Sam was so sexy! Just thinking about his body and how he… she wanted to fly home to him.

She was five months pregnant and about to celebrate her seventeenth birthday when Sam said,

'We must get married. This baby will have a proper name.'

'Really? I like it, and will you give me a ring?'

'Of course! A wedding ring.'

'When do we marry? '

'As soon as we can.'

'Ooh, Sam! I dreamt about my dress, the aisle with lots of flowers, the music, the-.'

'We are not having a religious ceremony. I couldn't. I'm sorry, but we'll be married in the registry office, my love.'

'But I planned it! Why can't we?'

He found it hard to explain he felt like Judas.

'Because I deceived God, and I will not be welcome in His house.'

'Oh? Fine then, as you wish. As long as we marry, it will be great!' she said, brightening.

In her voice crept disappointment, but nothing seemed able

to shift his thoughts of self-commiseration. Samuel did not set foot in a church after leaving the priesthood and planned never to do so again. Only by forgetting what he had been, his life with Lucy would be achievable. Did he have any regrets? To dwell on the past was a mistake. She filled his life, his days, and in particular those incredible nights of passion and lovemaking so alien to him. *Oh, beautiful girl!* He was the luckiest of men at the thought that soon she would belong to him forever. Still, somewhere inside him woke an ache for the dog collar and the black and white simplicity of the religious life, a wish to go back in time that gnawed at him. At last, he received the formal dispensation.

Their incomes allowed them to survive, but it meant keeping expenses to a minimum, to plan a life without luxuries. The dawn of his new life found him pacing outside the Registry Office, waiting for his bride. When she stepped out of the cab, he held his breath. A more stunning and angelic picture did not exist anywhere. Lucy had disguised her little bump under a simple, white long gown embroidered with pearls at the neckline. Her shiny red hair, adorned with miniature white roses matching her bouquet, cascaded in soft waves midway to her back. She wore nothing else except a beaming smile.

When he spoke his vows to his beloved, the memory of other promises dimmed his happiness. Nevertheless, those small mound-shaped breasts, the fluctuating flame of her hair, the gold in her almond-shaped brown eyes, and her moist lips belonged to him now. Oh, Lucy! so full of light. She might chase away the dark shadows lurking in his heart.

They invited a few people to their reception held in the

rented room of a small restaurant. She insisted on hiring a three-person band, and Sam surrendered to her will. Her grandparents, who acted as witnesses for both, were among the guests that included three of Lucy's men friends with their girls - and Sam's mother, who lived in Ireland, his home. Samuel had written to her about leaving the church. In her reply, she threatened to come and speak to the Bishop to stop her son from committing this terrible act of rebellion. He had phoned her, making clear he had made up his mind, and nothing would change it. His mother now seized this opportunity.

'I'm glad your father died, so he is not here to witness what you did, Samuel.'

'Sorry, you feel this way.'

'Is that all you can say? Once a young, introverted boy preferred to read the bible instead of playing with his friends. That boy had an inexhaustible thirst for learning. He said he wanted to help people walk on the right path and that his life had meaning only if guided by Him. I am sorry for you, Samuel, for making the biggest mistake ever because of that... that person! Do you see her? Listen to her empty talk! Observe her vanity, son! Are you sure this baby is yours? She flirts with any pair of trousers in sight!'

'Mother! Lucy is young and naive, but she's not a liar, and we love each other very much.'

'I thought that an intelligent, twenty-three-year-old man had summed her up by now. Please, there are always other ways of sorting things out without being so final.'

'Too late, is it not? Try to be kinder to her. Whether you like it or not, she is my wife!

'I remember something else in your past that you seem to have forgotten. I never told anyone, not even your father. Does she know yet?' Did she ever ask you about the marks on your forehead?

'No, mother. Those memories hurt me even more now,' he said, clouding over.

'I lost you, son, and all I can think of is the vocation you threw away. I'll never resign myself, but I will work on forgiving you. Goodbye, Samuel. May luck be on your side.'

She spoke these last words with tears in her voice, then left, hurrying away. Sam wished to chase her, to explain, but spotting Lucy and her beautiful, radiant face made him stop. Meanwhile, she succumbed to a similar lecture from her grandmother.

'I'll tell you this for free. You'll never be a happy woman. You're a devil who tempted a saintly man of the cloth, and you'll ruin his life as well as yours, the way you destroyed mine. I didn't want to be here. He forced me to come. Goodbye.' Annie left with her unwilling husband without giving the girl a chance to speak. Lucy faced the blow for a few seconds and then dismissed its effect. No one was going to spoil her wedding day. Two men approached her, but she recognised only one of them, who introduced the other.

'Do you mind Lucy? This is Harry.' Their eyes met. She liked him. They danced together, and the attraction flowing between them made her ignore her husband. Sam, still troubled by his mother's words, suffered for his wife's demeanor and wanted the party to end so that they could go home.

'Have you any black Russian?' Harry asked Lucy.

'What's that?'

'Don't you know? You smoke it.'

'Never knew of it, but it's good, yes?'

'Oh yes, great stuff. You haven't lived until you've tried it, my lovely.'

'Where do I get it?'

'You don't. A guy delivers it to me. I got some. When it's time to go, we three could move on to your house. My present.'

'Yes, Harry. Thanks!'

Turning to Sam, she said, 'He wants to come home with us for a while; he has a gift to deliver.'

'Not tonight, my darling… another time. It can wait.' She moved to embrace and kiss Sam passionately, and bending her head backward, she waited for his lips on her throat, smiling at Harry.

At midnight, a man and a woman in a long white dress hurried along a quiet street. Upon arrival, they disappeared among white walls, inhaling the strong smell of a new dark green carpet, and slumped on the rust-coloured fabric settee in front of a coffee table. She switched on the centre light.

'The table lamp's better. More relaxing,' said Sam.

'Tea?' Sam asked Lucy.

'The bubbly wine we received as a present. Lots of it, husband!'

He smiled and obeyed. The champagne they both drank for the first time had an electrifying result for both.

Lucy's painful back became a problem. Because of this, she had to give up her job.

'How are we going to manage, Sam? What can we do? Our money's gone.' Their initial happiness for the new arrival turned to anxiety.

'I'll find work, don't worry.'

It was time to be and act as an ordinary mortal, and for the first time, Samuel was facing the real world. What kind of job could suit him? All he had done in life was to pray, now scoring poorly even on that subject. Whom could he turn to for advice? His mother and Lucy's grandparents disapproved of the baby and their way of life. None of them wanted to get involved.

'I'm bored! I want to go out and enjoy myself. I'll go crazy stuck inside here,' she stated while carefully varnishing her nails.

I wonder what new shade of varnish is in vogue.

'I'll be working soon. We'll be fine, my darling. Be patient for a while.'

'And what will I do all day when you work? I'm lost when you are not here,' she said, sulking.

'Not here? I'm here most of the time, my girl!' He tickled her. She laughed. They made love.

'We need food, and don't forget, you will have this precious baby to look after. The fun can come later - Cinema, a fairground, whatever you fancy.

'Mmmm... We'll see, but I'm not staying in all day. I'm going out. If only I weren't in this condition! I'm so ugly! I can't even paint my toenails well.'

'But you can catch this!' he shouted, throwing a pillow at her. She caught it and hurled it back at him, running away with Sam in hot pursuit.

'I'll show you, you little imp. Wait until I get you!' Puffed, laughing, she stopped.

'My sweet, you couldn't ever be ugly. You're my beautiful bird of paradise.' He took her in his arms. She brushed his hair away and touched the scars on his forehead.

'You never told me about them. What happened?'

'A childhood accident. Come here, you...'

Again, he made love to her, listening with pleasure to her joyful little cries and dismissing his lie.

'I feel like Dante at the beginning of his journey,' he said, as they lay exhausted on the bed.

She asked, 'Is he a friend of yours? Where did he go?'

He smiled. 'Not precisely, more of an acquaintance. Dante was on his way to Heaven but had to start from Hell. Lucy…'

'Yes?'

'You'll be my Heaven.' At that moment, he spared no thought for the little book.

After registration in the Employment Exchange, Sam had been everywhere looking for a job. Exhausted, he sat on a wall with the head between his hands, unwilling to go home with bad news. Sam fully understood now the problems of his parishioners, those forced to steal to feed their families. What he told them then did not match how he felt now. Darkness fell blacker than his thoughts—time to go. A neon sign attracted his attention: Taxi Hire. He had tried to find work in the most unlikely places and decided to go in and ask there too. The man behind the desk lifted his head.

'Need to hire?'

'No, I need a job. I have a wife and a baby on the way.' Alfred, the boss, stared at him in silence for a while, sensing the young man's desperation.

'Can you drive? What was your job? Sit down and tell me about you.' He listened without interruptions.

'I'll give you a try, due to your honest past and ability to deal with all kinds of people. I will teach you to drive. Start tomorrow, eight, ok? Shake on it!'

'I… thank you, I'll be here.'

Sam learned to drive quickly, and his new life began. He liked to drive people around but disliked the sliding screen that reminded him of the past. He slowly acquired an extensive knowledge of the city. On the other hand, his mind centred on his wife, wondering what she was doing without him to keep her company. His absence made her miserable.

Lucy did some housework, then bored, went out to buy some food and for a stroll along the shopping arcade. Windows displaying expensive clothes, shoes, and furniture were her main attractions. Dreams then centred on a time when she would own the lovely things she desired above all else. Next, she went to the market for a nail varnish bottle, a cheap new blouse, and a little something for the baby. On her way back home, hyena-like laughter filled the air: it was Harry.

'I looked for you, my lovely. I still have your present. Do you want it?'

'Sure! What is it?'

'Not telling… a surprise. Is your husband home tonight?

'Yes, you can come after supper,' and she gave him the address.

To please her, Sam welcomed Harry, still smitten with Lucy since her wedding.

'Right then, here's my present for you both. Let's sit and smoke. You'll climb on top of the world, ready for anything.' He looked at Sam with a twinkle in his eyes.

'Smoke what?' asked Sam.

'Black Russian friend. The best, expensive, and the most fashionable road to happiness and trouble-free life. Don't you know?'

'I want to try,' she said.

The Flesh and the Spirit

Sam thought it was some kind of tobacco, and to please her, he gave in. Harry passed around the hand-rolled reefers. After a few choking attempts to inhale, they began to feel the effects of the drug. Their mood altered, they became very talkative, and laughter echoed in the room. The increasing sense of euphoria inspired them to outdo each other, and they performed the silliest actions. Sam took his clothes off, drank more wine, and his half-closed eyes followed Lucy. The latter opened another bottle giggling like crazy at his nakedness.

Harry seemed to be everywhere, moving to a non-existent tune until sleepy, he settled down on the floor with a moronic smile on his lips.

Lucy tickled Sam, and he undressed her. She switched on the record player. As the notes rose with a sweet smell, she danced, sinuous and sexy, filling the room with her presence. He joined in, his uncontrollable emotions responding to her advances. Unrestrained libido brought them to have sex like never before, while Harry glanced at them now and then. The morning found Samuel and Lucy naked on the sitting room carpet and Harry walking out of the bedroom. Who made love to her? She had very hazy memories of the events. Sam at least recollected some details of the wild happenings of the night and reminded her.

'Did you like it?' she asked.

'I... it's not right. What was in the cigarettes we smoked? '

'I don't know, but yes! I like the effect.' Even though disapproving of the night's events, his answer was honest.

'I must say, no thoughts, happy or otherwise, relaxing'

'Can we do it again?'

'I suppose so… if you want to.' He would ask Harry where to buy the tobacco before hurrying to work with a thick and sore head.

With Harry gone, she looked around at her second-hand furniture and cheap flooring already showing its threads. Dreams of a different life increased her depressed mood. In a world made of wishes, her feet sank in soft and deep carpets. Brocade curtains draped bay windows, and wardrobes burst with expensive clothes. On the dressing table, costly perfumes filled the air with their scent.

I want all of it. I want to be rich!

The evening meal consisted mainly of potatoes and mince or beans and rice, ready for Sam when he finished work. If she was not already in bed, Lucy poured on him all her boredom and nervous self-pity for the lack of money and the special cigarettes.

'I'm fed up. I don't know what to do, the baby's things are ready, and we can't even afford a smoke!'

'Be patient, go and see your friends. Time will pass quicker.' She knew a couple of women, but through their boyfriends. Resentment for the gradual transformation of her body caused her constant depression.

Look at you! You're not beautiful! Who wants you like this?

Sam gave in and worked overtime to pay Harry for the cannabis, which became a nightly occurrence. Sam's constant inner fights subsided then, and so did Lucy's feelings of dejection.

The little book gathering dust under the chest haunted Samuel, who found challenging its dismissal from his mind. During his trips in the outer reality, one that had become a cause for concern, the bible's ghost coexisted with other feelings.

Meanwhile, Lucy's sighs often culminated in tears.

I want me back. I want Lucy! Look what this baby is doing

to me!

On edge that day, she grabbed her bag, threw in lipstick, a mirror, a comb, and decided to visit Harry at home.

'My lovely! Come to give me what you owe?'

'Oh Harry! I need some. We'll give you money next week. He's working.'

'Come in. Shut the door. I'm no charity, but once is ok.'

She sat on the only uncluttered patch of the black and greasy vinyl settee. He rolled the reefer and curled on an ancient brown armchair with horsehair stuffing creeping out. While he prepared marijuana, she surveyed his lounge. A filthy mess of dishes, dirty clothes, and old newspapers was strewn everywhere on the threadbare green linoleum with cigarette burns all over it. Harry stood up and swept away the pile of junk from the sofa onto the floor with his hand. Sitting beside Lucy, he handed her a particular joint in which he had secretly blended another substance: opium.

She inhaled deeply. Harry had one already between his fingers. *He is handsome,* she thought, halfway through her cigarette. Her hand moved to his leg. She overlooked his dark and unctuous hair that fell limply to his shoulders, framing irregular bony features. The reek of his sweat drifted to her, who now ignored his stained vest, filthy trousers, and his glazed eyesight. Harry's smile made her forget all the rest, as his pure white, even teeth shone like pearls. His mouth ignited her desire. Hypnotised by it, she went closer, eager for his lips. He held her tight and pulled her down on the rubbish spread on the linoleum.

'Gorgeous girl!'

She giggled, and the shiny mass of her hair unravelled on a buttered and stale piece of bread.

What happened in the dazed time that followed, she could hardly remember. Lucy told Sam the truth, of course, and he became obsessed about leaving her alone. Did she? Or didn't she? He would never know, but along with this thought, his cravings for one of those cigarettes haunted him too, and his turmoil started again. He mulled over the past, priesthood, the pleasure derived by helping people, and over the certainty of things. Redemption was a possibility but only through the ultimate test. Although he adored her, only under the influence of the narcotics, he felt relaxed and content. Most of all, he needed to protect her. Therefore, he quit his job.

Sam's mother, a very wealthy woman, did not find it easy to forget about her son. To relieve her conscience, she sent him money every month that ended up fuelling their addiction. In a vision during one of his trips, Sam held an imaginary Holy Book, which burst into flames as soon as he opened it.

Notwithstanding her constant moans and the smoking of heavier drugs, Lucy gave birth to a healthy baby girl called Belinda, a fashionable and unusual name. The event thrilled them until faced with the demands the new-born made on their life. Sam needed to go back to work, but Lucy had to stay at home with the child.

.'We must stop this stuff for the baby's sake. We both need to make an effort.'

'You're right. Our child needs us. See? She's so cute, so tiny! Her little hands, the small nose, she is like you.' Her heart brimmed with love when she picked up the baby, tripped on a chair, and almost dropped her. He helped her up.

'She's as beautiful as her mother. Careful! Sit down. Give

her to me.' He watched his daughter with tenderness and held her for a while before laying her back in the cot.

Their addiction, already deep-rooted and unforgiving, did not let their intentions prevail. Within a short time, they realized that weak willpower was no match for it.

'I can't go on any longer, Sam. I need my fixes. I resent this baby, and I'm so unhappy!' While bottle-feeding, she told him about her nightmares, obsessions, fears, and the ever-present sick feeling.

'I notice your mood swings, my dear. You're very irritable.'

'We have no sex anymore, and I am unloved. I need you so much!'

'I'm here. Shall we call Harry for a delivery?'

'Yes. Now!'

Therefore, their descent into a mindless existence began anew, ending in an entangled world of experimentation and abuse for both, with only steep down slopes and jittery plateaus. The quantity of opium in the cigarettes increased along with their cravings. Harry's hook caught his fish. Lucy's patience with the child became non-existent. Their dependency demanded more potent narcotics, happily supplied by Harry. Sam went to see his boss, and promising to keep to his timetable, had his job back. He hoped Lucy would be fine alone with her daughter.

'Shut up! I can't take any more of your screams!' Lucy reached the cot on unsteady legs, almost falling inside it, dropping on the floor instead. She stayed there giggling, then stretched a hand between the cot's spindles and covered the baby's face with the sheet before crawling back to the sofa and inhaling deeply. She closed her eyes, wishing for the wailing to stop.

Her grandfather was the only one who went near them. Attracted by the constant cry so clear through walls and open windows, he went to see them and found eight-week-old Belinda shrieking incessantly at the top of her lungs. She had a purple face, held her breath because of tears, was cold and soaked in urine. He wrapped the baby in a dry blanket.

'Don't you care at all about this child?' he asked Lucy. Glazed eyes set on him with an empty stare.

'Yes...' She was adrift in a world of her own, and he took Belinda home, leaving a note of explanation for Sam, who read it after work.

'She is our daughter. You cannot ignore her. It is dangerous, do you understand, honey?'

'She cries all the time...I try...'

Sam then relied on grandpa to keep an eye on things, but very soon, the worry about his wife and baby and his need for drugs became unbearable.

'Sorry, but you must go, Sam. Whatever the matter with you, sort things out, then you can come back,' said his boss.

He found himself on the edge of an abyss, desperately trying not to fall in.

They could not survive without income. Harry only gave them a limited credit, and Lucy's constant moaning and withdrawal symptoms depressed Sam. Once more, he begged his boss, almost in tears, which moved the man to give him one last chance. Sam hoped Lucy would be the responsible mother their daughter deserved. His wages covered the bare necessities, and they needed to quit since unable to pay for their habit. He deluded himself they could function without that stuff for a while, but the drugs in their bloodstream and the constant itch that only smoking could satisfy commanded differently. Sleepless nights, withdrawal symptoms, shaking hands, and rows between them became unmanageable - they could not do without narcotics. He tried hard to hold on to his job, but he was in no condition to do so for long. His brain felt clouded over, he stared at people with a faraway gaze, and the tremor of his hands was unnatural. Sam expected his boss to question him about it any time.

At home, Lucy had her secrets. Controlled by her cravings, she left the baby with her grandpa and hurried to see her friend. *He'll give it to me. He understands.'*

'Harry, I need it so...'
'If you want it, you know the payment, my lovely.'
'Yes, but hurry!'
She had managed to keep him at bay a few times. Today, her craving had risen above any consideration.

Lucy started to undress, empty of any feelings. At the same time, he rolled a strong joint between long bony fingers, his hyena laugh sliding on the four tobacco-stained walls.

Sam's handsome and well-groomed appearance attracted women. His refined manners appealed to everyone, along with the smile that graced his full lips. The blond wavy hair he kept shoulder-length gave him a very distinguished air. Still, deep bags under his eyes, the tremor of his hands, and glazed eyes betrayed something abnormal. Faithful to his wife, now and then, he gave in to temptation and exchanged kisses with the ladies, but that beautiful woman wanted more than that.

One wintry Monday morning when he was on call, he found

her in front of the head office.

'I'm hiring you, Sam!' she said, jumping in the car. 'Drive to the park.'

The place appeared deserted, and she asked him to stop.

'Samuel, I can't wait any longer. Let's do it here.'

'I'm married, Liz. And we're too near my boss.' She interpreted his nervousness as excitement and desire. It drove her wild.

'Don't you like me at all?' she implored as wisps of her expensive perfume trailed towards him. He weakened and drew her slender body closer, kissing her moist lips. She unbuttoned his shirt, sliding the nails of one hand lightly along his spine, moving her other hand below his belt. He shivered, lifted her skirt, and touched her.

'Samuel! What on earth?' His boss knocked on the cab's window. How long had he been there? They hurriedly composed themselves, and when Sam opened the door, found a large barking dog and an angry man.

'Albert! Sorry, it won't happen again.'

'You bet it won't! You are no longer working for me. Who's this woman?'

'A client,' she intervened, 'my fault.'

'I don't give a shit. My firm's reputation is at stake here. I cannot condone this kind of thing. Come to my office when you're ready,' growled his boss, hinting at Samuel's trousers half-undone. Albert marched away with the German Shepard on the lead. The woman seemed upset, as her whim cost this man his job. She opened her handbag and took out a bunch of notes.

'Here, Samuel, this will help you until you find something else.' She closed his hand around it and vanished quickly beyond trees.

The situation at home deteriorated from bad to worse. Lucy neglected the baby so much that Granddad came one day to take the child away, with no intention of bringing her back.

'Shame on you both, how can you be so irresponsible? Your daughter could die, and you wouldn't even know it!' He was angry.

'Can't even feed ourselves, Sam. She better off... with him for now.'

'Right. Just for a while, uh? Until on our feet again. Soon, we'll stop.' They both floated again towards their unearthly cocoon. The money Liz had given him was gone.

'Why is that baby here?' asked Annie.

'Those two are not fit to look after her. We need to take over for a bit.'

'Really? How are we going to do that? I work, study, keep house, I have no time for anything else.' She sounded hysterical.

'Only for a few hours a day. I'll come home earlier at night, no overtime, and I will take over. You can study just the same. Is not the end of the world if you miss a few lessons?'

'But it is! The end of *my* world!' she screamed at him.

'We have no choice. You'll catch up.' He left her to feed the baby. She wished for somewhere to go away from there.

Samuel's mother died of cancer without getting in touch with her son. His unacceptable condition prevented him from going to the funeral. The pain for her loss mixed with the remorse for not going to her burial. His thoughts about her death bobbled among cannabis, opium, LSD, and other mixtures sprang forth from Harry's inventive mind. Mr Finnegan, the family lawyer, dealt with everything. Sam got a letter from him,

'Shortly, I will forward to you a considerable sum of money from your father's financial investments and the sale of your home, as per your mother's wishes.'

Perhaps now things will get the better, he thought.

'Lucy, a new life's ahead, we can afford to do something about our way of life. Do you agree?'

'Yes, anything. Let's go back to making love, the two of us. We take our baby.'

'We need to do something soon.'

'Yes....'

When Harry arrived with the usual 'delivery,' he also had news.

'You heard of the hippies?' He asked Sam.

'Who are they?'

'Dropouts from society. They have no jobs or careers. They are for openness, tolerance and are frank about sex. They're all for a tranquil life. They seek spiritual guidance and use hallucinogenic drugs to expand their consciousness. I'll join a group travelling all over the country to spread their message of peace. Do you want to come? Good people. Transport's needed, big enough to be home.' Samuel sat as attentive as the drug allowed.

'I can preach again. I know you're bored, but Belinda?' he asked.

'She's... fine with us. Travel? New people, yes!'

There seemed to be the hope of a new dawn after all. A few times more, the joint changed hands before Samuel's voice reached them from the distant place whence it came.

'Need a van-big - we get ready for - the road, Harry. I'll spread my words of faith - like...' He did not finish. In his scrambled brain, he believed this opportunity to be a sign from God, an exchange perhaps, to allow him to atone for his weaknesses. He had to follow his destiny.

'Great! I'll tell them. They'll be happy.'

At that point, Harry left the real world for one in a twilight corner where they all now lived.

Using some of the large fortune received, Samuel bought a camper, soon transformed into a self-contained living space for three adults and a baby. The brightly painted flowers and hearts roughly executed by Harry stood out on the dark green exterior, very similar to the other vehicles they were joining. The time came for Lucy to tell Mark of their departure, explaining they would take Belinda along.

'We're going to get cured. Somewhere, far from here. Right, Sam?'

'Yes. We won't be back for a while. Only when we're better. All planned.'

'Your daughter will need you both. Write to me and let me know when you're coming back. Promise? Sort yourself out, Lucy.'

'Yes, for Belinda's sake. Bye for now.'

Annie was not present. Mark's face expressed concern when she hugged him. They were ready. Before locking the door, Sam fetched the bible under the chest of drawers, and she saw him caress it lovingly.

'That silly old book! I don't want anything to do with it. I hate it!' Lucy yelled at him. She had been jealous of it, perhaps rightly so, since the day of its discovery.

The Gospel of Lucy represented Sam's daytime doctrine. The

bible had become his 'mistress,' the thing to hide, the source of his every day's humiliation. At last, he thought, his 'mission' was about to begin, and they would be a proper family again.

Their first night among strangers gave them a taste of their life to be. The tongues of the fire rose in the breezy spring air. Their red light shone on smiling people, on hands passing pills, a small piece of paper that someone would lick avidly, or a drink made with the 'magic' mushroom. Stories came to life about their 'movement' and the different ways it affected people, making them conscious of a peaceful, worry-free experience leading to a happy existence. Sam did not agree with some aspects of these beliefs, especially concerning free sex. Yet their apparent search for spiritual meaning filled him with hope.

Every night the group sat beside the fire. Discussions took place, and opinions bounced around. Sam started to preach his hazy theories about the human spirit.

'...It has to be in touch with the divine to achieve the mutual unity upon which the beliefs of this community seem to rest.' Did anyone listen? The consensus was they all aimed at finding the connecting thread between body and soul. They could only achieve this through a drug-induced outlet for the subconscious, which brought inner serenity and love. Everyone needed to understand and absorb this credo. People had to integrate within these joyful, problem-free ways following the famous motto: "One for all and all for one."

During one of these discussions, someone mentioned hearing about a church in a desert where people thrived on a particular drug, a place of peace and love.

'I wish I remembered where this place is...' the man said,

scratching his head. Sam just listened, half-believing his words.

Lucy went along with any decision. In the group were two other youngsters aged two and three years. When bedtime came, mothers helped each other to settle the children. Belinda slept inside a basket in a corner of the camper, usually fed and changed by another woman. Lucy's drug problem seemed worse than his, and without the help received from the other women, she would not have been able to cope. Sam spent some time with his daughter during the day, and the guilt that once corroded him lifted a little.

The group kept moving from place to place, not staying too long anywhere. They all helped one another, and Lucy, free to indulge in her habit, seemed much calmer. Their efforts to bond with baby Belinda had shaky foundations, and neither parent managed it. Sam's public, washed out and doubtful 'sermons' deluded him into believing they would bear fruit, helping a little his self-respect. Then Lucy gave him unexpected news.

'I'm with child.'

'Oh, no! We cannot go away. My work is too important. What are we going to do, love?'

'All I know is that I want to have fun. I'm young! I feel trapped, and I don't like it. Best if I go home to have the baby, then come back.'

'Are you planning to leave it with them? We can't cope with two babies, and there's no room left. And we are still on...'

'I'll take Belinda. She's better off with them until we go back soon. Do you agree?" He thought about it.

'Yes, you're right. No life for a small child here, we'll return home. Tell them it's for a little while.'

'Is there another solution?' she asked vaguely.

'We are what we are, I think, my angel. We tried. It didn't

work, did it? But we'll have to go back, my sweet, to look after our kids. We'll go and get help, what do you say? '

'Yes... and all will be hunky-dory, huh?'

'For sure, we'll be a happy family one day.'

'We've sorted everything, then. I'll go home when the time is near. I'll be back as soon as I can. Can I count on Harry for a stash to take with me?'

'I'll arrange it, ' he said.

Three weeks before the birth, she left carrying her eleven-month-old daughter in a made-up sling. She arrived at her grandparents' house with a hungry and wet child screaming to the top of her lungs. Mark was amazed at their sight.

'Lucy! Belinda! Where have you been? No news from you for eight months.' His wife came into the room. She just glanced at Lucy's belly.

'I see...', she said, quickly retreating to the kitchen without another word.

'Is there a brew going? And something to eat, Annie!' He shouted.

She started to prepare some sandwiches, unconcerned about slicing her fingers with the carving knife she kept bashing about on the wooden block while cutting the ham.

'When are you due? Are you well enough to have another baby? Where is Sam?' With Belinda on his knees, he waited for answers. She explained it all in fits and bouts, and he paled.

'Annie has started a course.'

'We can't look after our kids yet. It's only for a while. There's nothing else we can do.'

'I'll talk to her. I have my job. She has to study and works a few hours a week. Annie would have to give it all up, but for a short time, perhaps we can do it.'

'I'm counting on you, granddad. Thanks!'

That instant, Annie walked in. She had caught the last words and the plate with the sandwiches split in two when she banged it on the table. Lucy grabbed a sandwich, left her daughter, and hurried to her house to get a fix.

'Tell me what's going on,' said his wife with a harsh tone and red in the face. Mark started to feed the child, but he had to tell her.

'You got to quit college until they come back. It will be very soon. We cannot do anything else.'

It hit her like a bullet – her visions of a new life, reduced to smithereens within minutes once again.

'Mark, I am not going to quit college. I've waited too many years for this opportunity. I am not doing it.' His wife's defiant answer amazed him.

'We have no choice. Only for a short time.'

'Not even for one day.'

"Well, resign yourself. It's going to happen.'

'I'm going away then.' Her words made him stare at her in disbelief.

'Really? Where will you go? No money, no home, and folks talking about you!'

Nothing she could say would improve anything. He did not seem too bothered by the fact, but Annie added her resentment to the one she had accumulated inside for such a long time. It was a tale repeating itself; she had to step aside once more. What had she done so wrong to deserve this fate? The love for her husband had gone years before, along with his for her. They had been strangers in every way, and now there was no hope and no time for the slightest change.

Lucy tried hard to keep away from the more potent substances Harry had procured. And a week later, a tiny boy named Thomas made his entrance into the world. Hands shaking, she looked at him with love.

'My baby... I am not able yet, soon.'

Mark pitied all of them: Lucy, Belinda, the newborn, and his wife, with the sudden weight of two children on her shoulders. Self- recriminations still dominated his life and surfaced again, only to make him drown in remorse.

'You two are killing yourself with that junk. Couldn't you try?' Lucy shook her head.

'When we come back, Samuel says we'll be cured. I'm going back in a few days. Can I talk to Grandma?'

'You'd better not see her. I told her you'd soon be home, right?' She nodded. To abandon her children was not easy, but she had no option.

Only for a while.

A week later, she was ready to go back. With a last kiss, inhaling the unique fragrance of her baby's skin and with a caress to her daughter's curls, she left.

The cab stopped near their site late in the evening. A few people still moved around. Anxious to share a reefer with Sam and tell him about Thomas, Lucy opened the door without noise. In the quasi-darkness, she made out two shapes huddled together asleep in her bed.

Oh, Harry! Not again, she thought, turning on the torchlight.

Harry was not in, but a woman slept in Sam's arms, one she had seen going into other vans often enough.

'Sam...' She collapsed to the floor without a sound. Her limbs ached. It had been a long trip by bus and cab so soon after giving birth. Before taking off her clothes, she smoked a cigarette, then slipping into Harry's bed fell asleep, only to wake briefly with his weight on her. When her husband woke in the morning, he glimpsed at the woman beside him and then saw Lucy with Harry.

What have I done?

Still in bed, barely awake, Lucy was about to pounce. But Harry held back the tiger.

'Well, Mr. Saint, well! Lonesome, were you? Did you enjoy her? Did you fucking enjoy her?' She screamed at him,

'Sorry, my love, I don't know what...'

'But I do! I do! And me wanting to come home to you, to Mr. Bloody Saint! Belinda and Thomas say hello! Our children, who will call us Auntie and Uncle it seems!'

'What are you saying? How are you? And the baby?'

'I want to go home, with or without you.'

'Fine, love. Sorry, I didn't know what-'

'Neither did I. We are even. Let's forget about it.'

The woman beside Sam flung a shawl on her naked body and vanished like a ghost. For the first time since their marriage, she realized that he could be unfaithful, too. He was as guilty as she was. It made her very unhappy.

'No more kids, love. We can't. We must go back soon to see ours.' Samuel said to her sometime later. But 'soon' never came.

Two years went by without them worrying about anything else. Now and then, during a drug-induced stupor, distorted images of their children surfaced, and a deep depression overcame them both.

Due to the chill in the spring air, the men lit a roaring fire, and most people sat to smoke around it. Now and then, someone strumming a guitar or a few words interrupted the tranquillity of the night. A young man, unsteady on his feet, started to dance near the fire. People laughed. Some egged him on.

'That's it, Bert. Show us your steps. Quick, and we'll join you!'

He became increasingly daring in his pirouettes. Moving to the sound of imaginary music, he went faster, dangerously close to the fire, and stumbled. Lucy observed the scene in front of her as if in a dream. Her state of insensibility suffocated the scream inside her throat. At the same time, her eyes tried to connect with the other faces around. Everyone saw Bert fall into the flames. He screamed, but nobody lifted a finger to help. They all remained stock, still watching the human torch in a daze, wondering what to do as the man ran into the field, crazed with pain and the stink of his burning flesh. He collapsed, and by the time others got to him, he was dead. Some felt guilty, others hardly remembered, but nobody admitted that a cocktail of new drugs passed around could have been the cause of Ben's "accident." From that moment, the friendly atmosphere, music, and chatter ceased to be. A few departed, and the rest appeared to have lost the sparkle in their lives. The horror of that night left an indelible mark on everyone. After the police investigation, Lucy, Sam, and Harry decided to go back home.

The Flesh and the Spirit

CHAPTER 3

1957

'Thomas! Belinda! Come here! Meet your Uncle Sam and Auntie Lucy.' The children shrank away, giving them an indifferent glance.

'Do as I tell you,' said Annie in a commanding tone of voice. 'Come and kiss them.'

Lucy produced a bag of sweets and the girl, now three years old, took her two-year-old brother by the hand approaching her shyly. Thomas pulled the bag from Lucy.

'Can I hug you now?' Lucy asked.

The children accepted without enthusiasm. Sam received the same treatment.

'Don't eat them all. Give them to me, Belinda,' said Mark.

'Yes, Daddy,' Obeying promptly, she took the bag gently from her brother's hand, but only after the removal of a handful of sweets she shared with Thomas. Two beautiful little strangers, greeting a couple of visitors. Granddad took Lucy aside.

'They call us Mum and Dad, and you're Uncle and Auntie. Do you understand? Before it's too late, do you want to set the record straight?'

'Why? It would only confuse them. Better to leave things as they are.'

'Then you can never tell them, do you agree?'

'Agreed. We can have the kids when we're home anyway.'

'How long are you going to stay this time before you all go?' Annie asked coldly.

'Some time, I think. We can't say yet,' Sam said.

'And will you take them with you now?'

'Can they come to us any time?' said Lucy.

'Up to you really,' said Mark.

'Of course, they can take them! If they can keep away from that rubbish long enough to feel human, that is,' said Annie vehemently.

'We've got to go now. Bye, kids. Till later.' They left with a hug, going home to welcome Harry, who would be staying with them temporarily until he found a place of his own.

As their dependency progressed, they experimented with other drugs. They soon experienced their full effect, each adrift in an absurd reality impossible to escape. At one point, Harry ran towards what he conceived to be a door, only to fall out of their window on the first floor. He landed onto the grass below, ending up with a very sore head, a broken leg, arm, and two ribs. After a time in the hospital, he went back to them with an unchanged attitude to his mixtures. Nonetheless, one evening life changed for Sam.

The whirlwind of his chaotic experience transported him somewhere with the sick and the rejects, urging him to comfort and help. Throughout the entire blurred and wildly coloured vision, he was conscious of a light enveloping what he saw. He believed it to be God lifting him higher above himself and even heard His thundering voice.

'Go, Samuel, into the desert.'

'Yes, I will. I will.'

'Find me there. They need you!'

'I will. I will.'

His words rang in his ears like a hundred hammering bells. The next day, when both as far away from the side effects as manageable, he said to his wife,

'I want to go, love. I must. You coming with me?'

'Where, Sam?'

'I'm not sure.. to a corner of the world where they need me.'

'We're... not going back to the peace people?'

'No. The kids. I understand if you want to stay, but I have a lot of work to do.'

'So! You plan to leave me behind?'

'If you wish it. I don't know where I'll be going yet.'

'Ha! You'll travel and enjoy yourself, and me? I can't cope. We're Uncle and Auntie.' '

'Not going for fun. You know what my mission is. I told you.'

'Well, Mr. Saint, where you go, I go - as long as we've dope.'

'Don't call me that! I hate it!'

'When do we leave?

'I'm waiting for inspiration.'

'Can you find it in another dose, huh? And some love for me?' He ignored her.

'Got to try and stay clean. I need to think clearly,' he said aloud to himself.

'Mmmmm, you'll have to hurry then.' She drifted to Harry-with-the-broken-leg, stretched on the floor, and inhaled the smoke from his cigarette before snatching it from his dirty fingers. Then, she turned to Sam,

'And Harry?'

'He can stay here, Lucy. He needs to take care of our place.'

'Good, but I'll miss him. He understands.'

'So do I, and we'll be just fine.' He knew - more than suspicion, but had to let it go. The overwhelming feeling of his disloyalty to the Almighty had prevented him from enjoying his wife physically for quite some time. Cancerous guilt had steadily penetrated his subconscious, where lodged the regrets and the ruthless betrayal of everything that had been sacred to him.

You are a priest forever. That line from Hebrews 7:17 persecuted him, and the voice inside him did not abate. It gained impetus, imprisoned him in past vows of obedience and chastity. His resolution to be chaste once more overcame all else - the first step of a ladder he determined to climb. If Lucy kissed him, he did not respond, for it was a 'dirty' thing, the tongue-in-the mouth-type, which he substituted with a simple peck on her lips. She became an endless temptation. The drugs for him were Satan's instrument to his total perdition, to hell on earth, and to the one waiting beyond the mortal gates.

'I... am... unloved...' she often said to him.

'I do love you. Wait, I can't...'

'Fed up... I need...'

'I know.'

'Go! Go to your bible! Kiss her! Fuck her,' and with these words, she floated to embrace her friend passionately while Sam left the room, guilty. His fault - but it burned inside.

During their two months at home, the children visited briefly a couple of times accompanied by Mark, who took them back due to the state in which he found the three of them.

'Try this, Sam... The best, just got it today.'

'No. I'm going to pass tonight.' He needed that stuff badly. The sweat and the shakes of his body commanded him to accept, but he had to control his willpower, win this battle, or it would be too late. Sam did not intend to submit, but the various mixtures had too strong a hold on him, and he found himself roaming in weird places. His body's temperature felt so high he expected to burst into flames. When all ended in relentless pain, Samuel locked himself in the bathroom. He filled the bath with cold water and submerged up to his neck until the craving eased off enough to allow him some respite.

Fine, Samuel. You will get there. Fight this evil, or you will not be able to do His will.

He understood the extent of Lucy's addiction to be worse than his, and he knew that to wean her from it was impossible. In her eyes, he discovered contempt for him, and Harry was her-better-to-ignoring what he was. To change things, they had to remove themselves from that way of life. He had to escape the powerful voice inside him that repeated,

You're a failure! Sinner, sinner, sinner! Bad man! Bad, bad, bad.

When Sam's atrocious attacks slowed down, he began the search for the kind of work that would fulfil his newly discovered calling. "In a desert," He had said. Where to start? Then he remembered that someone in the group had mentioned a place where people used a drug all the time for spiritual understanding and as an all-encompassing panacea. After a visit to the library, he finally found his destiny among the dusty racks.

"The Peyote Church is a place where peace reigns supreme, and everyone is a brother or sister. People that join this self-sufficient community exchange their labours for a life of absolute bliss and enlightenment. They help needy people, and with the aid of the peyote plant from which they extract the same name's substance, they progress on the path of true life and fulfilment. Rituals, a straightforward way of living and its regular consumption benefit the residents greatly."

A drug to help people! I must go there as soon as I can. I have the money. He is showing me the way.

Studying the map printed under the article let him know

that reaching the church signified a journey to Mexico: to the ferociously hot desert area of the remote Aravaida wilderness.

Destiny is calling, Samuel. Go!

'Lucy? It will not be an easy life for you where I am going. Do you understand?' He shook his head.

'I'm going with you....'

'Very well, but no smoking for me now. I must think.'

Although wanting to succeed more than anything else, he found giving up difficult. Cannabis became his only aid from the all-invading symptoms, the demons sent by God to exact revenge on his body and soul. He took the small book in his hand - he had never touched it again, after its illusory burning - and it opened to this passage:

2 Peter 3:9

"The Lord is not slow to fulfil his promise as some count slowness, but is patient towards you, not wishing that any should perish, but that all should reach repentance."

Reading these passages on sinners reinvigorated his hopes. For the first time since leaving the priesthood, Sam knelt and prayed for guidance and strong moral fibre.

The Flesh and the Spirit

CHAPTER 4

1958

'Are you sure? Before buying the tickets, please, reconsider.'

'I can't cope.' Her glazed eyes stared at him. He needed to take care of her, but she represented constant temptations: lust and dope. He had almost succeeded in getting over the worst, but a long road still loomed ahead.

'Fine, then. I will buy two tickets for New York from London, then...'

'Yes! I'm going to fly away in the blue sky, over the clouds, like a bird!', while flapping her arms, she 'took off' from the settee, falling flat on her face and finding it hilarious.

'Listen to me, calm down. You need to know how far this place is. Just getting there is a challenge.' He shook her gently by the shoulders. 'Do you understand what I'm saying?'

'Yes, fine...' She sat pouting in the corner of the room like a naughty child, pulling her ears upwards as if to increase the field of hearing.

'From New York, we've to change twice on internal flights before arriving in Phoenix, Arizona. There we catch a bus to a town called Glide, a couple of hours away, and then we have to make our way to the Creek. '

'They know we... coming?' she asked.

'Anyone's welcome, of any credo and language. The door's always open.'

'They all use it?'

'Yes, the best stuff you could dream of and good for you.'

'I want to go, now!'

He smiled, and she went to embrace him, but he did not

respond to her advances.

'I can't, Lucy. Not yet,' he said, pushing her away gently. She gave him a piercing glare, a puzzling mixture of inability to comprehend and hate before drifting across the room to the reefer in the ashtray.

Lucy still slept when he woke up. A finger of dawn infiltrated between the curtains. It ignited the red of her hair, now almost ablaze on the white cushion, and the long lashes that framed her eyelids sparkled like the finest threads of gold. Small breasts jutted out of the sheet alive with soft orange shades. His ache urged him to kiss her all over. He wanted to hold her and let his manhood enter deep inside the warmth of her. But Lucy's delight, the smell of her skin, her moist lips would imprison him. That voice raged against him,

These impure thoughts obstruct your path. They steer you in the wrong direction. Are you so weak? Turn away from temptation.

Sam rose quickly. A couple of reefers were on her bedside table. He took one, held it between his fingers, peeked at her, and then with a cold sweat, crushed it in the palm of his hand before dropping it to the floor.

'What about the kids?' Mark asked when they made their plans known to him.

'I had a call from God. *He* wants me to go, and I must obey.' An attempt to dissuade him would be useless.

'And Lucy?'

'She can't stay here by herself. She needs looking after.'

He had to agree with Samuel. Belinda and Thomas were alien to them both and vice versa. Uncle and Auntie loomed over

The Flesh and the Spirit

them like ghosts that would leave negative imprints on their lives. Somewhere deep in the parents' heart lurked guilt but knowing their offspring was well and safe eased that sensation.

A couple of suitcases held all their belongings and a limited supply of cannabis. The time came to say goodbye to Harry. His trance-like condition, however, made him unable to understand what was happening. The man smiled, waved, and kept on smoking.

One goal alone occupied Sam's mind: to arrive at his destination. Still, Lucy had a different reason for wanting to go. To limit her use of drugs turned out to be a considerable task, and he became aware of people observing her unpredictability. Sam still smoked cannabis but nothing else and often suffered atrocious urges that gradually wore off. On the positive side, he started to control his habit and not the other way around.

Lucy slept on the train to London. After the taxi left them at Heathrow, she disappeared inside the toilet. The person who emerged sometime later could hardly stand up.

'Lucy! Oh, no! You promised!'

'I need it.'

He supported her by the arm and made his way to check-in, then helped her conquer the aircraft's passengers' stair. The tremor of his hands when he dried the cold droplets on his face told him how much he needed something.

'Is the lady well, sir? Can I be of assistance?' inquired the hostess concerned, as he managed, at last, to make Lucy sit down in the cabin.

'No, thank you, she must take her medication, and she'll be fine,' he said while locking her seat belt hoping she would remain quiet. The two empty seats near them provided some relaxation. A depressed and exhausted Lucy fought hard to keep her eyes open. Once they took off, her excitement to be above the clouds became a yo-yo with highs of laughter and lows of tears, happiness, and misery until she swallowed some tablets. Shudders, nonsensical phrases, and made-up words interrupted her rest for a long time. Relaxing a little, he fell into a quasi-stupor. When she woke up to ingest another dose, those white pellets seemed to him very innocent. Could he take a couple without side effects? Would they lead him back on the road he was leaving behind?

Please, God, help me.

He resisted his cravings - another minor victory that strengthened his determination.

An intense heat greeted them when the aeroplane landed in New York. Used to the much cooler English summer, they found the heat hard to bear. Inside the terminal, the two-hour wait for their connection to Los Angeles seemed endless.

'Please, don't take any more tablets,' he pleaded, conscious of people eyeing her with curiosity. Slumped on the seat, she looked ready to pass out at any moment. To not attract attention, he appeared unconcerned, or someone would have offered help, and he could not risk a doctor's visit. Sam put his arm over her shoulders.

'Our flight will not be too long, my dear. Wait until we're on board, agreed?'

'Yes. I need the toilet.' He sustained her remaining outside, but after a while, there was no sign of her. The time for departure approached, and she did not appear. Ladies went in and out, and he had no choice but to go in. The women viewed him doubtfully about to say something, and he called her.

'Where are you? Lucy!' The shakes.

He spotted a foot protruding from under a door - her shoe. He pushed the door open. She was on the floor, head leaning against the toilet and unconscious.

'Up, darling, up. We need to go!' He made her stand up, heading to the boarding gate.

'You need help, sir?' asked the steward.

'No, thank you. My wife will be fine. Her medicine and a good rest are all she needs. We've been travelling for hours. We come from England.'

'Very well, ' he replied with a dubious peek.

The plane took off, and she put her arm under Sam's, stroking his leg and kissing his neck, giggling.

'Kiss me... I want you to kiss me...'

'People are looking. Not now, please.' He had pressed the wrong button, it seemed, and jack-in-the-box sprang up. Her sweet and sexy voice changed into a scream.

'Not now! Not ever! You never kiss me! Never fuck me! Anybody wanna fuck me? Mr. Saint here can't manage it. Ssshh! God's watching!'

She slumped on her seat while heads turned in disbelief, amused, horrified, and open-mouthed. Sam wanted to disappear. She was quiet for the rest of their flight, dozing.

Once in Los Angeles, after long queues, at last, they stepped outside the terminal. Exhausted, he took care of the luggage, Lucy and her whims, afraid she would fall if he let go of her arm. A cab left them at the hotel nearest to the airport. This trip could have been exciting for both under normal circumstances, but 'normality' was still unknown to either of them. She seemed to have sunk to a deep level of depression, but in the coolness of their room, she revived.

'I'm so tired! So thirsty!'

She pulled him by the arm with a mischievous expression and stretched on the bed.

'I want you... now. It's been a long time.'

'I can't. The aftermath of the drugs, I think. Be patient.'

'Try, please! I am unloved! At least if Harry was here... Take off your clothes, and mine!' she demanded.

He undressed, shying away from his nakedness, unbuttoned her blouse, her bra, and saw those magnificent breasts waiting for him to touch them.

No, I made a vow to God. I cannot ever break it. He's watching me.

He attempted to cover her nudity with the sheet, which she cast aside, pulling him on top of her.

'Kiss me,' she commanded angrily while her hands wandered all over his skin. An electric current passed through him, and he leaped to his feet.

'Not now, love. Let's eat first and then sleep. We're exhausted, and tomorrow will be a long day too.'

She stood up, pacing to the French window. Her white, perfect body outlined against the sunset's violent colors: a shining dove framed by the timeless cycle of the night after day. He took each step in slow motion, his body eager to reach her. A few seconds, paces that seemed to last forever until she moved away, hurrying to grab her handbag and locking herself in the darkness of the closet. He dampened a towel with the drinking water and wiped himself all over, wishing for relief from the humid heat. How could he tell her of his decision?

Not now. When the time's right, but not now.

'Lucy, love! We need food and lots of water. Open the door.'

'Not hungry. Let me be! I'll come out when I'm ready.'

After a while, the well-known smell filtered through. The temptation was strong.

Just a little. No, I need a clear head. I must look after her, and our destination is near. I must resist.

The waiter knocked with the food he had ordered. He took the tray from him, swallowed a significant amount of cold water, and ate a beef sandwich. Very soon, overcome by tiredness and the hot climate, he fell asleep. Lucy's high-pitched monologues from the bathroom penetrated his vivid nightmares.

The dawn found her half-human in speech and demeanour, but Sam ready to go. He forced her to eat a little, to drink, and helped her with her clothes. The temperature had not reached its peak yet when he hailed a taxi. They boarded the craft to Phoenix after a long wait, but the brief flight found both very agitated.

'We there? I don't want to travel! I want to go back.'

'Not long now. Have a little patience.' He talked to her as to a child.

'It's all you say! Patience, patience! I got none.'

Tenderly caressing her forehead, he tucked a lock of hair behind her small ear. She regarded him with pleading eyes.

'Can we go… home? I'm so tired!'

'Our new home's not far. We are almost there,' and he touched the little book in his pocket.

On arrival, they took a cab to the bus station. Sam let go of Lucy to purchase the tickets to Glide and a couple of tortillas. In her stiletto heels, she tripped and fell a few times on the gravel, scratching her arm and cutting the side of her leg badly. She started to cry like a baby, and people stared at them, increasing his discomfort. The scene attracted a kind Mexican woman who handed him a strip of linen as a temporary bandage. Once in her seat, she finally gave way to her usual tormented slumber, sobbing and needing a fix.

The sweaty driver descended.

'Final de Carrera,' he said, wiping his deeply wrinkled brow. He sat their cases on the ground, ready to depart. Nobody else alighted in Glide, and Sam helped Lucy off the omnibus. She had complained of dizziness and a splitting headache throughout. He checked his surroundings. The town, baking under the sun, sprawled in front of him in a jumbled collection of small white buildings close together and some tall constructions emerging among the rooftops.

'Sir, what transport goes to Aravaida Creek?' Sam did not speak Spanish, but perhaps his knowledge of Latin might help him.

'Horse y el wagon,' he answered with a toothless grin at the ignorance of these people. When he looked at Lucy, her obvious pain moved him.

'There... go... water,' ' he said, pointing a chubby finger at a small cabin.

'Tell Maria. Me, Pedro, sent you. Woman no well needs medico. You foreign, yes?' He produced a green bottle, took a swig, rinsed his mouth, and spat it out.

'Yes, thank you. We'll be fine.'

The conversation, helped by gestures, had been understood by both. Sam picked up both bags, and with Lucy limping and hopping, he reached the yellow building the driver had indicated. A scantily dressed woman arrived, dragging her bare feet on the dusty stone floor, and he asked for water. She obliged by bringing a sizeable cool carafe and two glasses to a rickety table where they sat down.

'I'm so sick... my leg and arm are sore. I want to go home.' She started to cry.

'We're close, love—one last trip. When we arrive, they'll help you. I'm sure of it.'

She fell silent, sobbing lightly and trembling. Sam went to ask the woman,

'Maria?'

'Si, señor.'

'Pedro... cart, caballo? Peyote church, Aravaida Creek,' he said.

'Mi son.' Then two fingers went up, and she said, 'doscientos,' waiting for the money. He gave her the two hundred pesos. The woman called 'Jose!' A short young man with a thin moustache and a wide sombrero emerged from behind a piece of red material replacing a door. He glanced at them. Maria exchanged a few words with him, who filled half a dozen flask-type tins with water and took them outside. His mother stared inquisitively at Lucy. Jose came back and gestured for them to follow him. He secured the water with a rope inside an old wooden cart. A sizeable overhanging umbrella provided shade and a bench fixed to the boards functioned as a seat. Lucy and Sam accommodated themselves on it as best as possible, placing one bag at each side. Jose tied the hat under his chin, then urged the horse into a trot. Nobody spoke. Lucy's dejection steadily increased, attributable in part to the incredible warmth. She was faint and uninterested in her new surroundings.

'Let me see your leg, love. I'll wash it.'

Ignoring her protests, he removed the bandage, discovering

infected wounds: a hopeless plight. He poured some water on the cuts and bandaged them again with the cloth. She put her legs over one bag, rested her head on his knees, took another of her pills, and then dozed off. Samuel's irritation made him restless: it was all wrong.

What am I doing here? If only I could smoke.

Soon after, another voice said,

Just a puff. Go on. The cigarettes are in her handbag. Who would know?

His hand slid inside it. The hardness of the cigarette case reassured him, and he anticipated the relief he would experience. His hand was halfway out when a voice thundered,

No! You swore. Are you going to let me down again?

That voice was so angry he withdrew his empty hand.

They journeyed on under the shade of the shaky cover, aware of every bump on the ground. The hot air stifled them, and the glare of the sun penetrated through their sunglasses. It was becoming a nightmare. Although glad that Lucy just lay with her eyes closed, he worried about her breathing and evident state. Helpless in doing anything else, he gave her water frequently and reassured her with his words.

About to doze off, his eyes took in the scenery around him in amazement. His expectation of an arid desert, invaded only by cactus, had been wrong. He saw a surprising diversity of vegetation spread all over, with clumps of orange flowers glowing against the dark soil due to the intense brightness. Numbed by the heat and sunlight, by the novelty of it all and the uncomfortable seating, he also slept, waking now and then to make sure they both were hydrated. He had not felt this bad for quite a while. The waves of craving for a cigarette

The Flesh and the Spirit

took advantage of his weakened mind. They invaded his brain and precluded any other thought, overriding his reason and willpower. He held his book and read the passage about Christ in the wilderness:

"... Man shall not live by bread alone, but by every word that proceeds from the mouth of God."

He had succumbed to his temptations. However, this time, the Devil had to wait because he had reached the land of his salvation.

CHAPTER 5

Jose stopped near a giant cactus to water the horse, and once its thirst was satisfied, he jumped on the cart without a word. Nobody spoke, but occasionally he turned around to look at them. Unwilling to wake her up, Sam did not dare to move, aware by now that the potent pills she took induced sleep when unable to smoke. Grateful for it, he surveyed around in awe. A variety of cacti populated the desert. The very tall ones embraced the sun with their thorny and distinct arms. Others, shaped like sizeable balls, were ready to roll on the ground, while bush-like growths resembled fleshy ears rimmed by small spikes and tiny red blooms. Overcome by the sheer greatness of his surroundings, a reverential feeling transformed his experience into a soul-stirring one.

As they went further, the landscape nearer the stream became greener. A river flowed through the canyon, and dumbfounded, Sam concluded this 'desert' did not compare to any arid wilderness - it was a unique and scenic expanse. Many trees' varieties flourished on the river's banks, and different kinds of birds flew in the cloudless and deep blue sky. Fish jumped in the clear, slow-flowing water, and when caught by sunrays, sparkled like jewels. In this place of magnificence and utter peace, he forgot about the dreadful state of his body. His wife moved.

'Lucy! Look! So much beauty around us! It's scorching but so amazing!' She raised her head, eyes trying to focus but not finding it easy. He gave her water - it tasted warm and stale.

'Are... we... there?'

'Almost, I think,' he said, looking at his watch. They had been going for two hours. Jose crossed the creek at a low point, and the splashes of water made Sam wanting to dive in, but a short distance away, Jose turned to him.

'There!', he said, pointing at the opening of another canyon. Sam's heart missed a beat. On a great plateau, jutting out of the rocky hill stood a building, similar to a squat white ghost dropped on the brown soil. As it happens in a mirage, the intense heat rising from the earth distorted its outline. An uphill path of dark red stones led up to it. A long and broad porch extended its size, with an arched entrance dripping with purple flowers. Green leafy plants grew on the ground where they stood, and lichens clung to the scattered boulders. Then more cactus, clumps of bright red, orange, and pink blooms along with more greenery. Sam fell instantly in love.

'We're here! It's amazing!' He shook her by the shoulders, attempting to bring Lucy out of her hypnotic condition. He lifted her, stepped down, and tried to make her stand, but a very swollen leg, a dizzy head, and glazed eyesight prevented her. She hardly glanced around before closing her eyes again, leaning on him.

'Home... Home, Sam,' she said faintly.

Jose placed the bags on the ground and, with a wave accompanied by 'Adios!', turned the cart around.

Lucy spoke to Sam in a dreamy-sounding voice.

'Where are we? We never get home. I don't know where we are. Where am I?'

He realized that her panic was real, like a child's irrational terror of being lost, of finding herself tricked into reality when all around her seemed unreal.

'It hurts, can't move,' she added, whining and about to faint, managing to hold on to him while he made a makeshift bed with their luggage. He placed her on it, sprinkled water over her face, and forced her to drink. A yellow liquid oozed from the cloth covering her leg.

'You can stay here, love. I'm going to call for help.'

'Yes... I...' She dozed off again while he hurried under the hot sun, off-balance and with stiff legs. Worried, often turning to watch her, he had almost reached the entrance when a man opened the door and rushed towards him, speaking Spanish. Sam conveyed urgency through gestures. The short, chubby man followed him, glanced at Lucy, and called others at the top of his voice. Another two men ran outside and carried her between them. The first one to appear took the luggage and gestured him to follow. Sam's dizziness grew worse, but upon entering the building, a pleasant coolness welcomed him. A woman arrived with two cups and a pitcher of water. He gulped it down, then followed the men. They took his wife to a small room and settled her down on a wide paillasse in a corner. The man with a fixed and toothless smile brought in their belongings. The woman offered him more water, then lifted Lucy's head murmuring in Mexican and poured some in her mouth. Lucy gazed at that face puzzled, moaning loudly and scratching her leg furiously. The filthy piece of linen came off in her hand as she shivered with fever caused by the infection and the lack of drugs. When the woman saw her wounds, her calm changed into alarm, and she left talking aloud, with words he did not understand. Bewildered, he sat on the floor with Lucy's hand in his, trying to soothe her and cooling her face with water. She needed a doctor.

God help us. I beg you! Don't let anything happen to her. Take it all out on me! He prayed.

An old man with sallow, desiccated skin and bent on a

The Flesh and the Spirit

knobbly wooden staff appeared. He regarded the newcomers briefly before going to Lucy to inspect her wounds. He touched her forehead, saying in perfect English,

'She's very ill, dangerously so, and needs some medicine for her temperature. I'm going to fetch what I need. I'm Ben, welcome to Wirikuta.' Sam was astounded that he spoke English and shook his hand, somewhat reassured.

'I'm Sam, and this is Lucy, my wife. We came hoping to stay. I'm so glad you speak our language! Can you help her?' he asked anxiously. 'Our travels coming here were never-ending. We're exhausted.'

'No one comes to this place for a visit, only to remain. Brother and sister, we are ready to be your family. You both need a rest now.' At this point, a tearful Lucy pleaded,

'I need a fix... a smoke, a pill. Please!'

Sam understood a greedy pain demanded all her attention, and she needed to escape it. Her cries echoed loud and long as waves of agony mixed with them. He focused on the man, ashamed of her request, but his words eased Sam's agitation.

'Don't give her anything. I have all that is necessary just now. I'll be back with Yesenia,' he declared in a gravel-like voice, wheezing badly.

The muffled sound of his stick on the stone floor remained the only noise in the silent building. Lucy went on screaming at Sam, demanding her fixes. A short time later, the woman called Yesenia came back with Ben. She had a tray with something milky, a dark liquid, a brown paste in a jar, and some cloth pieces.

'She is my assistant, with a very gentle touch. Don't worry, we'll cure her leg, and she'll be fine in a few days, but she must drink this - not a pleasant beverage but will make her rest and clear the blood from the poison, very important she drinks it all.'

Sam brought the bowl to her lips, but she spat it out after tasting it, coughing and shouting.

'I can't! Give me my pills!'

He looked at Ben in dismay.

'If she doesn't take it, she might die,' said the man loud enough for Lucy to hear him.

'Help me, please,' Sam asked the woman, who exchanged some words with Ben.

'If you hold her down, she will force it into her mouth. There's no other way.'

Due to Lucy's frail condition, the struggle was brief. Yesenia succeeded in pouring it down her throat, making her swallow all of it. Afterward, she washed the wounds with the milky and smelly substance, dried them, spread the ointment, and wrapped the leg in a strip of thin material. Lucy calmed down.

'She'll be out for a long time, best for her. Are you hungry? If not, take this. It will make you sleep and recover your strength. What's it going to be?' He waited patiently for an answer handing him the bowl, which he emptied of its foul-tasting content wanting to please him. When Ben left, he stretched dazed near his wife. She stared at him with half-open eyes - the last thing he remembered.

When Sam woke up, the flaming colours of sunset filtered through the shutters of the small window. He stroked Lucy gently without the slightest response as she laid still beside him. Panicking, he called her, shook her forcibly, but no movement or sound came to reassure him. She appeared white, cold, and lifeless. *Could it be? Was she?* He panicked and darted along the corridor, calling for Ben, who shuffled towards him.

'Quick, I think she is...' That scary thought made him leave the sentence unfinished. Ben went to her with his slow gait, felt her pulse, inspected her eyes, and put an ear to her lips.

'She's fine and over the worst. Thank your God and the peyote plant. Let her be for now. You slept solid from yesterday afternoon until now. It's the magic hour, and you need some food. I'll send Alma. Eat, rest, and ask questions later. I'll be back.'

Ben had made the right decision as his stomach rumbled and the dizzy spells increased. His heart sank when he glimpsed Lucy's still and ghostly face.

'I'm so sorry, love, ' he said, not knowing whether she could hear him.

A young woman left a bowl of steaming, delicious smelling food and water. First, he drank the water, then he devoured the fish stew and dozed again, waking when darkness had taken over the room. The girl came back with a lamp that she hung on a hook in the wall. She peaked at Lucy and smiled at him. The unmistakable sound of the walking stick on the floor announced Ben's hunched figure.

'Is she awake yet? And how are you, my boy?'

The words took him by surprise, as they implied a great deal of familiarity, but they sounded natural spoken by Ben. His father had never called him 'my boy,' he had never been interested in anything except making money.

'She's not awake yet. Is that normal?'

Going to Sam's wife, Ben called her name repeatedly, catching his breath in between.

'Wake up. Come back, Lucy!' She stirred, and Sam kissed her cold cheeks.

'Darling, I'm here. We're safe, and we're home.'

She opened her eyes and stared at him with an unknowing gaze. Taking in everything around her, she whispered, 'Home? No.'

'Love, this is Ben. He saved your life and mine, I think. We did not wake for more than a day. How are you?'

'The leg? Can't feel it.'

'Very well,' intervened Ben, 'she needs nourishment. I'll see to it. Make sure you eat something, little lady. Tomorrow, I shall tell you everything you want to know, son. I'm going to rest now.'

He hobbled away. Soon after, Alma left another tray with the same food as the previous one. He thanked her, and she answered,

'De nada,' scurrying away with a smile on her lips.

'Sam?'

'Yes, I'm here. Eat to get well,' and spooned a little sauce into her mouth. She was so thin! The eyes seemed huge on her small face with the child-like air. At first, Lucy almost choked and then very slowly ate half of the food.

'How's your leg?'

'Not painful.'

He wanted to tell her all about Ben, Yesenia, and Alma. Yet he held back, waiting for her to recover enough to be intrigued.

CHAPTER 6

Sam woke up and examined the surroundings. A long wooden box occupied one wall, and apart from a hanging lamp and the paillasse, the room contained nothing else. The stone floor's coolness under his feet and the room's temperature made the heat bearable. Lucy was still asleep. He walked to the window, and as soon as he opened the shutters, an intense warm wave engulfed his body. When his eyes grew accustomed to the extreme glare, Sam felt sure to be dreaming: his sight set on a perfect, fantastic garden. It displayed neat rows of peas, beans on canes, patches of ground with various bushes, and plants climbing up its enclosing white walls. In the centre of this Eden stood the most tempting apple tree one could imagine. Exceptional deep golden fruits hung heavily from its branches without dropping as if held there by magic. Shiny, emerald green leaves crowned each perfect globe. A pergola-like construction covered with dried-up vegetation shaded the whole area, where narrow pathways headed in every direction. He turned to see if Lucy had woken and found her staring at the white ceiling. She heard the excitement in his voice when he spoke,

'Love! Come and look at this.'

She surveyed him with eyes lacking sparkle, shaking.

'Can I walk?'

'You don't need to. I'll carry you.' He lifted her light frame and brought her to the window.

'So hot...' she whispered, but after a peep emitted a little joyful sound, threw her arms around his neck, and kissed him repeatedly. Her closeness disturbed him. He yearned to hold her tight against his body, to kiss her soft mouth, her delicate throat, to possess her. A range of different sensations almost conquered him, but he refused to accept them aware of their human source.

'How lovely, so green!' she said listlessly.

'Does your leg hurt? Can you walk?'

She tried but failed. 'Perhaps if I lean on you... I need it, Sam.' No fantastic views could defeat the state of her mind and body.

'If you wait a while, I'm sure Ben will have a solution.'

'I can't. I need it now!'

'Please, love. He knows, and he will help you.'

He held her tight in his arms and attempted to soothe her. The tremor in his hands had almost gone, and he hoped to resist his physical cravings. He felt good today - better than he had for a long time. The tapping on the floor announced Ben's arrival.

His long silver hair, now gathered in a ponytail, exposed every detail of a face that reminded him of brown corrugated cardboard in colour and texture. On his white poncho, red, yellow, and green designs appeared faded by time and use. A pair of disintegrating leather sandals completed his attire.

'You're both up. Good. How's the little lady?' he asked in a tone as cheerful as he could manage.

'She needs some of her stuff. We still have some and...'

'Do you want to cure her?' he asked Sam, then turning to Lucy, 'Do you want to heal, my child?'

'I tried, but I can't.' She sounded sorrowful. Ben's grating voice thundered.

'Three days into the abyss, but when you come back, you'll be on the way to being addiction-free. Or you can live in hell for the rest of your life.'

'Please love, I believe he can cure you. We're safe now,

Lucy.' Shaking like a leaf, she said,

'Yes ...'

'Well then, this room will be your world. Alma will bring you food, but you must take what she will give you each morning and night. The right result depends on this or is pointless even to try. Your husband can stay somewhere else during this time. Is that alright, my boy?' He wheezed severely.

'Yes, Ben. Whatever you say.'

'We start now. One of the women will provide what the little lady needs. Come with me.' Sitting Lucy down, Sam kissed her forehead.

'Darling, you'll be fine. I'm sure they saved both our lives, and they will help you now.' Smiling tenderly at her, he left with Ben.

The woman came in with a tray of food, a clean cloth, a jar of ointment, and a dark liquid cup. She knew what to expect and was ready.

'I'm Alma. You, Lucy, yes?' Very gently, her nimble fingers cleaned the wounds and replaced the bandage. Lucy's agitation increased to the point that spasms tightened her body inside and out.

'My bag! Give it to me!' She ordered, pointing at the chest.

She understood and said, 'No! Eat,' and helped her swallow a few spoonsful until Lucy pushed it aside, refusing more. When the woman brought the bowl to her lips, she spat it out after tasting its content.

'Horrible! I don't want this poison.'

Alma acted right away. She tied her hands with a piece of cord, held her head, and retrieving a small funnel from her pocket, she pinned Lucy down with her knees and inserted it into her mouth. She poured the liquid down her throat a little at the time but without mercy. When Lucy started to choke, she stopped saying,

'I help, or you do!'

Although about to retch after each sip, she had no choice but to swallow the foul-tasting tea, yielding to the inflexible Alma, who once done, retrieved a pot from outside the door and bits of material. She left them both on the floor, then removed the tray and her handbag.

'Not that! Please, you can have money, anything you want, but give me the bag.'

'No, señora. Bad for you,' and she left, latching the door.

Lucy's body contractions intensified, and in the utter silence, her sobs echoed. She called her husband at the top of her voice for as long as she could, but no one came. Burning and taken by strong convulsions, under the influence of the beverage, she fell asleep.

Behind Ben, Sam noticed quite a few doors along the corridor. They entered into a sizeable kitchen-dining room with tables and chairs neatly arranged in the middle of the floor. White cupboards decorated in bold red, green, and blue Aztec patterns ran one wall's entire length. Along another wall, two broad shelves used as worktops flanked a stove fired by wood. Everything was spotless.

'We all come here to eat together. There are twenty of us men now and three women, Alma, Yesenia, and Mariana, all wonderful cooks. They make baskets, pottery and mats to sell. The men do all the rest. They catch our fish, tend the garden, the goats, the hens, and draw the water from the river.' He gasped, 'we are self-sufficient, my boy. The upkeep of it all is backbreaking in this heat, but the work is done willingly and with joy.'

Sam followed him across the room to a door leading outside. Once open, the sudden temperature difference made him dizzy.

'Here we keep the animals,' and he pointed his bony finger at the goats inside a pen, shaded by a trellis similar to the one he had seen. The two men milking and watering lifted their heads,

'Hola, Ben. Hola, Sam,' they grinned and went on with their tasks. Back to the passage, another door gave access to the dream-like sight from the window in his room.

Not with-standing the intense hot conditions, a feeling of coolness permeated the air. Some of the men tended to the plants, a few watered, and others picked and filled their baskets with vegetables.

'Hola, Sam. Hola, Ben,' they said with a grin, then continued with the work at hand.

'Who are these people? Where do they come from? They all seem so happy!'

'They are now. These men and women were lost and looking for something.'

'Did they find it here?'

'Yes, my boy. Through the years, people came and went. They stay a long time or short, but they all leave only when their search is over.'

'What are they seeking? What is the religion of this place?'

'The founder called it a church, as it is a refuge for anyone, of any creed. Under this roof, there are no religious icons, and we never discuss individual beliefs. Our only tenet is cooperation, harmony, love, brotherhood, and respect for each other and nature.'

'How long have you been here?'

Ben hesitated before answering, 'Thirty years. When my wife died after thirty-five years of happiness, I could not cope with life or people. I wanted to disappear, vanish from the world. I was fifty-five then, a botanist and student of the ancient Mexican language. My journeys had no purpose, and I arrived here by chance. I never left. This place was different, but its goal never altered. Let me sit down. I get so weary.' He slumped on a small stool, still holding on to his stick and catching his breath.

'What are people searching for here?'

'What have you lost, Sam? What did you come to find?'

'I lost my God, and I came to find Him,' he replied sadly.

'Search, and you'll find. There's an inscription in the old language carved on the stone above the entrance that says, "Search for the self," which is the most fulfilling journey of a lifetime. Some never find the right path. Some abandon it halfway, and some go astray. Who perseveres and reaches his destination will live knowing. Through that knowledge, he'll be reborn, achieve the impossible and exist forever.'

'I was a priest once, walking on my rightful path. I lost sight of it, Ben, and I am searching again. The fortress I once accessed is now impregnable. I am outside, waiting to be allowed in.'

'You're lost, my boy. With the help of our magic cactus, you can find your true self again. Your wife will receive what she requires as well.'

'I'm not too sure. We've different needs. Do you think you can free her from this addiction? I almost succeeded myself, but there are other issues.'

He did not know yet when or how he would tell Lucy of his resolution and wondered about her reaction. He believed to be in love with her, yet he lacked the compassion, maturity, and

The Flesh and the Spirit

knowledge that came easy to him in other areas of his ministry.

'Your wife might change too, here. Wait! The next three days will be overwhelming for her, and she'll try every trick to get what she wants. Better if you stay away. The women will care for her. Trust me.'

'I do, and I understand that I can only find if I search by myself, which I intend to do, but tell me about this magic peyote plant. Is it a drug?'

'Not exactly, but a bit of everything. A panacea for all the ills of body and soul, used for more than five thousand years. The only secret is in its dosage and dilution, depending on its purpose. You can drink, spread, even ingest it in its natural form or mixed with other medicinal herbs. But its principal use has always been - and still is - a plant of metaphysical and spiritual identity.'

'But where does it come from?'

Ben paused for a while, trying to breathe again, which at times he seemed unable to do.

'Forgive me… My chest. Not to worry. I suffered this for many years. Well then, what is peyote, you asked? A small and spineless cactus, with disc-shaped buttons growing close to the ground, chewed or soaked in water to produce a liquid. When taken orally, its effect varies according to the person's expectations, mood and surroundings, and varying potency.'

'A special experience then.'

'Yes, but not always positive. Sometimes enjoyable, other times terrifying, causing all sorts of bad fears. A very enigmatic outcome.'

'When do you take it?'

'Once a week. We gather in the hut at the bottom of the garden and have a ceremonial ritual with peyote. Do you want to come tonight?'

'Yes, very much.'

'I'll send someone to call you. I'm tired, my boy. Too hot for me, even here. Pedro!' he called to one of the men, 'show him another room, tell him about our daily routines and where he can be of help.'

'Pedro understands English,' and as he wobbled away, Sam shouted behind him,

'Is the name of this place Wirikuta?' He stopped a moment to answer him.

'Not really, but for the Huichol people of Mexico, Wirikuta means heaven -- a desolate but magical desert valley. A very suitable name, I think.' Then, he was gone.

From Carlos, Sam learned to milk the goats, then he met Francisco, the cheesemaker, who showed him how to make soft and hard cheese. Pedro said,

'You like to do this, Sam? It can be your job.'

'Yes, I'll be happy to do this.' He was confused. Why did the Lord want him to come here to this paradise instead of punishing him with hell on earth? It was not a place of worship, so what good could he possibly do?

Don't ask God for reasons, Sam.

He must punish me, and I must suffer and resist temptation as He did. I must pay for my betrayal. I am unclean. Perhaps one day, You will take me to your bosom again and show me the way forward. I am the lamb that strayed. Please, come and find me.

Sam needed to get used to the climate, as he only found some relief inside the building. When mealtime arrived, he met all the people living there, as if he already knew each of them. They talked to him either in their language or with a few English words, and Pedro always translated.

'Why is it much cooler among these walls?'

'Señor, these are blocks of stone two feet thick. Bueno in summer, warmer on cold nights. Just keep window and main door closed.'

They ate cheese, vegetables, and bread, and after the washing up, everyone retired for a *siesta,* to relax, or for a snooze. Pedro showed him to a room smaller than the one he was in with Lucy but with the same content. Worn out by the heat, he lay down on the paillasse and thought about what waited ahead. Poor girl!

Sleep soon came. Waking up, Sam decided to go out and explore. After filling a small terracotta flask with water from the container in the kitchen, he borrowed an umbrella made of straw from a bucket near the door and quietly stepped outside. Remembering Ben's words, he gazed above the door, read the engraved inscription on the arch, and reflected on it while keeping to the downhill pathway.

Ahead the canyon widened, ending up where the inlet was flowing. The rich odours released by the vegetation clung to the nostrils, and he inhaled the moist and penetrating mixtures. Sam observed the immense wonders around him with boundless admiration. After rushing to paddle like a child, he sat under a tree and let his sight climb in awe the incredible height of the majestic peaks flanking the creek. Birds' calls crowded the air. Fish darted out of the water like silver blades, and a wild goat on the opposite bank came to satisfy its thirst.

A potent magician had performed spellbinding and lasting tricks on the stage of nature, and the silence taught him to listen to murmurs others could not hear. His mind crossed the threshold of an untold passage where this beauty drew him in, as possessive as another - Lucy. A compulsion to belong took hold of him, and he envisioned to be gravel on the riverbed, a wing skimming the water's surface, the reflection of an overhanging branch. He was a rock in the stream of existence, one tiny molecule within forces controlling the creation of all. A voice calling compelled him to pull away, and he saw Pedro.

'Tlamatini asks to talk to you. Coming, Sam?'

'Who's Tlamatini?'

'Ben is Tlamatini, "the wise man" in the Nahuatl language of my ancestors.'

Ben met him at the entrance.

'Did you like what you saw?'

'I have no words. How's Lucy?'

'Going through the worst, but coping. Come, after our meal, I want to show you something before dark.'

Alma brought to the table a thick omelette filled with cheese and vegetables accompanied by fragrant tortillas,

'Sam, Lucy is well. She drinks medicine,' she said, carrying on with her duties.

'Everyone speaks some English here. I need to learn their language. Will you teach me?'

'Yes, my son, with pleasure.'

A chatty and happy atmosphere pervaded the dining room. After the meal, Ben and Sam strolled into the garden.

'I want to show you something. We sit and wait for the exact moment when afternoon and evening suspend in perfect equilibrium in mid-heaven. What do you think of life here, son?'

'I love it, and I wish to help with some work here. I'm going

   The Flesh and the Spirit

to be a cheese-maker!'

'Mmm... I'll not eat cheese for a while then.' Ben meant to laugh, but a cough shook his frame to the core.

'Not to worry, my potions helped until now. They will for a few more years, I hope. Come, Sam, the time is now.' Ben approached the apple tree.

'Here. Stand just here. As soon as the sun comes into view below the trellis, behold it carefully.'

Both stood and waited. When the flaming rays engulfed the tree, the fruits became red, luminous, surrounded by a golden halo. A unique moment he would never forget.

'The apples shine with the radiance of a glorious sunset, like in the garden of the Hesperides. The sunset's goddesses graced us with their tree. I nurtured it from its birth. I shall do so until I die, and after.'

Moved, he answered, 'I will always look after it, Ben. I promise.'

The old man put one hand on his arm, and his veiled sight fixed on Sam,

'I know my boy... I know,' and the wave of his genuine love reached Samuel's heart.

CHAPTER 7

The stars were flickering as he entered the wooden construction with all the residents of Wirikuta. That name fascinated him, as it embodied the whole meaning of the place. Ben explained what would happen during the ritual and warned him that his perceptions might not be what he expected. Those present sat in silence cross-legged on the ground, and Ben began chanting in the Huichol tongue.

One of the men kept beating on a drum, and Ben drew lines on the earth with his staff in the middle of a circle, where he also placed a bone whistle and a feather fan. The light hanging from a beam transformed the shadowed faces, modified their appearance, and made them spectators waiting to be engrossed in another world. Mariana passed a container of squishy cactus. Each of the participants dipped a hand, coming up with a fistful of small pellets, which they ate. Its awful taste almost made him retch, but Sam succeeded in swallowing the lumps. Everyone drank this mixture, then a different one passed from one hand to another, a disgusting and very bitter liquid. Each person sipped some of it. Mariana filled the container three more times. Ben's words, unfathomable to him, blended in with the other's chants. Sam›s head became heavy.

A little at a time, he sensed his separation into two different halves. One-half stayed fixed to one spot, but the other rotated at a vertiginous speed towards a black hole. Once through it, indescribable patterns of coloured lights darted all around him, strange shapes of plants, clouds, mountains of impossible size, red, blue suns in a green sky, and voices. A cacophony of sounds towered above all, enclosing him in a vacuum.

'Go, go!' they repeated threateningly.

The din increased, hurting his ears up there, among the giant carnivorous blooms and the black starlight. The coils of a giant snake then trapped him, and his mind reunited with his body.

He woke up on his bed with sunlight filtering through the shutters, still fully dressed and ready to fly. Flashbacks invaded his brain, and they lingered with sounds lasting all day.

Lucy. How was she?

He had not seen her, but the women referred to him that her "illness"- as everyone called it, was improving. Soon he would find out, and even though the thought of her had never left him, he had no idea of his wife's plight during that time.

For three days, Lucy's mind wandered on a series of plateaus in the peyote-induced half-sleep. She teetered on the edge of an abyss experiencing horrors so real that her screams reached a long way along the corridor. She always shook with a fever-like tremor when sweat poured down her face, and insane thoughts infiltrated her mind. Alma cleaned her, restrained her when it became necessary, forced her to swallow the tea, and dismissed the pleas for her bag. On the fourth day, Ben allowed Sam to see her.

Very apprehensive, he found her standing near the window.

'How are you, honey?' he embraced her tenderly.

She clung to him before answering,

'You never came,' and with a hangdog expression that bore into his soul, she added,

'I need you. Will you love me?'

That emaciated and pathetic figure with deep bags under her eyes and matted hair was his wife. Overflowing with pity, he caressed her ghostly face, and only when Ben walked in, he felt safe.

'Little lady, are you better? All you need now is good food, and to drink what I'll give you, then...'

'I'm not going to swallow that poison ever again! Tell him, Sam. Please, help me! I can't do it anymore!'

Ben displayed a toothless grin,

'You won't have to. This other tea is not bad, but you must keep taking it twice a day for another month. Then you will be cured. Guaranteed.' He said, in the gentlest voice he could muster.

She stared at him inquisitively before saying,

'You can't even guess what I went through. Never again.'

'I know all of it, but now you're in the recovery stage. The potion will help your body to adjust without too many symptoms. What do you say?'

She examined her hands. The shaking of the past days had diminished. Her head was clear. Her body, although still weak, more energetic at the same time. The bandage on her leg had gone.

'I think I'm going to be well.' Holding on tightly to Sam, she gave him a grateful look. For the first time, what he caught in Lucy's expression shook him to the core: an intense, grown-up, and very tender love.

'Little lady, Alma, and Mariana will show you where to wash and eat, and then, they will take you around the place. Go and meet your new family. We all want you to be well.'

Very subdued, she eyed the two women who came in. They handed her a blue pot with a red orchid plant.

'Welcome, sister!' said Mariana.

Lucy uttered a surprised, 'Thank you,' and mustering strength still unknown to her, she deposited it on the chest. The bare room came alive with colour - not alien and hostile to her any longer, but welcoming and friendly.

'Leave her in the capable hands of the women, my boy. You'll see her later.'

'Shall I go now, then Lucy? You know the girls.'

'Yes, Sam. Go.'

They met in the evening at mealtime. The hot climate had painted Lucy's cheeks with a rosy glow; a red flame danced on the shiny hair now gathered in a ponytail, and she wore a spotless, plain yellow cotton dress. He gazed at Lucy as if they had just met. Without makeup, her face was that of an innocent child. Long lashes framed her big brown eyes, now amazingly bright, and she befriended everyone, whether they understood her or not, causing general hilarity. A different person had blossomed, one Sam never knew before. A beautiful creature who attracted him like a magnet. Sunset was spreading on the horizon when she asked him,

'Will you take me to the garden? I would love it.'

'Yes, come.' He placed his arm around her shoulders. Hand in hand then, they sat, inhaling the sweet smells of the cooling air. They watched as the view began to slumber under the velvety sky. Their eyes feasted on red flowers that, catching the last of the light, burned like lingering, smouldering embers. Clusters of petals released an intoxicating scent, mixed with the desert's earthy smell after a hot day. Both succumbed to the enchantment of that moment.

She moved closer to him and kissed him passionately. His lips responded, and he held her tight, losing himself in a desperate need for all of Lucy. His passion equalled hers, his heart palpitated, his breathing accelerated. Then a brief mental excursion into sinful images compelled him to descend from the heights reached. He pushed her aside with intonations full of urgency.

'No, I can't wait,' he murmured. He took her to their room, where he sat in silence on the box with the head between his hands.

'Sam, do you love me?' She asked sweetly, prising his fingers apart. His rejection flared her emotions.

'Look at me. I am here.'

Sinuously, as if moving to the music of Ravel's Bolero, she took off her dress, standing naked in front of him but half-dressed by the shadows of the lamp.

'I love you, and I need you. Touch me. I'm back, Sam. I'm here for you.' She knelt and held his hand on her breast, pressing along, aware of its blazing trail.

He weakened, hardly breathing, but when about to kiss her, he distanced himself.

'No, Lucy, please.'

She moved closer, searching, playing with his body.

'Let's wait. I am not ready.'

'When Sam? When will you be? I think you have changed and don't love me any longer. Is that so?' The incredible tenderness in her voice increased the torment inside him.

'I do love you, but in a way you might not comprehend. I'll tell you if I succeed in achieving what I came here to do.'

'What, Sam? What is it that you came here to do?'

'My purification. Of the body and the spirit. That's why I can't make love to you, do you understand? If I give in to temptation now, I'll never make it.'

'What, darling? We're husband and wife, yet we have not been close to each other for so long! I want your body, along with your heart, isn't it normal?'

She had called him "darling" and had spoken about wanting his heart too. He delighted in the new meaning interwoven with those words, but *that* voice was so loud, he could not ignore it. Very calm he answered,

'I can't say any more yet. Let's wait.' The knot in his throat made him almost sick.

'Until after your "purification"?'

'Yes. I must do what's right. Try to understand.'

No, she did not know what it all meant, but after his "purification," all would be well again between them. She needed to wait. Lucy lay down on the paillasse without another word, sobbing until the tea already drunk deadened her pain and desires.

He peeked at her body with love, lust, and concern.

I must go away now, tomorrow, before it is too late. Lord, help my weaknesses.

Tired from the hard work of the day, he tried to get some rest, but his mind kept straying and asking questions he could not yet answer. From then on, the supreme peace that reigned in Wirikuta became a stark contrast to the storms gathering inside his mind.

Sam found Ben with a bowl of milk in the dining room. A few others gradually joined for breakfast.

'I must talk to you. It's time for me to do what I must,' he said in a sombre tone of voice.

'Yes, my boy. I understand. How can we help you?'

'I'm going to the desert alone. Is there a place where I can shelter? The sun will be my enemy. For the rest, I only need enough peyote to last me a while and nothing else.'

'Son, you're a stranger to this place, on your own, and

without food or water, you'll not survive long. Why like this, Sam?'

'I'm here because He sent me to find Him. I must prove to Him that the pure love I gave Him once is still there intact and that I'm ready now to give Him all of me forever. The cactus will help me.'

'It can be dangerous. You are not experienced enough to take it freely.'

'Advise me on how often and how much Ben, and about a refuge from sunrays. I want to go as soon as I can.'

'Sam, there are all sorts of dangers out there. I don't want to lose you, my son.'

'I'll be fine. I can't go on like this. I am like Hamlet, but torn between two loves: Christ's and Lucy's.'

'Yes, I can tell. Come to my room after lunch to find out about the plant and the environment unknown to you.'

Two weeks went by, a time that Sam spent with Ben. The more they were together, the more he admired the man whose mind, despite his ninety years, was sharper than most. In his life, Sam had never been as close to anyone, apart from God. He listened attentively to anything he said, appreciating the reason they called him the wise man. His knowledge and wisdom stretched far beyond the common. It turned out to be a fantastic experience for Sam, who relished every minute with this source of constant learning.

A table, two chairs, the usual paillasse, and a long chest adorned Ben's room. Around the walls, shelves from floor to ceiling displayed books on any subject, kept in a particular order.

'If you want to read, come and help yourself, but when you

finish, put them back in their place.' That was all he ever asked of anyone who wanted to borrow them. In a section, Sam found volumes in many different languages. Wishing to learn Spanish, he borrowed a few.

Inside Lucy's head, unable to grasp the meaning of Sam's words about his "purification," ruled an endless confusion. He had asked her to wait, but she had waited too long for him to resume a normal relationship, to make her feel wanted and loved. The smoothness of the wall he had erected between them prevented her from climbing it. She understood to be the enemy of his goal, whatever that goal might be. Admitting a temporary defeat decreased her pain, along with the thought that after his "purification," he would go back to love her. While dealing with his rejection, she also filled her heart with hope.

I'm still the same person he loved - she thought piteously unhappy. *Perhaps even a better one because I sense that I've grown up.*

What Lucy had experienced during the three days locked in her room, although shocking, had unsealed a door to a life of new sensations. Ben's continuous potions had treated her body and her mind, where a curtain gradually lifted, revealing the person behind it. She needed time to find out who she had become.

The women took over Lucy and taught her to weave and make pottery. Every passing day, helped by the 'medicine,' she became more relaxed, learned Spanish words, and chatted with them. After a while, the chat revolved around their private lives and their prolonged stay. Alma, the youngest, spoke first.

'I had to... prostitution, very young. I not want that life. I hear of church. I run away. Here's my familia and pacifico life.'

'Sad. I'm happy you here. Me...' said Yesenia as her mood altered to an unhappy one, 'I escaped from village to hide. My mother, dos children, killed by "gringos" that wanted my outlaw husband. I knew of this place. I come to heal and save me life.' The woman's deep suntan and lined skin made her much older than her years. She betrayed profound pain, and the rest closed around her with a hug.

'Me, a tramp most of me vida. One day, time to root somewhere, belong to community. Here I find all, and more.'

'But what about men? Don't you miss...' asked Lucy.

'We don't need them! We are friends here. We work, laugh, and stay happy. Men are like brothers. But you married.'

'I might as well be by myself. Sam...' on the edge of a revelation, her voice quivered, and her eyes brimmed with tears. She stopped. Thoughts of Sam caused her suffering, more so for his refusal to provide a proper reason for his conduct.

Sam devised an excuse to keep away from her. Often, when Lucy's tempting advances became hard to bear, he went to sleep in the smaller room, saying he was studying. Lost in a sea of uncertainties, Lucy explained his actions by telling herself perhaps it was her fault if he did not love her any longer. Yet there were times when she read a different, unforgettable message in his eyes and hope. There was hope.

Samuel was about to embark on his journey, deeming himself ready for whatever the next few days had in store. Not wishing to face Lucy, before Ben's lingering embrace, he asked him to say goodbye to her.

'My last few words to help you with your quest: let your

eyes be like an eagle's, your heart like a lion's, and your hand steady so the arrow can travel to its target. Dreams are but a reality in disguise. Clothe them with your cloth. Peyote will give you the dreams. It is up to you what you make of them. Pedro will come to ferry you back in a week. Be safe, my son.' His voice shook as he pronounced the last sentence that faded into a mutter. Then he wobbled away as quickly as he could. Pedro was waiting for Sam.

'Did you forget your bags? I go and get them.'

'No. I have this,' he said, patting the pouch he carried.

'But you go to the desert with no food? Water? You die!'

'No, I'll live.'

Pedro launched him a puzzled look then a worried one, but he would faithfully follow Ben's instructions. Walking through the archway, Sam lifted his eyes to read the inscription on the stone above the door: "Search for the self."

I'm going to search for Samuel.

CHAPTER 8

The first light of sunrise found Sam and Pedro near the wide entrance of another canyon. They followed the bank for a while until they found a small boat covered by branches on a piece of stony ground. Pedro had two full water containers, Sam knew what to expect from then on, and as Pedro rowed in silence, he thought about Charon, who ferried the souls to Hell. Yet unlike the damned, there might be a chance of his coming back. As the sun climbed fast in the sky, they landed on the opposite bank. They left their transport under the shade of bushes.

'Come, Sam. We hurry.' They kept going for some time, leaving behind the lush vegetation to find a desolate plane where cacti alone survived. The heat became suffocating, and Pedro made him drink often. Ahead of them was a high rocky mass.

'We almost there. You can't see the cave now, hidden by shadows,' said Pedro. With straw hats and drinking plenty, the walk under the fiery sun was bearable. At last, they reached the cavern in the rock.

'I leave you. We drink first. I am back in seven days.' Sam asked him to take the water, and Pedro headed back, shaking his head and muttering to himself. He explored the deep rocky inlet that would be his home. Cold sweat and anxiety indexed how he truly felt, then thinking of Christ, he smiled:

He went through it all as a man, not as a God, and survived.

Sam intended to try until his last breath. He sat on a stone inside the cave in deep concentration until the contemplative mood came to an abrupt halt. His eyes set on the horizon – still indistinguishable due to haze and distance, and he watched the darkness spill into the light.

All of a sudden, Lucy's absence seemed to reach everywhere: a presence without sound, without life, until her face lengthened among the shadows of the cacti outside. He needed to be grateful to her, as a different way of life had forced him to discover the cracks in his vocation. On the once calm waters of his life, her tempestuous current had led him to land there, to find his true self.

He touched the scars on his forehead, and all came back: a twelve-year-old boy gazing at the crucifix hypnotised by Christ's crown of thorns. He wanted to experience *His* pain, to understand it, and to be close to Him. On his way back home from school, he had picked a few branches from a blackthorn bush, and shaping them into a kind of circle, had hidden it in the school satchel. At home, in front of the mirror in his room, he eased the crown of thorns on his head. While bearing the stinging pain, tears flooded his face, soon mixing with blood and dripping down on his clothes. The more he pushed the thorns, the closer he felt to Him.

At last, he screamed. His mother took him to the doctor, explaining it with a fall on a thorny bush. She was the only one who knew. When he told her the reason for what he had done, she cried with joy. Her son's future would be in the hands of Christ, and from then on, Sam belonged solely to Him.

As the night descended, Lucy's image faded into the desert's sunset. Sam regressed from his reverie. He found a niche in the rock and a stone with a flat top he used as a seat. He gathered several thick pieces of wood and chunks of dried cactus blown inside by the wind and lit a small fire. Ben made sure he took matches, as he would need protection from the cold and unwanted animal guests. Sam retreated to the niche, folded his poncho beneath him, and sat down with his back against the wall. He concentrated on the flames a short distance away.

Aided by the almost tangible silence, he cleared his mind of all thoughts, deposited some of the buttons beside him, and chewed them. His stomach refused the substance. He started to be sick but continued to chew until he took the amount Ben advised, soon slipping into a profound meditation. When his consciousness returned, the night appeared unusually black. Yet the sky sparkled with stars so close to him as to appear hanging on the hook of darkness. Sam fixed his eyes up there, where a giant white flower blossomed. Rainbows live with vibrations intermingled with giant trees and half-human animals in a speedy succession of running images unknown to him. He ate more cactus, visualizing horrid shapes. An odd sensation invaded him. Although grasping where he was, he experienced a disconnection between his physical and spiritual form. The latter now integrated with the vibrating rock. He then flew over enormous pure white spineless cacti, over sweeping seas, trees growing to outlandish dimensions, running at vertiginous speeds through the seasons before disappearing. After ingesting more peyote, he found himself staring at the monstrous apparition of a gigantic dog outside the cave with three heads and eyes of fire: Cerberus, who blocked the exit. Guardian of the gates of Hell, it never let anyone emerge from that dominion. Sam needed to get out of there, but the infernal being kept him, prisoner, inside the cave. The dog's blazing eyes began to grow out of its skull. They covered the opening with a curtain of flames, searching for Sam, now wandering in a blue and cold desert wearing a coat made of dust and gathering wood for the fire. A million faces in the sky disappeared in blazes of colours, but he felt safe inside an enormous plant.

The nightmares slowed down. Feeling very tired, he stretched on the ground halfway between the real and unreal world. Throughout the insensibility periods, his dreams came forth from a three-dimensional reality and weird planes of existence.

He woke up sweating profusely, hungry, and with sore bones. Shielding his eyes from the glare of daylight, he glanced at the small mound of ash. The heat around him increased steadily, along with his thirst. The sun in the heavens marked the time allowing new interpretations. Not a single thought troubled his hibernating brain when he reached for the cactus. The daily dosage kept body cravings at bay and helped his meditations. As the drug penetrated deep into his system, the visions became more frightening, with mind and body unaware of their surroundings. He woke from his profound, altered perception when darkness had fallen and returned to the material plane only to light a fire and follow the previous day's pattern.

On the positive side, his hallucinations decreased a little, giving him time to see and think better. To exit the cave was a priority, but Hell's mastiff still guarded the entrance. After three whole days between reality and fantasy, the three-headed beast's significance was clear: the past, the present, and the future. He wanted the dog removed to break free from his past and present life with Lucy. But what about the future? His only chance of fleeing from Cerberus lay ahead, on the path he had to travel to the end to triumph over human appetites. In his imaginary sights, he followed a Christ who seemed to shrink further away from him. Yet while the body weakened, his spirit freed itself of earthly burdens. The serenity he had chased for so long became the little beacon granting him to survive the ordeal he was undergoing.

On the fifth day, Sam did not react to the bite on his foot. When at night he tried to stand up and light the small fire, he collapsed in pain. Touching where it hurt, he felt the swelling on his leg, now unable to hold his weight. After chewing some buttons to soften them, he rubbed the pulp on the small holes before eating a much bigger dose. For a while, a sort of numbness took him over. Starting to 'see' the poison spreading in his blood, he invoked the Almighty to help him. Overpowered by a high fever, Sam slipped into unconsciousness, waking up at daylight, reflecting this could be the end, as now he did not feel like a human being.

Please, help me! Don't let me die like this. I want to be near You.

He was incapable of standing and unsure about the marks' origin. Sam made the cactus into pulp again and left it to dry on the punctures, eating the rest.

To defeat the fear conquering him became a priority. He had an idea of the passing time by using the sunbeams' shadow on the walls like a sundial. His life hung on a thread, and the following sunrise or sunset might witness his last breath on this earth. In the morning, the swelling and the pain escalated. His stomach ached, and he doubted whether his head was still attached to the body. One last dose left, then oblivion for Sam.

Imaginary demons surrounded him, attacking him frenetically. They tore his ears, pulled out his eyes, sniffed, hungering for his flesh, touching his body with lust, and their number continually multiplied. He felt helpless and overpowered by the tormenting fiends until he became aware of an incredible force. He believed to be standing up, fighting them like a heroic knight, but not with a weapon made out of metal. He held a sword in the shape of the only word that could save him, and between screams, he repeated – God! God! God! - Until he fainted.

Samuel came round feeling tossed to the other side of mysterious gates, towards an alien territory where few men ever roamed. It resulted in the uneasy thrill of one with a power unfamiliar to him. With tremendous effort, he succeeded in dragging himself to sit down. Cerberus had left the cave. Hell's gate now lay open in front of him.

Is it too late? Pedro. When is he coming? Perhaps I can make it. Or will he find a lifeless body?

He swallowed the last few bits of the plant and fainted.

Pedro arrived while the sunrise stretched on the horizon. When Sam's body came into view, with bones sticking out, eyes closed, and huddled motionless on the ground with a very swollen leg, the man thought he was dead. Sam remained unresponsive to his calls. Alarmed, Pedro checked his breathing staring at the ashen face underneath the redness of the exposure to the heat.

'Sam! I'm here with water. Do you live?' He shook him repeatedly without much hope. But then, a sound came from his cracked lips. Pedro kept calling him, pouring a little water in his parched mouth.

'Sam, not too hot yet.' Carrying the worn-out body in his muscly arms, he tried to hurry back to the boat. After laying him down, he rowed to where Ben waited with others to take him back to Wirikuta.

He sensed the shape of a room around him and hovered dimly on the rim of memory.

'A scorpion. As weak as you were, without peyote in your system and on the wound, you would not have lasted that length of time. I wasn't sure I could save you with my ointments and potions.' Ben stood beside him. Lucy held his hand and touched his forehead.

'You were unconscious for the whole day, son. The foot seems to be better. How are you? Ready for some of Yesenia's food?'

'I'm starving, and so thirsty! How did I come here?'

'Pedro found you almost dead. He carried you to the boat.'

'Why did you do it, Sam?' There was anxiety in Lucy's voice. Sleepless, with endless agitation, she had waited for his safe return, still needing answers to her questions.

'Perhaps some men must fulfil predestined lives. I had to find out for sure. Now, I'm at peace. I know where I'm going, Lucy.'

'Are you leaving?' she asked, worried.

'In a way. I have forsaken my old life. You might not understand it.'

She had not understood him for a long time, but it never seemed the right moment to ask.

Ben moved Sam into the small room to recover. In that silence, he began an introspective voyage, leading to a firm purpose. Early that particular morning, as Yesenia opened the window, he sampled a lungful of the chilled air, breathing in a bright, fresh world where he could now start over.

Lucy did not leave him throughout the days of his healing, during which time he kept a fixed frown. Now aware of a full recovery and seeing him walk in the room, she asked,

'Darling, when are you going to come back to our bed? Please,' she begged, but Sam knew he would never share a bed with her again. It was time to tell Lucy. It would be difficult to make her accept the facts. He sat on the chest, thinking, and she joined him.

'Let me explain. My feelings for you have changed to brotherly love. '

'Samuel! What are you saying? What do you--' she said with eyebrows drown together.

'Don't interrupt me, please. I must tell you what has happened to me.'

She touched his hand, and he pulled away.

'When I met you, I weakened and let the flesh take me over. It was wrong because I had given myself completely to God, and I betrayed Him. I lived with overwhelming remorse that tore me up inside. I trusted my love for you would be enough, but my vows started to persecute me, the vow of chastity, especially. My training taught me to discard sexual urges and believe in my body's total purity, a temple that God would favour. I grasped later that you filled a physical need taking me over. I went to the desert to find out about myself and to regain the innocence of the man I once was.'

'But I love you! We've children waiting for us. You're their father. Isn't that important to you?'

'They can have a mother now who is fit for them.'

'I'm confused. You mean to say that we aren't husband and wife any longer?'

'Yes, but only in spirit. Each of us must achieve his fate.'

'I can't do without you! I need you!'

'Darling, physically, you must let me go. I'm not telling you to stay if you don't want to. You decide. I'll never leave Wirikuta.'

'Don't you care for me at all? Not even a little? You *are* my husband, not a priest! Why can't we be together? I'm lost without your love. Let's live like a married couple again!'

'You don't understand. I can't blame you, but I can't go back on this decision, ever.'

'I'll try to find a meaning,' she said rushing away to hide her tears. His words hung in the air, then dropped on her like salt on an open sore. The wall between them had no aperture big enough to let her through to the other side. She ran to the river, where near the slow-flowing waters, she had often found inner serenity. Now deep thoughts swept her away.

He does not want me, does not love me, and never did. The truth is, he's married to a bible. The way he cherished it, how he stroked it, was I blind? That book has always been my enemy. I should have destroyed it from the start.

Her heart throbbed with agony. Her wailing lasted throughout the night as she tried to face reality.

Sam, asleep in the small room, did not hear her. With his emotions frayed at the edges, he confided in God to help her to understand.

Lucy's inner loneliness became unendurable. The ambivalence was tearing at her like a ragged blade. At first, she lost herself in a maze of doubts and questions: is *it my fault? Did I cause this to happen?* To which followed a throbbing silence, allowing her to assess her plight.

Sam. What shall I do without you? For you, I don't exist any longer. I am alone. I don't fit anywhere in your new life.

His words burned inside her like a flame. They avoided each other after his speech. Still, one last time, she needed to make sure before the inevitable outcome. When he went out in the garden with a basket, she followed him.

'Sam...'

He was kneeling to pick some vegetables, and her voice startled him. Standing up, he stared at her motionless, without expression, waiting.

'I can't go on like this.'

'Lucy, you must understand, my dear. Trust in God.'

Emotionless, he knelt again and went on picking the onions. First, she froze then reacted to his indifference.

'Why? Look at what He's done to you and me! He's taken your heart along with all the love for anyone else but Him. Look at me!' She was hysterical, shaking.

He continued picking. The love inside her exploded.

'I hate you, Samuel,' and she ran away.

Sam and Ben spent most of their time together. The man seemed determined to pass on to him all his wisdom and skills. The young man's eagerness to learn meant a partnership in unison, a perfect match becoming increasingly like an intimate father-son relationship. Once Ben asked him,

'Do you want to spend the rest of your life here? You might be bored and decide to leave.

'I'm going to tell you what Wirikuta represents for me. I've found my Shangri-La. That beautiful and mystical valley where people were immortal, remember? But if removed from their city, they immediately turned to dust. I believe if I ever left this enchanted place, my spirit would die as Wirikuta has absorbed it.'

'I know what you mean exactly. At my death, I'll be buried here and belong to it.

After the episode with Sam in the garden, Lucy worked even harder at weaving and pottery making. From her friends, she received some of the affection and comfort she craved and found courage in the peyote rituals. She was grateful to Sam because here, they had cured her drug addiction, and she had learned values and aspects of life once thought of as valueless. The calm sense of well-being in this blossoming new person now overrun the suffering and torment in her heart. *Who am I? What are my plans?* She thought, like a child waking up to the world for the first time.

Our past will hit him like a boomerang, and he'll spend the rest of his miserable life regretting it. I hate you, Sam. One day you'll beg me as I begged you. I'm alive. I love life, and I'm not going to live it here. The image of her children flickered in her mind. *I'm going back to be a mother.* She sighed, aware of a past she had to account for. With those thoughts spiralling in her head, she decided Sam and Wirikuta had to remain the dream she was stirring from, ready to face the world.

'I'm going home to our children. I'll never come back here.' Sam noticed her indifference.

'You'll be doing the right thing. I'm delighted, but don't destroy their life by telling them who their real parents are.'

'Not planning to just now. Perhaps when they are older. Goodbye! Enjoy your "fate" as I will mine.' Without another word, she turned to go, leaving a stranger behind.

'Wait.' He went to the chest, coming back with a packet.

'Here's most of the money we have. Take it, I don't need it but you do. It will be enough for fares and initial expenses. Will you manage the travel arrangements and...'

'Don't worry. I'll get there. Thank you.' She took what he handed her and left.

Sam knelt to pray for her.

Pedro attached a little cart to the donkey. Controlling her

emotions, Lucy said her goodbyes and hugged Ben. She took the same bag and clothes she had arrived with and began her long trip back, eager to leave behind the heat and Sam.

Speaking the language a little made everything easier. Once on her flight home, she briefly thought about her past life in Wirikuta. Haunting memories, worn clothing, and an old melted lipstick were all she had left behind. When the aeroplane landed, and she touched English soil, the winter wind brushed her face, and the drizzle welcomed her with its wet misery. She filled her lungs with that air, shivering with the cold but happy.

Everything's so different, so strange.

The taxi took her home, and, sure of herself and excited, she knocked at her grandfather's door. Since there was no answer, she headed to her flat. Would Harry still be there? Lucy hoped he had left, or she would tell him to find somewhere else to live. With the key in the lock, some images ran through her mind in quick succession. She hesitated. Then pushed the door open and froze. Filth reigned everywhere. Yellow and brown tobacco stains smeared the walls, and metal buckets overflowed with rubbish. Greasy papers, empty cans, bottles, and mouldy food mixed to cigarette butts, charred remains, and grey ash littered the carpet. An acrid and awful smell saturated the air making her want to throw up. She pinched her nose and stepped carefully onto that mass of trash, going to open the windows. Next, she walked away and locked the door, intending to wait on her grandparents' steps. Nervous about seeing the children again, her heart ached because of past actions. The idea of running away occurred to her, but as she stood up, ready to go, she heard voices.

Annie looked at her as if witnessing a ghostly apparition. The children's faces betrayed curiosity.

'Lucy, what are you doing here? Where's Sam?' she asked, minimally interested. Her words and gestures lacked any warmth.

'I'm alone. He stayed behind. Hi, kids!' Her voice shook.

'Belinda, Tom, say hello to your Auntie.' They obeyed, and she bent to kiss those lovely alien beings three and four years old. Once inside her grandparents' home, she noticed nothing had changed. Annie left her standing in the hall.

'I've been home, Grandma. Did you see my home? Where's Harry?'

'He died of an overdose two months ago, and I locked up the flat right away. I'm too busy with these two to look after and everything else going on.'

Lucy did not know. How could she? Sam and herself had never bothered to write, too immersed in sorting out their lives, too selfishly involved with their problems, without a thought for anybody else.

'Where is Granddad?'

'In the hospital, very ill, and they say he'll not last another week. I'm just back from there.' Again, only a cold indifference transpired from her words.

'I'll go and see him first thing tomorrow. I feel drained right now. Can I stay here tonight? I can't face my home again today,' she said, thinking of poor Harry.

'He made your room into a workroom.' Annie was relieved, she could tell.

'I'll go then. What's the name of the hospital?'

'St. Luke.'

It was apparent she was an unwelcome stranger, and after a last glance at the children, she went home. Lucy piled up some of the rubbish with a broom, closed the windows, and switched on the fire, but there was no gas. She spread a couple of towels on the floor from her suitcase and bundled up, fully dressed with her coat on. The thought of Harry's dead body in there terrified her. That whole place revived visions of a screaming baby, along with a life she had wanted to scrub away.

Granddad's likely death towered and lingered in her heart. He was the only person who cared and whom she had always loved. Unable to sleep, her frantic mind kept spinning towards dawn, making plans for the day ahead.

I'll see him first. Next, I will sort out this flat for the kids - they can come whenever they wish. My little children, so tall! In time we'll know each other, and I am not short of time.

She arrived early in the morning, and the nurse allowed her to see Mark. Approaching his bed, she felt a pang in her heart.

'Granddad! It's me, Lucy.' She kissed him and held his arthritic hand between hers. The lines on his worn-out face and the thinning hair made him older than his fifty years. To the sound of her voice, he opened his eyes.

'What are you doing here? Where's Sam? When did you arrive? Where have you been? Tell me, darling! I thought about you every day, but no news, ever!' he said feebly.

'I couldn't get in touch where I was; they cured me, and I'm here to stay. Sam's not coming.'

'I don't have long to live. Before I go, I must tell you.'

'You're going to be well, and it can wait. Now rest. I'll come back later tomorrow.'

When she bent to kiss him on the cheek, he murmured in her ear, 'I wanted to tell you for a long time. Don't go yet.'

'What is it?'

'Your mother... She didn't die in childbirth.'

Now her attention focused entirely on his words.

'What? What are you saying?'

'It's all my fault, Lucy. All of it! I'm bad. I don't deserve your love, or your children's.' His face showed distress. His voice became agitated and fitful. She remained silent.

'You're my daughter, not my granddaughter. And your mother...' A tear made its way from the corner of his eye, leaving a snail-like trail that vanished in his ear.

She observed the shiny streak spellbound, then let his hand drop as if it were burning coal before saying with a thread of voice,

'My... mother?'

'She... submitted to my perverse need... only once. You were born, and she couldn't help hating you. She didn't want you and gave you to us. She lived with a man for a while, and after his death, she disappeared. We never heard from her again.'

I'm his daughter. Is my mother not dead? Who am I? A shocking secret. Lies! All my life is a lie! Sam. He would look at me like dirt. Daughter of sin. Children of sin. All lies! The man on that bed is a monster.

She sprung up and strode away with his words trailing behind her.

'Never tell Annie, please, she never ...'

The world evaporated around her, now catapulted into a long black tunnel without exit. Trapped in this cold and empty space without light, she heard an echo repeating,

'You're nobody—a woman with a fake past and an artificial future. Your mother hates you. Your grandmother hates you. Your husband doesn't want you. The children are too young to understand, to have their fantasy world destroyed. You're nothing to them. Who loves you, Lucy? No one.

Her pain howled inside her, but she fought to remain in control, not to panic, not to break into pieces. She hurried in the street without direction, dizzy with her knowledge, preventing herself from crying.

At home, she sat sobbing for a long time, going over his words repeatedly. She rummaged in the past, remembering every detail, understanding the reasons for his and grandma's silence. The present ceased to exist until she saw Jean smiling at her, caressing her hair. Lucy felt her love, gained strength, and threw her past and present in the bonfire created by her mind. The future was waiting.

Far away. Oh, to be someone else! These gaping wounds will never heal. I have secrets to guard.

Her daily drink would be the poison Mark had left in her life.

That man! He will go to hell, leaving me to mine. If only Harry were here! The children? Pull yourself together, Lucy. For them, you will need to carry mountains of despair with a smile.

She started to clean the house in a frenzy. There still was a great deal of money in the packet, and she purchased presents for Belinda and Thomas, a settee, beds, and a cheap carpet. Lastly, she bought a bunch of flowers on her way to the graveyard. The caretaker found the little patch of the buried ashes and his name on a wooden cross. She stared at the dark earth for a long time, suffering.

'My only friend, I do miss you. If only you were here. Think of the good times we could have! Now we're both alone. Goodbye, Harry.' She scattered the yellow chrysanthemums on the ground - the only thing she left alive behind her.

To bring her home back to normal did not take Lucy long.

She plunged in that task with great impetus, but it was over too soon. Afterward, time trickled away. Each day her grandparents' unanswered questions surfaced anew. Those two people should have sunk in the swamp of their deceit. While searching for an elusive way out, she strayed in a labyrinth of self-torture. Lucy felt invisible, empty, trapped in her present. All her dreams remained sealed in a cell of her mind. Drying her eyes, she waited for a demon to exhale his last breath. Maybe then, her children's friendship could give her a reason for going on living. At that moment, she did not wish to have them around.

I need one of Harry's cigarettes, badly.

Haunted by the wish for drugs, she felt ill but ignored where to buy them.

For a whole week, Lucy stayed at home alone, anxious for news that would mean the end of her life and the start of another. Empty of all emotions except hate, she heard a knock at the door and motivated herself to open it: Annie stood there.

'I thought you might like to know that this last operation saved his life. He's not going to die after all. I need to go.' She disappeared, abandoning Lucy to a reality she was not able to face.

I must go away, far away, now.

Wasting no time, she booked tickets for the only place in the world where at least she could forget herself, but not without slipping a note under Annie's door with the address. Throughout her journey back, sinister visions of the truth stopped her from any kind of rest. Hate became a driving force. It filled her mind and her heart, sparing a small corner where her mother's life remained separate and dormant.

Part II

Bradford 1937

Behind the closed door

CHAPTER 9

Her eyes did not want to see. Her body did not want to feel. Her mind did not want to understand. She gripped the dark wooden headboard, where the roses she had attempted to paint as a child, although faded by time, were still visible. Then she was running on a golden field bursting with sunshine and flowers. The air vibrated with bird songs, and butterflies rushed to meet her. The wind whooshed through her hair and the smells of the earth - intense, moist, and warm, made her dizzy.

The pain brought her back to reality and forced silent tears to flood her pillow, but she was going to discard it on her meadow. The wetness on her neck and hair added to the one between her legs. She kept her eyes shut while he, getting up from the bed, hastened to put on his trousers, saying,

'It will not happen again, Rose. Now you know what to expect. Go wash up.

In slow motion, she heard the floorboards creaking under the weight of his bulky size as he descended the stairs, then the slumming of the front door. Apart from her aching body, the focal point in her brain was disgust. She tried to numb her once-clear conscience, now stained forever, telling her that she had allowed something wrong to happen with the man she had loved and respected. Naked and in a daze, she managed to negotiate the stairway, crossed the sitting room, and staggered into the kitchen. Rose opened the back door, unhooked the tin bath hanging on the outside wall, and plodded inside. Ignoring the hot water simmering in a big pot on the coal range, she got hold of the tin jug and half-filled the tub with cold water from the tap. Rose immersed herself in the freezing pool, shivering, and scrubbed her small and fragile body with the carbolic soap to a bleeding point. She was punishing Rose, who was not Rose any longer but someone she now hated.

I'll never hear his pleas again or see the torment on his face - finally over - she thought, striving to appease herself.

Her emotions demanded tears, but her eyes stayed dry. She stood up, overcome by violent and uncontrollable tremors, stepped out of the tub, and let the water run down from her body onto the grey stone floor. For a time, her gaze fixed on the dark stains slowly disappearing through small gaps on its worn surface, and then she climbed upstairs to her room. She suppressed her reflection in the mirror on the wall by concealing it with a large red scarf her mother had knitted.

Erase it, Rose. Bury that memory deep in the golden meadow.

She dressed, hiding beneath three layers of clothing, with her skin still wet, shaking. Without a glimpse at the defiled white sheet, she pulled the mattress down and stripped it. She lifted the box of scented talcum powder, dipped the feathery pad in the pure white dust, and shook it all over it before dragging it back on its metal frame. Wrapped in the quilt, she lay on the floor with her eyes closed.

The meadow. You are there. Look at the butterflies, at the blue sky. No darkness, only sunlight.

Almost afraid to breathe, fearful nights followed when she focused on listening to the opening of a door, to footsteps on the squeaky boards of the landing getting closer. Before laying down, she pushed the heavy blanket chest in her room in front of the door, and she did not turn off the oil lamp, scared of the dark as she had been when a child - a time that now seemed so very long ago.

CHAPTER 10

When fourteen and like so many others at the time, she had found a job as frame spinner at the Moorside Mills, twisting together drawn-out strands of fibres to form the yarn. The wool industry provided work for most of the population - men, and women alike, with extended hours and little pay.

Inside the mill, a vast, rectangular four-storey building of light bricks with a clock tower, all the workers wore green overalls, and the looms made a fantastic amount of noise. Rose's home formed part of a long terrace and distanced about one mile from her workplace. The small hallway gave access to the front room and a separate kitchen with a door to the walled backyard. Inside a brick hut, a wooden seat with a bucket underneath served as a toilet. That yard had witnessed many children playing, bleeding knees and sprained wrists. It cemented life-long friendships and encouraged shy kisses in the dark. Also, in the hallway, a steep stair led to a landing and two bedrooms. Ackroyd Street, where they lived, seemed endless to her, with blocks of uninterrupted housing on either side built of the same red brick. During the cold months, the smoke from the coal fires discharged by umpteen chimneys contributed to the smog drifting in the air. Still, the smell of freshly baked bread from the bakery nearby filtrated through it for a while. Her father laboured as a painter in the railway, while her mother stayed at home ironing other people's laundry. Their combined efforts ensured a paid rent, nourishing meals, and affordable clothing.

Betty worked beside Rose. They usually laughed and chatted during tea breaks - but that happened *before*. There was no laughter or idle talk any longer, not a twinkle in Rose's eyes.

Just a lasting depression. Her hidden agony fell like a mist on her pretty face, and people thought the world weighed on her young shoulders. It did. Her whole world lay shattered by the actions of a man who gave her life. No protest had been valid. No struggle or screams sufficient to stop him.

'Your mother must never hear of this,' he had said, hastening out of her room.

The younger men at work admired her looks. She was keen on one in particular. *Before.* Everyone's eyes now seemed resting on her, as if probing to unveil her guilty secret, condemning her.

'What's wrong with you? You're too quiet! You all right? You in love by any chance? I think he has the hots for you!' said chubby Betty, smiling and hinting with her head at the good-looking boy drinking tea during the break and talking to a male worker. Rose's face turned purple.

'Don't be daft. Not so. I don't give a chuff.'

'But you cared! What's new? You seem like another person!'

True. Once, the young man's gentleness, deep black eyes, and respectful manners had attracted Rose. *Before.*

'I'm not too well,' she answered, weaving in some truth.

'Go to the doc. Maybe you caught something that passes on. Keep away, ya germ breeder!'

Betty laughed, but Rose's expression did not betray any feelings. Betty's words did not affect her.

'He's so shy that one...a few of the girls would do backflips to catch his eye. Mary told me how hard she tried.'

Her friend expected her to show some interest, yet none came and sighing, Betty resigned herself to Rose's mood. However, only one girl occupied the mind of the young 'Handsome

John,' as the women called him, and a couple of weeks later, he dared to follow Rose on her way home.

'I cannot help watching you, Rose. You're so sad lately. Would you go out with me? Maybe on Sunday, for a walk? I like you a lot.'

She peeked at his face, at the unruly black curls on his forehead. His voice was sincere, and his hand reached for hers. She let him, in desperate need of someone to lean on.

'If you want, tomorrow, behind the church,' but her words lacked enthusiasm.

He nodded. They parted.

She opened and shut the front door quickly and heard her mother's voice.

'Rose, is that you?'

'Yes, mum.' She hung her coat and went to the kitchen, where a short, plump, black-haired woman in her thirties was preparing dinner.

'Your father will be late again. As usual, I'll wait for him. You eat.'

She sat at the table without a word pecking at the food, glad her mother was busy tidying up.

'I'm not too hungry, just tired. I'm going to bed.'

'Fine. Night.'

'Night.' She was trying to avoid her mother, not to meet her eyes, just in case...

In her bedroom, she undressed, dropping her black skirt and jumper over the small rocking chair- a gift from her parents when she was four - making sure it was out of her sight. She thought briefly about John with a cold heart.

Take it all in your stride, Rose, and never think.

She slipped her nightdress over heavy underwear then

   The Flesh and the Spirit

stretched on the carpet with the quilt up to her eyes. Her bed, now covered by a dark blanket, towered beside her like a malignant presence. Whether awake or asleep, she endured each day the invisible mass of her shame, and although exhausted from a day's work, her turmoil did not let her settle. What could she have done more to stop him? Alone in the house with him, no one to help or hear. *He* was supposed to love her. Love? A nauseating word now erased from her vocabulary. Another tormented night loomed ahead.

Behind the church, near the cemetery, her thoughts went to those people at peace. John was kissing her, holding her. Did he call her 'my darling'? Her lips did not respond. With arms limp at her sides, she kept still, a marble statue without a heart. Invited by her stillness, his hot and sticky hands wandered everywhere, searching.

'No need to be tense, Rose. I like you - the prettiest girl at work.'

His husky voice reminded her of *his* when… A glimpse of her "first time" drained the colour from her face. Her hands shook.

'No,' she said, pulling away from him, racing home as if the devil was chasing her, with '*his*' words still in her ears:

"*now you know what to expect.*"

Yes, she did, and she hated it with all her might.

When she started to vomit every morning, Rose had no idea of what was wrong with her until she revealed it to Betty at work.

'Oh my, sounds like you're pregnant! You been with that fella there?' she questioned in jest, pointing at 'Handsome John.'

Rose's face turned crimson, and the girl gaped at her. She found it hard to believe in that possibility. Both of them always agreed they would not have sex before marriage.

'Hellfire! Did you really? Is it true? Did you say anything at home? What you going to do?'

Very agitated, Rose implored her,

'Don't breathe a word to anyone. Keep it to yourself.'

'I understand. John's so gorgeous! My mouth is sealed, but soon they will guess.'

What to say? *Can I trust her*? She thought for a second. *No.* She could never tell, as the truth was even uglier now and impossible to admit. But was it true? Her friend interpreted the changes in her body already apparent: the rounder hips, the bulging stomach. Betty seemed sure. Soon on the girls' lips, Rose saw impish smiles. Some made rude gestures, and one of them even put a bag of wool on her belly under the apron, laughing. Rose hurried to the bathroom and vomited once more. One of the women had hung a mirror on the wall. After catching a glimpse of her ghastly face, she took stock of the situation. Only one way out appealed to her, as there would be no explaining to do, no humiliations to endure, or the birth of a baby to detest. She despised this seed growing inside her. This invader made her sick, sleepless, reduced her to a state of constant anxiety. There would be no lies to tell. It was the only solution, and she returned to work in a daze.

'Betty, I must go out right now,' she announced with a haunted air on her face, dropping the thread from the bobbin.

'What's wrong? You don't look well.'

'Got to go, tell the overlooker.'

Without another word, she went to take off her apron that fell to the floor. She ignored her coat on the peg and, insensitive to all, stepped out into the winter air. An icy wind gusted about her exposed neck, and driving rain soaked her long brown curls, drenching her. Still, Rose marched on, a small figure oblivious to all, swiftly following the path towards deliverance. With its dark clouds, the afternoon sky showed a hazy shape now part of the menacing scenery. She stopped on the bridge, high up from the tumultuous black waters below. No thoughts invaded her head. Calm, unafraid, inches from the tranquillity of mind and body, she lifted one leg onto the low parapet. Her heart drummed, her blood swirled like the rushing river - a deep breath, the other leg almost over, and an arm grabbed her, pulling her back.

'Rose! What on earth? You mad? Why do you want to jump?'

She held her gaze on him as if staring at a ghost and struggled to break free from his grip, anxious to grab the parapet, to dive into oblivion.

'Stop! Come here. Don't be a fool! I care about you.'

Why does he interfere? I'm nothing. I deserve nothing.

'I'm with child,' she said, without looking at him.

John took a while to recover from the surprise, then dragging her away from the railings, he asked,

'Did you tell the father? He'll marry you, I'm sure. All will be well.'

'He's married. I don't want this baby.'

'Rose, let me help you. I want to be your friend. We will sort it.'

Help. Friendship.

'I'll never want this child,' she uttered, shaking all over from the cold and her anguish. Worried she would slip away, he held her tight to protect her.

'A baby's always God-sent, and no one has the right to kill it.'

'I'll never want it. I hate it.'

'Then you could have it adopted. Someone will look after it.'

From his words, she received a glimmer of hope. Perhaps she could act upon them, see it through. Still quivering, she stated with indifference,

'I'll be your friend, if you want me.'

Happy to hold the girl of his dreams, the one he wanted close, he enfolded her in his arms. Once, his stupid attitude had made her run away, and he wished to make amends. He took Rose home, and as she inserted the key in the lock, he said,

'Go and warm up. I'll see you at work, love. Don't worry. It'll turn out fine, you'll see.' He smiled at her. Ignoring him, she opened the door and disappeared.

The young man went home with his mind and heart in a whirl, thanking Betty under his breath for telling him of her concern about Rose.

There was no time to waste, as she still breathed in the land of the living. A temporary 'thing' was invading her body, but an escape now seemed possible.

I'm going to make sure, she kept on thinking, ready to coerce him to accept. *That* day her soul had departed, leaving an icy shell, and unable to deal with her guilt, she determined to get rid of it.

Rose walked into the kitchen, where her mother was making dinner. She followed the movements of this simple, hard-working woman going about her tasks with almost mechanical actions. A dark blue housecoat protected her mother's clothes from spills and stains, and tortoiseshell combs held her black hair in place on the back of her head. In Annie's world, life was either black or white, with no shades or compromises in between. She focused on her motherly and wifely duties and personified respectability. She noticed her daughter's white face and peaked appearance.

'How's you lass?'

'Not too good, ma.'

Oh, mother! Don't ask me why I am pale, why I am so silent, why I hardly rest. I could never tell you.

Soundless words addressed to her mother that, if feeling alive, would have pierced her heart—this new person performed with difficulty even her daily chores. The sensitive, young girl that once existed had vanished forever.

'Eat first, then go to bed,' said her mother decisively, handing her a plate of mince and potatoes. She sat down but did not touch the food.

'What time is father home tonight?' she asked casually.

'Not long now,' her mother said with a glance at the cuckoo clock on the whitewashed wall yellowed by age and grease from the cooking. Her father now came home late at night, and she rarely saw him. Strengthened by her decision, Rose could wait. What would she say to him? Since *that* day, their eyes never met. She thought about what she intended to say. An unusual calm took over her tension, replacing it with a great sense of relief. Gazing at her mother, she was sure of the outcome.

'You picked a bad time to be ill! Your father wants me home, but yesterday I got work for six hours daily, early morning in the grocer's shop. I'm not having anyone tell me what I can't do. I start in the morning. You'll have to help more.' She said nothing.

The front door opened and then closed. He hung the coat on the hooks of the round hallstand, left the shoes, and went into the kitchen.

'Now then,' said Annie.

'Get kettle on,' he said to his wife, trudging in without looking at anyone.

'Take the weight off your feet. The Yorkshire puddings are in the oven.'

'Smells good, I'm famished,' he said, collapsing on a chair at the table.

Since the episode in Rose's bedroom, he never went near or was ever alone with her. That avoidance remained mutual.

'I'm not hungry just now. I'm going to rest.'

Getting up, Rose glanced at his bent head where the silver mixed to his black hair. He did not move. She went to her room, where since *that* day she had slept on the carpet.

Every night she traced the green and yellow leaves with her finger, counted the pink flowers' petals in the pattern, and waited for some rest. She sat on the bed as if a part of her, waiting for him. To become stronger and to reinforce her decision, she needed to experience his guilt as well as her own. Her memories came to life once again, with words branded on her mind, *'Come here, my darling...'* Sitting on the bed, he had taken her hand in his. She knew what he would say after hearing it many times during the past year. While growing up, she was also aware of the strange way he looked at her and the tremor in his hands whenever he touched her. Now his imploring words spoken in a murmur hunted her again, *'I need you so much.'* She would never forget the expression on his face at *that* time, one she had not seen before. There was sadness in his voice but later enjoyment in his actions, and Rose recoiled. She had adored, trusted, and confided in her father.

'I want you to recognize what a man's love is - the caring, loving way. You're sixteen and must learn before someone comes along to spoil it all for you,' he whispered.

'But it's wrong, isn't it? I'm afraid.' She implored him with tears in her eyes.

'In a way, it is. Why do you think I'm suffering? Don't be scared. I'm the only one who can teach you. You'll understand true love when it comes then. One day you'll thank me for this. I'm going to make you feel what love is. I'm doing this for you.'

'Why can't I learn from another man?' He took no notice of her innocent plea.

'Because it would be awful for you the first time, like for all women. It is for your good, to save you a lot of pain later.'

She almost believed him. He would not lie to her. But something made her rebel against it, to fight and scream and implore with all her might until, crushed under his weight, she laid still with eyes shut.

That Sunday at confession, she summoned up all her bravery to lighten her burden on God through His forgiveness. Her turn came.

'Father, three days ago... I couldn't stop him... I tried...''

'What happened? Tell me. Do not fear, only God's listening.'

'He...he...

'Who, my daughter?'

'My father...he did it to me...' she murmured, shaking.

'Are you saying that your father interfered with you sexually?'

'Ye...yes...' she was unwell now.

'What a terrible sin!'

In his voice, she detected shock, unbelief, and condemnation. The warnings and absolution had come with the recital of three

Holy Mary and five Lord Prayers. Yet Rose did not absolve herself. She vowed never to set foot in there again, as Father Luke's words about the "terrible sin" resounded in her mind.

I'm going to be free at last, she repeated like a chant, to gather courage. She was about to call her father to come up.

Downstairs, with dinner over, while doing the washing up, Annie said to Mark,

'Go up and ask her how she is. I think she's got the flu.'

'You go. I need a rest.'

'So do I, and you'll not lift a finger to help,' she said, hinting at the pile of dishes that needed tackling.

He obeyed and plodded upstairs, not wanting or daring to go in. His daughter's room was out of bounds now, and the thought she might tell someone terrified him. Outside her door, with the head against the doorpost and short of breath, he knocked lightly.

This unexpected sound startled her, and she managed to say,

'Come in,' her voice reached him loud and clear.

'Are you alright?' he asked on edge, opening the door and leaving it wide open. Rose was sitting on the bed, but before he could utter a word,

'Sit down!' she ordered in a harsh voice, unlike her own.

'I'll stand here. Your mother asked me...'

'I'm pregnant.' A long, silent pause, then his face turned scarlet, and he shut the door.

'Who? Does he know? How long?'

'You know it all. It was made on this bed, remember?'

'You crazy? You're lying.' His voice trembled now. 'Who is the father?'

'It's yours. I don't want it.'

   The Flesh and the Spirit

'It can't be true.'

'No lies. No more. I want nothing to do with this. It's all yours.'

'What do you mean?'

'I would kill it if I could. I tried to, but I failed. You will have it.'

'How did you try? Don't you know that it's a mortal sin to kill an unborn child?'

'And what you did? Is that not a sin?' "*...a terrible sin...*"

'What about your mother? She will never agree. We can't do this,' he said with a pleading voice.

'You'll make her take care of this baby or I shall tell her.'

'She wouldn't believe you.'

'We'll see. Call her now.'

'No! Promise you'll never tell.' His agitation caused his hands to shake.

'As long as you'll do what I ask, no one will ever know.'

'You give me no choice.'

'You didn't give me one either,' she said, adding, 'I loved you too much as a daughter. I'll never forgive myself for it.'

'Rose, it was for you,' he said humbly.

'Well then, this is for you,' she replied with irony touching her belly, in command for the first time.

'To sort it out, I must think of something for your mother. You tell her you're having a baby. For the rest, you got to invent a man.'

'I've already thought of that,' she said coldly.

'Who?' he asked, disconcerted.

'My business.'

The inflexibility in her voice surprised him.

CHAPTER 11

Retribution day. For the first time, he felt almost remorseful. To tell his wife about her decision and that the baby's father - Rose's boyfriend - wanted nothing to do with the child was not going to be an easy task. Annie would insist on talking to the boy, but he needed to make her believe that, after speaking to him, the outcome yielded no hope. His reasons? That he was too young. It would ruin his life, and he earned just enough to feed himself. Mark told her the man was adamant about his resolution: a truly hopeless situation. It was clear no one could do or say anything to make him change his mind, and he did not wish to talk about it ever again.

'Your daughter doesn't want any part in this birth. She hates this baby. We must take care of the nipper, Annie,' he pleaded in a resolute tone.

'You can't be serious. I don't want to hear it! My child-rearing days are over. That girl is a sinful and heartless bitch. We can have it adopted.'

'She is our daughter. We cannot abandon her.'

'I can't even bear to look at that brazen hussy now. I'll have to put up with the whispers of the whole neighbourhood. She's a black stain, Mark, one that will take a very long time to wash out, if ever.'

'Let folks talk. I don't give a jot.'

'But I do! To forgive her and for everyone else to forget, we can't keep a constant reminder. There's my job to think about, and I have plans for the future too.'

Silence fell, then staring at her, he said,

'My mind is made up. We'll keep the baby. After all, it is our grandchild!' The stubbornness in his voice conveyed to her a final decision.

'Never!' said Annie, banging the pot she was holding on the table.

'Don't make me do...destroy our family. Can you, just once in your life, do as I ask? I'm determined, no matter what the cost. Give up your job. I'll work longer hours. There's plenty to do.'

His wife paled, and her hands shook when she brought them up to her face saying,

'What would you do?'

He did not answer.

'My wishes don't count, do they?' she said.

'Not this time.' He knew that, from then on, his married life would never be the same again.

CHAPTER 12

The two of them went out often. Rose's plan gave John peace of mind and relief from his worries, knowing the extent of her hate for this unborn child. He tried his best to reassure her, and when holding her hand, he hoped that through that single gesture, he could make her understand just how much he cared.

She began to appreciate his solicitous manner whenever she felt sick at work. As a treat, he brought her empire biscuits fresh from the bakery. He took her home every day and did all he could to encourage her to be less severe in her outlook.

'Don't get worked up. You'll see, all will be well in the end,' he always repeated.

At home, her mother ended up ignoring her. Mark was hardly there now, working overtime just to be away from the resentment of his wife and his daughter's intimidating presence.

As Rose's condition became evident, she suffered the whispers around her and understood everyone labelled John as the father.

Poor man! He is the scapegoat, she thought, *and without even agreeing either.*

He let people believe it, hoping to stop the gossip.

'Don't worry. It doesn't matter what people think. It will pass...' his soft and tender tone became her soothing balm. She never detected any accusations or judgment, only understanding her predicament and his wish to help her.

'Look at her, Miss Proper. You'd think butter wouldn't melt.'

He heard the comments at work and turned to them with a reddening face.

'Let her be! She's worth ten of you!'

The girls hushed up, but as soon as he turned his back, the gossip started again,

'Look at him, besotted.' one whispered.

'Not as guilty as she's, of course, with him a man and a handsome one at that,' said another.

Not one girl spared a sympathetic thought for Rose, as they believed her to be John's steady girlfriend, which stirred a jealous wave among them. The only one who spoke to her was Betty, who never knew Rose's reason for leaving in such a hurry that day. She was not the prying kind. She waited for either of them to tell her.

Rose succeeded in keeping her meetings with John a secret. He took her to the cinema and for walks, held her hand, kissed her on the cheek and the young man fell in love with the quiet, petite and lovely girl who never smiled. Her face was as beautiful as the statue of the Madonna in the orphanage. He worried about her and determined to see her happy, to force out the deep sadness in her eyes. John never dared ask her any questions about the child's paternity, understanding her unwillingness to explain or to talk about it. He also ignored her intolerable situation at home.

The air in her house was thick with Annie's and Mark's silence. Annie did not hide her contempt for her daughter or the anger for her husband's selfish and unbending decision. The ebb tide of pain had washed away Rose's feelings. Since *that* time, she faced life with indifference and apathy.

Seven months later, after a difficult pregnancy, she went to the hospital as an emergency. They advised her about the dangers of this birth.

'We shall have to remove your womb. There might be

complications. '

'Do you mean I might die?' She hoped.

'My dear, we cannot foresee what's ahead. Try not to get upset.'

'I'm not worried,' she asserted, emotionless.

'There will be intravenous anaesthesia. The operation will not be painful, as we're putting you to sleep.'

They took her to the operating theatre. Two doctors and three nurses waited, plus the anaesthetist, who fixed a mask on her mouth.

I don't want to wake up, was her last thought.

As the effect of the anaesthetic decreased, her suffering increased. She was sick a few times and then heard a male voice.

'It's a miracle. The baby's fine. A girl, she weighs 4 lb, small but perfect. The bad news is that you will not be able to have any more children.' The sympathetic tone of the doctor reached her from the fog in her brain. He was holding her hand.

I'm still alive.

'I don't care,' she replied without any reaction.

The nurse came in, pushing a trolley with the tiny bundle in a small glass cot connected to a machine.

'Look at this beautiful girl. Congratulations!' she announced.

'Take her away! Give her to my parents,' she said without even a glance. 'They're adopting her.'

Speechless, the nurse gazed at the doctor.

'Don't you even want to see her?' he insisted. But Rose's words still hang in the air, and she turned her head to the wall.

A wasteland inside Rose's heart prevented her from any emotion. She dealt with all the thoughts in her mind through rejection, relieved her body was again her own. Soon any external trace of the pregnancy would be hidden away and disappear under her clothing.

No, you must never cry. You're strong. It never happened. Go on living until you die.

She needed to remove herself from the pain, to disassociate from that place. Hence, she emerged on her beautiful meadow, chasing the pure heart of her childhood. She ran and kept running until the smell of the earth mixed with the one of a hospital room, the songs of twittering birds with a beeping noise, and the blue sky became a white ceiling. In an attempt to escape her surroundings, she rose in agony from the bed and collapsed on the floor.

When John arrived, Rose's pallor and stern countenance cut him deeply. She had been and was going through a great deal. Everyone in the ward knew of her wishes: no visitors throughout except him.

'How are you feeling? How's the baby?'

He put some grapes on the bedside table, then took her hand in his stroking it gently, waiting for an answer.

'All fine,' she said before he asked.

'When are you going home?

'I can't go back home. I don't want anything to do with the two of them,' she vowed with determination.

'Let me think about a solution, Rose.'

At last, John's search for affordable accommodation brought him to the house of a middle-aged owner, Mrs. Hirst, who laid down the law right away.

'For a while, you say? Until you and your sister can rent two separate rooms. No pets, and no guests to stay until late. I hope you will both appreciate how lucky you're here. My husband added the bathroom on the landing with the cold water and even hot from the fire back boiler downstairs. He converted the loft, but there is no water. You must bring it up from the bathroom and wash the dishes in there. Clean up after yourselves. I've included the electricity in the rent. Mine is a reputable home in a decent area. Make sure she behaves. I shall count on you paying weekly without delay. Does it suit you?'

'Fine Mrs. Hirst. Thank you.'

'I will let you be if you don't bother me. All we share is the stairs. I use the bathroom after you've gone in the morning.'

He gave her the deposit right away and went to see Rose with a hopeful heart.

'I... asked the landlady if my sister could come and stay with me for a while - his face was on fire as he spoke - until she found something else. She agreed as long as I give her more money. Is it all right with you? Do you mind sharing a room with me? With both our wages, we can pay for it and afford to live.'

'Thank you.' The icy cold tone of her voice could freeze anyone's caring heart. He worshipped her, but since that time behind the church, he sensed something wrong and was scared to touch her. Perhaps by living together, she would get used to him and maybe someday love him. He ignored whether she cared for him at all. Rose looked tired, and although wishing to remain longer, he cut his visit short.

I am not coming home, she declared in a note to her parents. *I'll be back at work as soon as I can to help him pay for our place. I have told the doctor about the adoption, and you can go and collect her. They'll let you know when. I don't ever want to hear about this child or from you,'* she added, knowing they

The Flesh and the Spirit

would try to convince her to keep the baby. The love for her mother was intact, but she would never go back on any of her decisions. The inner metamorphosis that took possession of Rose placed her father on a level far below contempt.

When John arrived at Rose's house to collect her personal belongings, he found them gathered in one half-broken suitcase on the steps. On the top was a note:

'Leave an address. We might need it.' He knew Rose would disapprove, but thinking about the child, he scribbled it in a hurry, left it in their post slot, picked up the case, and brought it to the room ready for them.

A week later, the hospital discharged her, and he took Rose to their new home, hoping she would be pleased with the accommodation. Her expression of indifference did not change when she walked into the room. A glance around without a word and a glimpse at her bag on the bare floorboards was enough.

'Do you like it? All we can afford but a peaceful place.' He said humbly.

'Right.'

Expecting nothing more from her, he did not resent the curt answer. John had found the two single beds joined when he had moved in a few days before. He had separated them to comply with Rose's unspoken wishes, that by now, he understood.

The week after moving in, she received a short letter from her parents to inform her they had called the baby Lucy.

How did they find out where I am?

John did not mention the note he had left, afraid it would upset her. She flung the piece of paper in the refuse bucket where her past belonged. Then she forced her guilt, remorse, resentment, and self-hate back into her private hell.

The work in the mill was demanding for both of them. Besides, since Rose's co-workers' questions remained unanswered, it caused all sorts of malignant speculations, and they shunned her.

She cooked their frugal meals in the room on two electric rings. The aroma of food lingered in that space, clinging to the bare, dark wooden-panelled walls, rafters, and floor. While cooking, she kept the door to the landing open wide, as the two windows on the ceiling remained permanently sealed. Without heating in the room - that they would not be able to afford, both looked forward to the warmer season. A night's rest after the long working day became all they needed.

Three months went by, during which time the landlady asked a few times about John's "sister" finding accommodation,

'I would prefer she moved out. You might give people the wrong impression.'

'Mrs. Hirst, my sister did not find a place she can afford by herself. Her wages are not enough. Where can she go?'

'Have you no family?'

'We are orphans.'

'Well, I keep no heart to throw her out. She can stay. Such a quiet, nice girl.'

Rose's state of mind seemed improved a little. Still, when she washed or dressed in the bathroom, her fingers traced the line of the large abdominal scar in the tarnished mirror, reminding her of what she longed to forget. Then the hate she had managed to keep under control acquired a life of its own: for *him,* for herself, for father Luke, and the prayers he told her to recite to purify and absolve her soul, but what about her body? Above anything, she wanted it as pure as it had been. The future now did not hold exciting promises. The only dream she remembered recurred every night: an image of herself running on a golden meadow.

Nevertheless, no flower blossomed there, the butterflies had vanished, and heavy black clouds chased each other in a stormy sky. An icy wind pushed her into racing fast. Exhausted, unable to go further, she threw herself on the ground, anguished, touching her big belly, trying to get rid of it through her breathlessness.

When awake, she could recall every detail. Then the pain throbbing inside her wanted to emerge, to sensitize her to what she refused to acknowledge. She never let it happen and suppressed it with the tears she could not shed - in the deepest part of her.

She came out of the baker shop and froze. Her mother was crossing the road pushing the pram. Panic-stricken, she rushed to hide inside the grocer. Annie parked the child outside the butcher and went in. Her first instinct told her to leave, but something stirred in her heart, now beating furiously, and she approached the pram. Rose stared at the lovely little creature with a soft pink bonnet, asleep with her tiny hands at the side of the head. A few instants seemed an eternity. She hurried away, about to choke from the knot in her throat. That image stuck to her mind, impossible to dismiss, and as time passed, she hoped for a new casual encounter. There was even a temptation to... no! Going too close to her mother's house would be dangerous.

Forget she exists. It's the only way you can survive.

When John was ten years old, the nuns gave him a violin donated by a former musician. He showed a great interest in music during services. After this gift, he never wished for anything else. That instrument became his life, his friend, his companion from the beginning. Being a perfectionist, he practised with passion for years. The results had transformed screeches into soul-filled pieces of exceptional quality.

When he played in their room, each sweet note seeped into the darkness of Rose's soul, then the fear and self-loathing for the past trapped inside her abated a little, bequeathing some peace. He played whenever he could. His deep black eyes fixed on her face as if trying to penetrate her impenetrable shield through the vibrating chords and the echoing melodies.

They were unique moments for them both. They brought John dreams of how it could be if she loved him. He imagined her pale naked body close to his, the music and all the love inside him cascading on her, washing away her torment. He never saw her undress. Rose always took her clothes off in the dark or the bathroom.

'Good night John. Sleep well,' she said, freeing her long, curly hair from the combs she used to keep it in place and turning the other way.

'Good night Rose. Rest well,' he answered.

More often lately, mostly when she slept, his thoughts wandered,

'Oh, Rose, what would it be like to hold you, to exchange kisses, to touch you?'

He would fall asleep with these images. Nonetheless, afraid of Rose's reaction to any affectionate gesture, he tried to reject his need of her as a woman and concentrated on accepting friendship alone.

One night, the moonbeams cascaded into the room through the window above her bed made her glow with unearthly beauty.

Rose's hair spread on the cushion like a mandala. He lingered on the small, still face in the centre - now white and perfectly etched in a cameo fashion. He progressed to the delicate neck and uncovered shoulders. She was sleeping as restless as ever, and he felt compelled to be near her. With his heart beating fast, he went to kneel on the floor beside her bed. He touched her lips softly and listened to her irregular breathing, mesmerized by the scent of her skin, adoring her very presence. She woke up and, with a scream, darted to the furthest corner of the room, where she crouched down, shaking.

'It's me...don't be afraid,' he murmured. 'I just wanted to caress your face, to mix your breath with mine. Come to me, please.'

His words were incredibly tender. Rose ignored his outstretched hand, but when he sat on her bed, the moonbeams that engulfed him worked their magic. She shuffled towards John, slowly unsealing the door to mysterious sensations. She needed to be safe, someone to hold her, and kneeling, nested herself in his arms. He enclosed her in to protect and shield this fragile girl from her unrelenting, gnawing feelings. Reassured by his closeness, when she lifted her head to him, she was ready. He slowly removed her nightgown and held her naked body with love and anticipation, prepared to stop if she wished. John and nature released human responses imprisoned inside her, setting her free in a foreign dominion. There she discovered physical reactions to his soft touch and understood she could not control them by willpower. His caresses did not cause her to shrink away like their first time. She let him kiss her, anticipating what she expected - pain, disgust - although willing to submit to please him. His warm lips brushed her neck, her ears.

'Love me forever, Rose, as I will love you.'

She closed her eyes, not running but gliding on that meadow where his breath was thawing her senses - and the flame of passion melted the ice in her heart. Rose's movements responded to his. She opened her eyes and caught a glimpse of his face irradiated by the moonbeams, captured all the love it expressed.

'John, yes,' ' she whispered, enfolding him in her embrace. She exchanged his kisses, surging under him and relinquishing mind, body, and soul into his to be one forever. They tasted the Gods' nectar in their union, and its sweetness lingered, inebriating both. Her pillow moistened with tears of relief, joy, and life-giving pleasure.

CHAPTER 13

'Are you home, my love?' He was trying to hide the surprise from her.

'No, it's a ghost. It made tea as well.'

'It must be a good cook. I could smell it all the way home!'

'You silly man! Don't exaggerate. Today, it could only afford a little mince, potatoes, and onions!' Laughing, she went to kiss and embrace him.

He kept the hands behind his back.

'What's wrong? Don't you want my kisses?'

'Well...I've something better for you.'

'Better than my kisses? Never!'

'You might change your mind,' he said, closing her hands on a box of chocolates.

'Are you mad? They're expensive.'

'I thought of your sweetness and couldn't help myself.'

'I forgive you. Nice to eat these in bed tonight.'

He saw the twinkle in her eyes. Her love was real.

Months of carefree days soon passed, filled with laughter, the energy of their bodies, the warmth in their hearts, and the pleasure of intimacy.

'I want to see you laugh, to see you happy. You're my whole world. Will you love me forever?'

'Forever my John, plus another forever,' she said, her eyes sparkling with love, hiding the ever-present sadness. Her happiness could never be complete. A little face in a pink bonnet haunted her, reminded her, and tortured her. But she learned how to smile, at least with her lips, stepping on the shore of her youth again.

'Rose, let's go dancing tonight! The church has organized it. We'll have fun!'

'What? I...'

By now, he knew how to dispel her doubts. Taking her in his arms, he quickly kissed her face all over,

'Say, 'yes John, I will go because I love you,' then he knelt as if praying. 'Please, my lady.'

She laughed.

'All right, you mad man, I'll come!'

That evening, she became the young girl of the past again. He was her miracle, the only joy she had ever known. They just aimed at pleasing each other.

'I like to bury my hands in the curls of your hair, so soft!'

'And I to feel them. I like it when you touch my face.'

He always traced the contours of her face as if to imprint them in his fingertips and inhaled the pleasurable scent of her sweaty body after making love. John wanted to see her happy and to hear her laughter.

I must find a way to remove the misery still in her eyes

'We'll take the train and go to Filey on Sunday, we'll have fun on the beach, and then we'll have fish and chips and ice cream in The Ice Parlour. What about it? A whole day away from here!'

'Let's go! Let's go!' She clapped her hands like a child and kissed him.

He had often worked overtime to make this happen.

Their loft conversion showed the rafters and contained nothing beautiful or cosy. Natural light brightened it through two small square roof windows when the sun shone above them. The shortage of furniture emphasised its size and bareness. The furnishings included necessary basics: a couple of chairs, a rickety wooden table, an old oak wardrobe with a collapsing door, a metal table with an electric two-ring cooker on top, and the two iron-framed single beds. Yet to them both, it was a peaceful haven. Rose made it brighter by the daffodils she picked in the field on her way home from work or by the wildflowers during a walk or the holly branches with the red berries that she hung on the walls.

On their first Christmas together, she gave him a new shirt, and he bought her a box of watercolours, as she had mentioned how much she loved painting as a young girl.

'Thank you, John.' Words pronounced with a deep sadness shining in her eyes.

She was no longer that girl. He could not understand her reaction but avoided any questions, waiting for Rose to tell him whatever raged inside her.

One day, during John's overtime, she took the box and placed it on the table. She stared at it, almost afraid to touch it, while the past came streaming back. A twelve-year-old girl held a pastry brush, dipped it into a tumbler of water, into red powder, and painted miniature roses on her wooden headboard. Since the watery combination kept running, learning by her mistakes, Rose had wiped it out, starting anew. The petals then acquired a shape and formed flowers in full bloom, adding colour to her straightforward child's room and life. Later on, they had witnessed...

No! *John, my darling!*

She poured some water in a glass, but her hands shook when she opened the paint box and held the paintbrush. A piece of white linen torn from an old sheet became her canvas where she began to trace roses like those she had painted once at home. When she tried to recapture the blooms of her childhood, her tears fell freely, purged and liberated. By mixing with the pinks, reds, and greens, they diluted the intensity of the shades. In the end, she finished her artwork.

John, I love you.

He was her escape.

Rose stuck the painting on the dark wooden panelling, and the whole place gained an airy and light appearance, almost as she felt - *almost.* That black area inside her remained unreachable, an everlasting fight between love and hate, veiling memories that would never lessen or disappear.

A newborn baby carried away, an image impossible to erase.

My John, you're my life. I can't hide the truth from you any longer. In your eyes, I read the questions you don't ask. You must know.

When he arrived, he spotted right away the difference in the room. Above all, in the woman who kissed him hard on the lips with a sparkle in her eyes. The future with his "flower" now seemed even more beautiful.

Today marked a particular occasion: John's birthday and Rose took a day off. He would come home earlier, knowing she waited for him. By saving a little money every week, she had enough to buy him a present at last. She would purchase the Swiss waterproof watch he liked, but could not afford to buy. Rose stopped outside the jeweller's shop a little apprehensive, searching inside the sparkling glass window. It was still there. Without hesitation, she pushed the door, and the unexpected sound of the bell startled her. A man appeared from the back of the room and stared at her, surprised. Judging from her clothes, this attractive young girl did not seem wealthy. When she showed him what she wanted, he became uneasy.

'It is an expensive item. Are you sure? We've some cheaper versions.'

'No. That's the one I want. I saved a long time. How much is it? I need it engraved too.' He did not have the heart to charge her the total amount. His conscience prevented him, and he was sure she could not afford it. He thought of his daughter in a similar situation and decided to sell it to her at a cost price.

'I tell you what I'll do. I will give you a discount on this lucky day! I have the engraver in the back room. Is it a gift? I'll wrap it up for you with gift paper. How's that? The engraving will not take long. What wards would you like?'

She told him.

'Thank you. He'll be so pleased, I'm sure. It's his birthday. You're very kind.' She just managed to pay for it. Her radiant face filled the man's heart.

Rose thought about John at the sight of it and smiled. As an extra treat, she stopped at the butcher for two pieces of tender meat on the way home. She then thought of her new dress from the cheap clothes retailer around the corner, hanging in the musty old wardrobe. John intended to go to the cinema after dinner.

How beautiful life is!

She had also planned another special surprise.

I don't want secrets between us, and I will tell him the truth. Knowing will answer his unspoken questions.

She hoped it might even alleviate the heavy burden she carried alone and maybe shed some light on her dark places. She needed to tell her sweet, wonderful man the whole truth.

I'm sure he'll understand.

She glanced admiringly at the silver ring on her finger with a little blue gem. John gave it to her a few days earlier during a romantic walk. He seemed uncomfortable, but she was familiar with his shyness.

'Let's rest for a while,' he said, taking her by the hand to sit on a bench.

With his eyes fixed to the ground and his ears turning a deep scarlet - as it always happened when embarrassed - he managed to say,

'Rose, would you... will you marry me? Next month if you agree. I don't want to live in sin.'

Her response was immediate. She knew that his religious upbringing was the reason for the way he felt.

'Oh, John! There's nothing I want more than spending my life with you. I love you so much!' She kissed and embraced him passionately.

'We can't afford a church wedding, my sweet. Only a simple ceremony in the registry office. I'm sorry.'

'All the same,' she said, happier to know that it would not be an option.

John was an orphan brought up by the nuns from the age of four. The faded mages of his parents' consisted of his father's head bent on the cobbler's last and the dull sound a small hammer made when hitting the leather. Then the softness of her mother's voice when putting him to bed and the roughness of her hands from the washing of other people's clothes piled up in a basket. She pinned her very long black hair at the back of her head, and in summer, she washed and dried it in the sun. Its silky sheen still lived in his touch and his eyes. After his father's death, John had witnessed her endless tears, a sad face, and a constant cough. Both parents had died of tuberculosis at a year's distance from each other.

During his mother's illness, a kind and needy neighbour with four children took him in for a while, but the orphanage became his home after her death. At the age of fourteen, the nuns moved him to a tiny room of his own, and he started to work in the mill. He paid for his keep and saved the rest, which he used later as a deposit for their accommodation. The oversized loft room a short walk from the workplace in the two-storey, semi-detached red brick house suited them well.

John's timid nature had not changed growing up. When the time came to justify his "unholy" conduct to the nuns, he found it awkward and embarrassing. He decided it was easier to withhold some of the facts: about the baby and cohabiting with Rose. He also explained to them the impossibility of a church wedding, as they would spend their money more wisely. He did not like the lies, but she came first in his life, and he was doing all he could to protect her name.

She hurried home, with the precious little box inside her handbag wrapped in gold. She left a loving birthday note on the small and rickety wooden table, now covered by a white cotton cloth on which she had embroidered a red poppy. A piece of paper folded a few times and placed under the leg stopped it from wobbling. Two red candles inserted in eggcups and red napkins gave the table a unique romantic air. Rose started to warm up the electric rings, as they took a long time to come on. Soon, he would be home, and she wanted the meal ready. The gift was in her bag, prepared for him after dinner. She savoured the effect.

A quick change into her new light blue dress, an old overall to avoid splashes, hair tied with a white ribbon: the image in the bathroom's mirror pleased her. She browned the beef, leaving it to simmer in the gravy. Potatoes and carrots boiled in the pot, and she sliced a fresh loaf. Rose checked the clock on the wall, wondering why he was not there yet.

Half an hour later, her worry and unease grew into a panic. The food was cold. She grabbed her coat, ready to rush out with a horrible suspicion when, on opening the door to the landing, she found Betty about to knock. On her friend's face, she saw the sign of a tragic event.

'Rose...' she began

'Where's John? Did something happen to him? Where is he?' Still standing in the doorway, she screamed these words in her agitation while her stomach coiled like a spring about to release itself with force.

'Come and sit down.'

'Tell me! Where is John?'

'Go inside,' and she pushed her in, shutting the door behind them, but Rose remained standing there.

'I'm so sorry… so, so sorry!'

'Where's John? Tell me, or I'm going to the mill right now!'

'He was caught in the new machine at work.'

'How bad is it?' Her legs began to give way. She grabbed the door handle.

'He died almost immediately.'

Everything went black around her as she fainted. Betty put a cushion under her head, made her sniff the strong vinegar from the little bottle beside the cooker, and rubbed her nose with it.

'Rose! Wake up!' She called in a panic, shaking her.

She came round dazed, and in a tone precluding any arguments, she said,

'I'm going alone.'

Before her friend could prevent her, she had dashed out, and her hurried steps resounded on the wooden staircase.

At the hospital, she met some people - nameless people telling her she could not see him, not now, not yet. Rose was unstoppable.

'What happened? I want to know,' she calmly asked the doctor.

He looked at her pale and unemotional face.

'The accident took place while he installed a new piece of machinery. A chunk of metal fell on the back of his head - very sharp, very heavy. He could not survive.'

The man omitted to tell her that the object had almost severed John's head. He decided to spare her that knowledge, as the bandages were hiding the truth. She listened silently without tears or feelings, with the same numbness already experienced in the past.

'Can I be alone with him?' she asked in a harsh tone.

I need one last time

'Sorry, not allowed. Someone will be there with you,' the doctor answered before a call on the internal phone.

A porter came to guide her. The lift took them down to the basement, opening on a bare white-walled corridor. Without a glance or a word at her, he walked ahead, but from the sound of her heels on the tiled floor, he knew she was following him. When they entered the mortuary, her hands became uncontrollable. Her face turned as white as the sheet spread over the body on the trolley. On tiptoes, noiseless like a shadow, Rose approached the indistinct form.

Was it him? Could it be her John under that cover?

The porter surveyed her seemingly impassive face while uncovering his head. Strands of black hair stuck to his forehead, making a strange pattern. With the tip of her finger, she touched his cold brow and pulled the hair aside. When she spoke, the immense tenderness in her words altered her voice.

'My love, I have a present for you.'

She opened her bag, unwrapped the box. With John's gelid hand between hers, she placed the watch on his wrist, then whispered in his ear,

'The engraving says "yours forever." Time soon passes by, and I will not be very long, I promise.'

Rose closed her eyes and kissed him on the lips.

'Happy birthday, my love,' she said before running into the corridor.

The vice held her heart and squeezed.

Betty had waited for her to come home. Rose thought strange how the room looked so unadorned, immense, empty, yet filled by the aroma of fried meat clinging to the walls and the rafters. Like a mist, it had also deposited on John's clean change of clothes ready on the bed, and on every particle of the air she was breathing. She touched his freshly pressed navy blue trousers, the white shirt she had given him for Christmas, his new red tie. Their coldness made her shiver, but it did not matter now, did it? She folded them carefully, flattening out imaginary creases with the palm of her hand, caressing, remembering. Then she stored them away in the wardrobe. Betty insisted,

'I'm going to stay the night in case you need anything. I won't take no for an answer.' Rose ignored her. Betty left her alone and stretched on her friend's bed while she laid down on John's - both of them still wearing their coat. Rose's eyes remained open all night. Motionless, devoid of thoughts, she stared at the window on the ceiling all night. An unknown entity had ripped her insides out, leaving a perfectly clean container of skin and bone. Her mind drifted above in the dark universe, losing itself in it. No tears accompanied her state.

When the time came for John's funeral, void of any emotion, Rose did what she had to do. Only a few of his workmates attended. A telegram from her parents read, *'We are sorry.'* She tore it into very tiny pieces before burning it inside a pot. Due to the lack of money to bury him in the ground, she had him cremated. Afterward, she took him home with her in a small brass urn, never to part from him as long as she lived.

'I'm here with you, my darling. I will always be. No one can split us. Nothing can.'

Betty worried about her friend.

'Do you ever cry? It'd do you good instead of keeping it all in.'

'Cry? No,' and she carried on with her work like a piece of machinery programmed to do one task. Even her voice had changed.

'Do you eat? You're so thin!'

'Eat...'

Betty followed her friend's hands moving on the loom, her rigid body as absent as her mind. She gazed at her white face, at the lack of brightness in her eyes.

My friend, where are you?

This alien person belonged to another place where people were not alive. Betty understood that pain corroded Rose inside, and this world did not exist for her any longer. Nothing she could do or say reached the depth of her friend's misery. Rose found the new machine mesmerizing and kept looking at it as if expecting it to regurgitate her John.

At home, she talked to the urn containing his ashes.

'Come out, stop teasing me! I'm too tired to play hide-and-seek, my love. Let me find you!' Then she hunted for him under the bed, inside the wardrobe, in the bathroom.

'Where are you? Fine then, we can have a game later.'

She then caressed his violin, listening to his music - so beautiful, so sweet! For a while, it gave life to her soul. At bedtime, she waited for him to emerge from the shadows and lay with her. He cradled her in his arms and warmed her cold body with his as he had always done.

'I love you, Rose,' he repeated until the throbbing in her heart eased long enough to steer her towards a short and tormented sleep.

Four weeks later, while going home through a shortcut in the park, she heard music. A man was playing a familiar tune on the violin near the bronze statue of the horse she had admired with John. She was spellbound, unable to pull away. Like the few passers-by who stopped to listen, she threw a coin in the case on the ground. In doing so, she met his gaze.

'You're a beautiful creature, but your eyes lack fire,' he declared.

Rose stared in disbelief into his piercing black eyes. Along with the music, they reminded her of -- *No Rose, this is not John.* His gaze and that melody unsettled her. The man stopped playing as Rose was about to hasten away, and she heard him say,

'My name's Emilian. What's yours?'

Taken aback by this familiarity, she wished desperately to disappear. He took her by the arm, pulling gently.

'Stay, girl. You're safe with me.'

She did as he asked, as it happened from then on whenever she met his gaze. That's how it was from the start: his probing eyes resembled John's eyes. Compelled to look into them, spellbound by their intensity and brilliance, she tried to find John in them. Even the tiniest semblance of him, in whatever form, brought him back to her from the darkness into the light.

Rose was not interested in Emilian's thoughts. He disclosed just a few snippets about his travels a couple of times after his performance. A true gipsy and not a talkative man, he told her he was after a companion to share his vagabond lifestyle. Neither of them ever offered any information about their private lives. They asked each other no questions. With black hair and unfathomable age, the man always wore a very bright red scarf that contrasted with his dark brown skin. He tied it so tightly around his neck it seemed glued to it.

'I'm fed up of being alone, my girl. Do you want to come with me?'

Unable to afford the rent, set upon by memories, she only longed to leave her past behind, uncaring of where or with whom she was going. Yet, still haunted by that first and only sight of her daughter, she often hoped to see her again to determine whether they looked after her properly. Her wish grew more intense, but to what purpose? There could only be a negative outcome: too many secrets and lies.

Don't turn back, Rose, never. She decided.

'I'll come with you. When are you going?'

'In a week with my wagon.'

'I'll be ready.'

They fixed the time, and scribbled her address on a piece of greasy paper.

Rose packed a suitcase without telling anyone and left money on the table to pay for the room. She bumped the case down the steps and stood on the pavement. Shortly after, he arrived. Saying nothing, she let him help with her luggage, jumped beside him on the wagon, and, followed by curious stares from passers-by, disappeared with Emilian.

They kept going for some months from Bradford to Hull in his colourful transport, searching for somewhere to camp. Talk of a possible war already floated in the air, and fearing the imminent danger, he decided to move again. Emilian intended to make his way to stay with some cousins to live under the safer roof of a house should this future threat become real. After a long trip, they stopped near a brook and some trees.

'Here, woman, light a fire.'

'Yes, Emilian.'

'Get the food ready.'

'Yes, Emilian.'

'Don't fall into the water!'

'No, Emilian.'

'I'm going to get wood, woman.'

'Yes, Emilian.'

He never called her by any other name but 'woman.' Rose obeyed blindly, detached from everything. Always dressed in black, with hair cut close to the scalp, there were no more soft curls but matted, dirty clumps enhancing the white pallor of her face and the thinness of her frail limbs. She submitted to all his demands - except one. From the start, without speaking, she went through the motions of living day by day, not caring whether soaked or dry. At the beginning of their travels, he had tried to touch her,

'Come here, woman. I need some comfort, some warmth in my bed.'

He was about to pull her to him, hoping for a physical response, but her reaction was immediate. She grubbed a knife retreating into a corner like a trapped animal ready to pounce.

'If you try, I'll kill myself.'

From her cold gaze, he knew she meant it and decided to leave her alone. He slept on the bed and Rose on a filthy mattress on the floor. The man did not seem to mind, as he found self-gratification elsewhere. Rose became the obedient servant who cooked, washed, cleaned, and lit the fire without ever complaining. He liked her obedience and her silence that precluded any argument. He also learned the impossibility of exchanging even a few words with her.

Every night, under another layer of clothes, Rose always wore John's pyjamas. No thoughts invaded her mind, just a sense of being 'there' with him, wherever 'there' was. Still, when Emilian played the violin, he could never have guessed what took place inside Rose's forgotten soul. She was carried away to another world, to the only life she had ever had and cared for. By shutting her eyes, she found herself in 'their' room. John waited for her sitting on their bed, flooded by moonbeams that gave him a ghostly appearance. When the harmonious notes of his violin permeated the room, he shrouded her in his arms. She filled with longing then. For a fleeting moment, her human side surfaced again, she realized the insanity of her life. Then her heart cried the tears she was incapable of shedding.

They remained hidden in the same location, camouflaged by thick woodland near a small town for a while. Whenever possible, Emilian exhibited in public places, in restaurants and tearooms, anywhere in fact, where people gathered. Rose went around with his hat to pick up the few pennies thrown on the ground or handed over to her, enough for them to survive. That day, Emilian started to play in a café, but the owner asked him to stop, turning the radio on instead. After days of waiting for the outcome of political events, the whole nation heard the Prime Minister's dreaded words on the wireless.

"This country is at war with Germany."

The month was September, the year 1939.

'I need to move from here. I'll go to my cousins in Portsmouth who will put us up. It's safer there in their house. I must make my way as quickly as I can. Once there, I'll hide my wagon.'

She did not care one way or another.

In the general chaos, they embarked on their lengthy and cautious journey to Portsmouth. It took much longer than expected, as he travelled mainly at night time, not wanting to attract attention. It was daylight in Portsmouth when the roaring pandemonium in the sky started near the harbour. Emilian decided to leave the wagon under an archway and to search for cover when the air raid began. The bomb exploded. Among the debris and the bodies some distance away, a brass urn lay smashed on the ground.

Part III

Lucy – Her future

CHAPTER 14

1959

After the devastating revelations from her "grandfather," Lucy headed for the only safe place. Jose knew where to take this lovely girl with beautiful hair. He tried to exchange a few words with her, but she was not in a chatty vein, and he did not pursue it.

Only a vague recollection lingered in Lucy's mind about her first trip, and awareness of her surroundings lacked emotion, except for the eagerness to arrive. However, the weather made her sleepy, and for the first time in days, stretched on the bench, she slept soundly, waking up at her destination. Alma met her first.

'Lucy! She's back! Madre de Dios! Come see her!'

A little group hugged and embraced her with welcome words, but no trace of Sam or Ben. *Good,* she thought, but once inside, her husband came to greet her with an embrace.

'What are you doing here? How are you? The kids? How's everything?'

'Yes, everything's fine. The children don't need me. They're happy.'

She did not want to uncover the unholy wreckage of her life to him.

'Couldn't you stay?

'No.'

She did not volunteer any more answers. Aware of the sadness in her voice, Sam refrained from asking more questions. Something was not right. Perhaps she would tell him later.

Resuming her work and her life in the church, she only went

   The Flesh and the Spirit

through the motions and hardly talked to anyone. They all noticed the change in her personality, and Sam tried to find out what troubled her.

'I thought you went home for good. Is there anything wrong with the children?'

'They are fine.'

'What made you come back, Lucy? You are a different person.'

'I don't want to talk about it. I just need some peace.'

'But kids? Tell me about them.'

'Nothing to tell as they are better off where they are, not interested in Auntie Lucy. Oh, and by the way, Harry's dead.'

'I don't understand.'

'It makes a change! It used to be me who did not understand. I have no answers for you, so don't ask.'

He knew then not to insist, as they had become strangers. He spoke to Ben about it.

'She says there's nothing wrong, but she's a different person. I think she's mourning for Harry.'

'To quote from Shakespeare, "Smooth runs the water when the brook is deep." Who knows what is inside her heart, son. Wait and see.'

Sam kept his distance from Lucy, and she reciprocated, wanting to forget he existed. She had left him to God, whom she blamed along with Sam.

As time went by, Lucy became increasingly aloof and miserable.

I need someone who wants me, who lets me know that I exist as a woman.

In retrospect, the person she used to be filled her with doubts and uncertainties. This Lucy had to start a new life, forgetting everything she knew about a world where they had made her live under false pretences.

The old woman who comes with her cart to collect the pottery and the weaving is from the town. I will go with her.

Lucy confided her plan to no one and packed a bag ready to leave as soon as possible. On the day of the buyer's arrival, the women loaded their goods, which she would sell again in Glide. Hidden behind a boulder, Lucy peeked and waited.

'Ysenia, where's Lucy? She has a few things too. Go! Find her, or she'll miss Mona.' Lucy's heart raced. She waited for developments, hoping the girl would come back quickly, and she did.

'Can't find her. She'll have to keep things until next time,' she said in her language.

Once done, they disappeared inside the building. The aged horse began its slow advance under the heavy load, and Lucy came out of hiding, running after it. She startled the woman.

'Here, this money is for you if you take me to Glide,' she said in a hurry.

Mona dropped the few pesos in a small bag and moved along her seat to make a little space without speaking. She jumped beside her. The horse progressed at a steady pace, and Lucy glanced back. An emotional farewell hovered on her lips.

You never loved me, but I will show you, Sam. Nothing can stop me now. I am reborn.

Neither of them spoke. The sun was disappearing behind the horizon when they reached their destination.

'Can I stay the night? I will pay you.' The alternative would be to sleep under the stars.

Without a word, the woman showed her a corner in the one-roomed hut. A lamp hung from the ceiling, throwing a shadowed light on the paillasse, a chair, and a table.

'Tomorrow, market day,' she said, producing some bread and cheese out of a tin and a jug of stale water.

They ate in silence, and then she went outside, coming back with a narrow mattress which she pulled on the ground beside the other. A few minutes later, the snoring sound announced her slumber. Lucy stretched on it fully dressed, hoping for the night to go by fast. Her eyes closed, but her mind, like a waterwheel, kept lifting her thoughts until milled and bagged.

She smoothed down the creases on her light blue and sweaty cotton dress. In daylight, the room appeared even more dismal, and she stumbled outside. Mona was arranging her wares on red mats under a white awning a short distance away. Lucy surveyed the surroundings. Small buildings flanked a long and narrow street. Other sellers hastened about displaying their products on colourful blankets under canvasses sustained by sticks. Colours shone bright drenched in the dazzling light. She approached the woman who asked,

'You know my name, and you?'

'Lucy. Thank you for letting me stay the night. I need to find a cheap room. Can you tell me where to go?'

She shrugged and said,

'The tavern, end of the street, has a room on the back. Ask there.'

Lucy had very little money left and no idea of what the town had to offer. The people coming to the market and the houses nearby did not appear to have much. She fetched her bag and started to walk. The narrow road seemed to go on forever. Her stomach rumbled, her throat was on fire, and her feet hurt. At last, she ended up in a square with a small building in need of repair. A couple of tables and chairs outside the door and a collapsing board above the entrance with Taberna painted in faded green letters told her she had arrived. Desperate for a drink of water, she hurried inside. The man busy moving a few barrels raised his eyebrows, looking at her questioningly. She dropped her bag on the floor, saying in Spanish, 'Water, please. Water!'

He put a jug and a glass on the wooden counter. She thanked him and helped herself under his watchful eye.

'I need a room to rent,' she said, grateful for her slight knowledge of the language.

'Come, miss.'

She followed him to a door at the back of the Taberna. As soon as he opened it, the smell sickened her. Something scuttled across the floor, disappearing under a few sacks piled up in a corner, and Lucy stood on the threshold, afraid to go in. She gazed at the metal frame with a rolled and dirty paillasse, at the rusty metal basin on a metal stand, a chair, and a wooden chest with a broken lock. The light that found its way through a window thick with dirt altered its color to a rusty brown. She wanted to run away, then thinking of the few pesos left in her pocket, she asked,

'How much?'

He told her. She had enough for two nights and for something to eat. Lucy paid him, devouring the tortilla he brought her. She remained seated, drinking water under the gaze of the man behind the counter, obviously curious about this woman. He kept licking his lips under the thick moustache without a word. When the first customer came in, Lucy went to her room. Not daring to unroll the paillasse, she sat on the chair, and closed her eyes. Half-dozing, she felt sucked in a bottomless pit, where she remained until morning.

Not daring to immerse even a finger in the water of the rusty basin, Lucy went out determined to find out a little about the town and the possibility of earning money. Soon, however, she understood her search to be useless. The locals filled every kind of job, as life in that town revolved around survival. The idea of going back to the Taberna for another night made her cringe. For the first time in her life, she was hungry, unable to satisfy her hunger, exhausted and incapable of sleeping. Sitting on the steps of a church, she leaned in the shade of a wall and closed her eyes to protect them against the blinding sun.

'Sun strokes are for foreigners. Where are you from?'

Her eyes opened on a man watching her. As she stood up, his detailed scrutiny met her stare. He did not wear a poncho but a shirt and trousers. Nevertheless, he spoke and looked like a peasant. The heat and empty stomach made her feel about to faint, but he caught her just in time.

'Come with me. You'll feel better after a drink and out of this heat.'

He took her by the arm, guiding her to a place nearby selling nachos, sat her down, and ordered plenty of cold water. Lucy did not care who or what he was. When the smell of food reached her, the rumbling of her stomach told him she might be hungry. He asked her. She nodded in a hurry, and he ordered two nachos.

'Where do you stay?'

Lucy was not going to tell anyone. She wanted to forget about that place.

'Nowhere. I ran out of money.'

She wolfed down the food, and he said,

'I have a nice room. You want to share? I like you.'

Her teenage years hit her like a bolt of lightning. In a flash, she saw her payment for a perfume, a blouse, a movie, for her "services," for unnecessary and futile possessions without meaning, not worth the cost of her self-respect. Now her predicament gave her no choice but to accept the unthinkable. It was a matter of survival, and she wanted to live.

'I will share,' she said with tearful eyes.

Lucy went to collect her bag in the morning with a bruised body and mind, and a few pesos in her pocket. On arrival to the Taberna, she found her bag gone, stolen. Without thinking about it, she went back to Mona. Busy in the market, she did not appear surprised to see her. Lucy's voice shook when she asked,

'Can I stay with you for a little while?'

One look at her revealed the whole story to the woman.

'If you pay. Wash on the back. There's water and a basin. No bag?'

'Stolen. I'll wash what I'm wearing.'

The water cleansed her body and clothes, but not the filth of the previous night from her mind. In the sun, clothes dried in no time. She pulled the small paillasse inside the hut, curled herself into a ball, and fell into a deep sleep, only waking with Mona's voice saying,

'Come and help me, girl. My knees are sore.'

Lucy hurried outside, doing everything Mona could not manage.

'There is a tortilla in the tin. There's also cheese and bread. You can have half.'

   The Flesh and the Spirit

After eating, she felt half-human again.

Lucy spent the next few days helping Mona in the market, finding out the woman disliked talking. At times, when despair about tomorrow took hold of her, Lucy remembered what Jean had gone through in her lifetime. She began to think of her own life as a war she had to fight until the end. While this might be true, the outcome had to be victorious for everyone in this conflict, especially for her children.

When she set eyes on him, he beamed on her like the sun, and her spirit soared. He went over, bending to pick up a bowl but locking his eyes to hers. He asked her name, and she asked his.

'Rodrigo, señorita.'

She found his deep voice and full, smiling lips very appealing. He stood enthralled by her face, her hair.

'Do you want this bowl?' Mona asked him.

Without shifting his gaze from Lucy, he took some notes out of his pocket.

'I want six,' and gave her the money without counting it or turning his head.

'Is it enough?' He asked her, still lost in Lucy's eyes.

This mundane transaction became unimportant to him.

'Yes,' said Mona as the notes disappeared in her pocket.

Lucy broke the spell,

'Where do I go for food?' she asked her.

Unexpectedly, the answer came from Rodrigo,

'I'll show you. Not far, follow me.'

Conquered by the warmth in his authoritative voice, she agreed. Lucy followed his muscular body watching every move of his broad shoulders, of his delicate hands with long fingers, of his black and wavy hair ruffled by the breeze.

He is perfect.

When he stopped and turned to point at the stall, his straight nose and deep black eyes reinforced the spell.

'I'll wait for you, Lucy.'

So manly!

She imagined his skin soft and smooth under her fingers. In a whirlwind of physical excitement, her knees weakened. After a brief purchase of bread, tomatoes, and cheese, she went back to him. He read the message in her eyes, held her hand in his, and they took the road to paradise.

'Can we meet again? I must go now,' he said. 'Where do you stay?'

'With the old lady for a while.'

'I'll be here, señorita Lucy. You're muy hermosa.'

With her cheeks aflame, she caught the sparkle in his eyes. She had not felt "very beautiful" for a long time. He kissed her hand softly and strode away.

'Careful,' warned Mona, 'him rich guapo, but dangerous.'

She just smiled at the woman.

That night, a troubled mind prevented her from sleeping again.

What am I going to do? No money, no home.

That man, he was offering her a new beginning. She read it on his face and felt it in the touch of his hand. Sensations she thought suppressed came back. Ghosts from the past rose again.

Let go, Lucy.

In the twilight between sleep and consciousness, Rodrigo took centre stage with two children as a backdrop.

In the morning, he still possessed her mind. His glance alone

The Flesh and the Spirit

drew her like gravity. Her sunny mood seemed to reflect even on the shabby yellow dress that complemented her red hair wonderfully. He arrived driving a posh black car. The white of his clothes enhanced a dark skin that seemed to glow. His eyes regarded her admiringly.

'Jump in. Do you know this town? Where you from?'

'England. Here on holiday. I wanted to see the desert, and I saw it. It's too hot.'

'A long way to come, señorita. Are you alone?'

'Yes. I don't know this place at all.'

'I'll show you around, then. Not much to see during the day though, but at night the town comes to life.'

'At night? What's there?'

'Great places to eat, dance, music, the theatre. Would you go with me?'

Even to hell.

'Yes, Rodrigo, but someone stole my bag. I have no clothes.'

She found his face very close, and her mouth slowly drawn to his. When their lips touched, a bolt transfixed both. His strong arms held her as his breath accelerated into a spasm. His desire made her feel good.

The past is dead, girl. Enjoy your present.

Hungry for his kisses, his embrace, and his body, she was ready.

'Let's go to my home.'

'Yes, Rodrigo,' she answered with unbelievable anticipation.

He drove for a while in a maze of small streets that seemed identical. Squawking children, barking dogs, scrawny cats, and people with large hats and colourful ponchos went about their business at a slow pace. He stopped in front of a whitewashed bungalow standing on its piece of ground surrounded by a low wall.

'My home. Welcome, Lucy.'

He unlocked the heavy door, picked her up like a straw, and brought her inside. The coolness welcomed them in a room with closed shutters, but he did not stop there, heading for the bedroom. Contrary to the poor's custom, his bed was not a paillasse but a feathery mattress where he placed her as if holding a fragile figurine. He left her for a few seconds to drop his shirt and trousers to the floor. His nakedness revealed perfect muscles and a long, thin, white scar across his abdomen. When he turned, her excitement grew with the expression on his face. Taking his time, he removed her dress, tasting, kissing her skin, freeing her magnificent hair from the combs. His fingers entangled in its waves, and he buried his face in that red mass, moving to her mouth, open and waiting with longing for his lips and tongue. Burning with a fire she had not experienced what seemed forever, she unravelled in his arms like a ball of precious silk, winding around his senses. As he moved lower, she screamed with delight, tasting every inch of his body as he did with hers, both aware of their extreme desire. When her desperate needs overcame all else, she felt like a woman again.

'You're my beautiful doll. Will you stay here with me? Don't go back.'

His voice caressed her with the same gentleness of his hands.

'I want to be with you,' she said.

While lost in the kind of lust where each movement and gesture only aimed at pleasing the other, fingers entwined in moments of rapture, little cries took the place of words. He had sparked back to life a distant part of her.

After living three days through the most memorable times of their life, exploring and satisfying every secret wish, finally

The Flesh and the Spirit

satiated, they rested in each other's arms. Still on fire with their extraordinary lovemaking, he took her to buy a few dresses. When Mona saw them coming hand in hand, laughing, she shook her head.

'Good luck,' she said to her walking away.

In some areas, Glide gave the impression of a lovely place. Other parts of the city unveiled unappealing features: crumbling buildings, rows of washing hanging on ropes close to decaying dwellings, and half-naked dirty children running around. Most of the narrow roads converged onto squares graced either by a small church with a bell tower or by opulent structures and costly shops.

When hidden behind the unforgiving brightness of day, the town's lazy pace was transformed by dim lights settling long shadows over the alleys' and pathways' intricate nets. At night, the place became a drinking and gambling pit. Guitar music invaded every dark corner, mixing with the scent left behind by the heat. Those nostalgic notes struck a chord inside her soul and reached its deepest part merging with the remains of a woman called Lucy.

Rodrigo enjoyed showing his wealth and possessions, including 'his' woman. They became inseparable. Proud of her beauty, he was also eager for everyone to notice her devotion and sweet nature. He bought her the best of clothes and anything else she wanted.Only short absences kept him away from home, which he explained with, *"I'm going to do some work,"* coming back to her a few hours later. When she asked him what he did, and about the scar on his belly, she had to be satisfied with vague answers.

'What I do? I deliver some merchandise. I have enemies like everyone. It's a knife wound.'

He became her life, and their passion enslaved her. Every gesture, every fibre in her body, every action she performed aimed at pleasing him.

'You're the intoxicating scent of a rare desert's flower. You take my breath away,' he said to her.

Their insatiable appetite kept them at home during the day. Then something more began to shine in his eyes: a flame burning not only with desire but also with a unique warmth. Within that flame, she perceived a capacity for true love. Incapable of offering him her heart as well as her body, she feared his need for both. Lucy intended to plan a future for herself, one good enough for her children.

'We are two of a kind, my beautiful Lucy. You are the only one who understands me,' he said often.

They shared all, but neither of them ever talked about their past. Two strangers unified by lust and separated by lifetimes of experiences, memories, miseries, and secrets. She wondered what road Rodrigo had travelled and what he had left behind while drifting forward. He had never been seriously involved in his thirties, which summed up her knowledge of his life.

'This is a frontier town, a violent place to live in since 1885 when the gold rush began. The women I met were not exactly 'ladies' my hermosa. Drugs, greed, nobody like you, my rare flower.'

He took her everywhere, showing her around the place with unsuspected pride. The town's past surprised her. She admired the first famous train station built in the area and the beautiful theatre that still presented popular vaudeville entertainment. In particular, Cavitto, the oldest and most lavish jeweller in Glide

The Flesh and the Spirit

attracted her attention.

'We're going inside to choose anything you fancy. Don't check the price. I want only the best for you.'

'You're wonderful!'

She gazed into his eyes, drawing closer to him. Her breasts pressed on his chest. He pulled her to him so tightly she ceased to breathe.

'After, we go home,' he murmured in her ear, kissing her vehemently.

A gold chain with a pendant of three diamonds attracted her attention. He fastened the clasp around her neck, brushed it with his lips, and made her shiver. The jeweller smiled. Rodrigo took a wodge of notes from his pocket and paid without any fuss.

'Let's go, my hermosa.'

He spoiled her with presents and designer clothes. Lucy, of course, found this side of his character immensely enjoyable and exciting. Rodrigo's house had all the comforts of luxury. Patterned tapestries revived the whitewashed walls, and excellent hand-made mats covered the floors. Plush black sofas and carved small tables occupied the spacious entrance hall. Whenever they made love, their mutual physical attraction drifted almost tangible in the air. When their bodies joined, they found no barriers. On day, after making love, he got ready in a rush.

'I must go out, my flor. I'll be back when I can.'

One quick kiss and he was gone, leaving her to wonder where he was going and what he had to do in such haste, but she knew not to ask. Lucy feared upsetting the giver of the dream she was living. Incapable of shaking off her uneasiness, she waited for his return. A few hours later, he came back and handed her a small packet.

'I want you to hide this where no-one can find it. Don't even tell me.'

'What's in it?'

'Don't ask. Just do as I tell you and then get ready. I'm taking you out.'

Lucy obliged.

While he was in the bathroom, she went to the little patio at the back of the house and uprooted a desiccated plant from a large pot. She dug a deep hole with her hand, dropped the mysterious box inside, covered it up, and replaced everything precisely as before. He did not ask about its hiding place.

In the evening, Rodrigo took her to dine and dance in a new and smart club. The two men who came in caught Rodrigo's attention, and he stood up,

'Be back soon. Stay here, my love. I must talk to my friends.'

She glanced at the two well-dressed men. They had bumped accidentally into those people she disliked, and not for the first time.

'Who are they?' she asked when he returned.

'Just people I know.'

Rodrigo seemed troubled, but she did not question him further. If he wanted to tell her, he would do so without her asking. She stroked his leg under the table. He took her hand, rubbing it hard inside his thighs and their gazes spoke a silent dialogue.

Early next morning, a running engine woke her up, and she peered between the louvres shutters. From the green car parked in front of the house, alighted the two men she had seen the previous night. They came to the door and tried to force it

The Flesh and the Spirit

open a few times until their frustration gave way to angry kicks and knocks. Before she could wrap a towel on her naked body, Rodrigo shoved her aside.

'Stay here.'

She obeyed. Infuriated voices reached her, and a short time later, a car sped away. Had they left? He appeared soon after,

'I must go out, hermosa. When I come back, we'll get you something nice.'

She could tell his anxiety by the nervous tic in the corner of his mouth. While he threw on a shirt and trousers, she went to wash in the bathroom. First, she heard the now familiar engine, then thumping noises. Lucy hurried out in her towel just in time to see blood gushing down Rodrigo's arm and the same two individuals carrying him away unconscious. They raised their eyes to her with half a grin. She froze and then flew to grab a poncho to cover her naked body, but by the time she reached the door, a red trail and the vehicle driving away was all she saw.

What shall I do? Clean up, yes, and wait.

She busied herself for hours scrubbing the floor, washing away his blood, tidying up the house. Finally, she collapsed on the armchair. A sudden thought crossed her mind:

Will they come back? I saw them. I must go from here now.

Terrified by this idea, she threw a few things in a bag and took the wodge of money Rodrigo kept in a drawer rushing away . Opting for short cuts to avoid the main road, she took a room at the big hotel in town, locked herself in, and sat on the bed, thinking.

Rodrigo, where are you? What can I do? All that blood. Are you dead?

Not daring to leave the room, she curled up in bed, speculating on the events and unsure of what to do next.

For a whole week, she remained a prisoner inside the hotel, wondering about the nature of her lover's troubles. The hotel sent food and drink to her room. Then she thought of one possibility,

Perhaps Rodrigo has gone back home and is looking for me. I must go and make sure. Curbing her agitation, she ventured into the street.

Once she arrived at his house, her heart began to beat fast. First, she gave a darting look all around her. She licked off the droplets formed on her upper lip, experiencing the sweat of fear. Her hand reached for the handle, but she hesitated. Should she go in? What if? she lingered and withdrew her fingers. In the end, she turned the knob and found the door unlocked. With great caution, she pushed it wide open and stood there, shocked by what she witnessed. They had overlooked nothing in their search, even the furniture lay smashed, and the mattress's feather filling covered the place like snow. They had left nothing intact and no trace of Rodrigo. It seemed clear to her that they were desperately searching for something, but what was so important?

I must go. I am not safe here.

About to leave, she remembered the package and stepped onto the patio. The wind blew away the powdery dry earth from the smashed pots, obviously kicked in a rage. One of them had landed on the ground behind the patio's stone slabs, but although cracked and upturned, it seemed in one piece. Lucy recognised it from the faded red paint on the rim and turned the pot over. The packet emerged triumphant and intact on top of the pile of earth. She took it and hurried away.

CHAPTER 15

Back to the hotel, Lucy needed to find out the content of what she suspected to be the cause of all their troubles. The thick brown paper concealed a wooden box. With shaking hands, she opened it. A pile of uneven rough stones of various sizes varying in colour and shape fell on her bed, but that was all. What were they?

If those men were looking for them, they might be valuable.

Before going downstairs to the restaurant, she put everything under the mattress.

While waiting for food, her predicaments crowded her mind, asking for a solution. The anxiety for Rodrigo's whereabouts, always present, made her restless. She recalled their passionate times together, and her body ached for those special moments.

I owe him gratitude for his generosity and kindness. He never asked questions. He made me always feel wanted through his lovemaking. He was my saviour. Our affair kept the ghosts of my past from haunting me. Rodrigo, I miss you! But I must go on and build my life from here. My name? A new identity, a new woman. Yes!

She committed not to think about him. Emerging from the maze of her feelings, Lucy concentrated on her goals, knowing from then on, she had to interweave the cloth of a new life with lies.

A refined beauty attracted attention in a place like Glide. Her long hair highlighted by the sun enhanced the tanned skin. Long lashes framed deep brown eyes that sparkled as if sprinkled with golden powder, and her full lips disclosed perfect pearly teeth. Lucy's slim and elegant figure, always in high heels, moved gracefully, and her face and smile possessed the tender sweetness and innocence of a child. She inspired the wish to protect this fragile, gorgeous girl - appearing much younger than her age. She stepped into the restaurant with caution and gazed around, afraid someone would recognize her. Her choice was the table least exposed to the entrance in the furthest corner of the room. Absorbed in thought, Lucy disregarded the well-dressed, elderly man sitting alone. He watched her intently throughout the meal, his gaze fixed on her and every movement she made. A pleased expression then spread all over his wrinkled face and he proceeded towards her table.

'Hello, miss. Forgive my intrusion, but I'm bored with talking to myself. Would you be so kind as to let this grey-haired old man sit with you to keep you company for a while?' He waited for her to shake his hand. Who was this man with deep-set blue eyes, she wondered. Could she trust him? He was dignified, unlike those thugs friends of Rodrigo. She shook his hand,

'I'll be delighted, Mr.?'

'David Baxter, and you?'

'Susan. But I like to be called Susy,' and she smiled.

Unsure about that name, she decided to go with her instinct.

'Where are you from? I'm a New York man, here to visit my nephew,' he said with a marked American accent.

'I came from England to see the desert.'

No sense in lying. Her pronunciation betrayed her.

'A long way from home! When are you due back?'

'No hurry. Nobody's waiting for me there. I have no living family, only a distant uncle, but we lost touch. My home is a rented room,' she said candidly.

He felt sorry for her.

The Flesh and the Spirit

'My only relation is like a son to me. My wife died two years ago, and we had no children. I have a few good friends, though. Do you have any?'

'Not anymore, as they moved away.'

The conversation continued in light tones. She liked this man but began to wonder about his motives for befriending her. Lucy knew what men wanted from her, but this time she would be very cautious.

David admired her guts in journeying alone, so far away and knowing how to look after herself.

'Do you study? Work?' he asked.

'I'm manageress of a shoe shop. And you?'

There was some truth in her answer. She had always been obsessed with shoes.

'Retired lawyer, but still going to the office too often!'

'What's New York like? It must be huge! I'd love to go.'

'Well then, little Miss Susy. Would you like to trust me and come to visit my city? I live in an empty house in Manhattan. No strings, you can suit yourself.'

She thought about it. Was this the opportunity she needed? He seemed a decent sort of man, and she sensed he was as lonely as she felt. He read her thoughts.

'Alex will tell you I am an honourable man. All I want is some company.'

'I'll cook, clean, do your shopping if you like.'

'Not necessary. A maid does it all. We can go sightseeing. Please, be my companion. Are you financially sound? Maybe I could help a little.'

She thought of the money received from Rodrigo and the roll of notes taken from the drawer, but not enough to live on much longer. Perhaps what she had found inside the box might be valuable. She needed to find out, as Susy's life depended on it. Was this man truly offering something for nothing? Under the circumstances, she had no choice but to believe him, following her gut instinct. This stranger was unlocking the door to hope. She would walk through it then lock it behind her, opening another one for Susy instead. She smiled at him, bright with possibilities: her future waited.

'I will repay you, Mr. Baxter. I will find a job.'

He smiled.

'We'll see about that. I'm going to stay with my nephew for a week. Shall we meet here in a couple of days for lunch? You can tell me about your plans then. Be careful, my dear, and think of me as your grandfather.'

Shivers ran down her spine at that word. For a brief moment, she sensed the presence of her other self, the one imprisoned within her painful memories. Still, she nodded, shaking his hand with feeling. Before going, he surprised her with a hug. Her priority now was to make sense of the box.

Whom can I trust? If I meet those men, they will recognise me right away!

She locked the door of her room, studying what looked like uneven and dirty pebbles, more puzzled than ever.

I need a plan, but I must leave this place.

The night, although restless and interrupted by long sleepless spells, brought her counsel.

Early in the morning, she dressed in the peasant clothes bought in a market sometime before. With a long orange skirt, a white blouse, flat sandals, hair wrapped in a scarf under a straw hat, and sunglasses, she was ready and unrecognisable. Clutching the heavy box hidden in a deep pocket among the fullness of the material, she ventured into the street, forced to ask someone for directions. After meandering about for a while, she found the way to Mona's house, whose surprise spread all over her face.

'Lucy, people look for you from the church. I tell them you well?'

'No! Don't say anything about me, please, or my life will be in danger. I am going to show you something Rodrigo left me before disappearing. I will give you some money, but I need your help.'

'Si, señorita, bueno.'

The woman knew already to expect trouble and her expression changed hearing that name, but for Lucy, she was the only hope. Sitting on chair inside her home, she turned the box carefully upside down on her skirt.

'What are these, Mona?'

The woman's eyes opened wide.

'Put away, quick!' There was panic in her voice, fear even.

'What's the matter? What are they? Tell me!'

'They rough diamonds. Many, big, as they come out of the mine. I bring food to miners. Rodrigo sold them after men stole them. He kept some money, gave the rest to his boss. It made him very rich. Now go, no stay here. Go and show to nobody.'

With a brief 'thank you,' Lucy took some money from her purse and left it on the chair, making her way back fast. The word 'diamonds' echoed and bounced about in her head as she thought about the value of what she had. With one hand among the folds of the material to reassure herself, she arrived at the hotel.

In her room, she scouted around for a hiding place but found nowhere suitable. As a last resort, she lifted the mattress and slipped the box underneath it, changed her clothes and went to meet David for lunch as promised.

Is he my only way out of this mess? Play your cards right, be smart.

With a last survey around, she descended the two flights of stairs to the lobby and the eating area.

'Good day, Susy. You are lovely!'

He made a gesture of approval with his hands. They sat, ate, conversed and even laughed like old friends until he said,

'Well then, do you want to come and explore my city? You are safe with me, girl. You will also meet my nephew. He is the architect responsible for a few horrors round here!'

He grinned wholeheartedly before adding, 'not true, Alex is brilliant at his job. A great guy, honest and down to earth. I am very proud of him, my brother's son. His father passed away three years ago, after his mother.'

'To see that city is my dream! Thank you so much. Of course, I want to come. When are you leaving? By the way, I am sorting my finances, and I will pay.'

Susy is wealthy! All I have to do is sell them. I will find a way. That city is vast.

Still spellbound by Mona's words, she found herself unable to think of anything else. The difficulties she might encounter when selling the stones did not appear to enter her mind. David's voice interrupted her inner musing.

'Can you cook?'

'Yes, I can.'

Wake up, Susy. Play your part.

'Then all I ask of you is to teach my housekeeper. I am tired of eating the same food for months!'

She relaxed, as very soon, she was going to be out of harm's way. Wealthy and happy!

The Flesh and the Spirit

Hold on! I must sell the gems first!

A whole world of terrors then surfaced inside her head when she thought about the possibility that whoever was searching for them would not give up easily. How could they? She necessitated to make plans for her safety and to hide the treasure.

'Tomorrow for lunch then, if it suits you.'

His words penetrated her thoughts.

'Yes, Mr. Baxter. I'll be waiting.'

'Adios, Miss Susy. Call me David,'

He smiled and hugged her as usual before leaving. Lucy went to her room and locked the door.

Is it too late? She wondered.

Those men were bound to come after her any time now.

Disappear with that packet, Lucy.

Her life, her future depended on it.

A glance in the mirror made her decide the first step: disguise. The one she had adopted when going to Mona would be fine. After packing a bag, she left enough money to cover the hotel bill. About to go down the last flight of steps, she recognized the two men who had taken away Rodrigo. She would be next. Cold sweat and goosebumps preceded her walk into the lobby, where they were still busy talking to the porter.

Don't run. Calm down. No one will recognise you.

She passed the men and braved the streets, wondering where to go. Remembering a little derelict house seen when out with Rodrigo, she headed that way.

The tiny building stood by itself on a small plot of parched land. When she disturbed the rickety door, a loud and creaking sound echoed in the air as she struggled to push it open on its rusty hinges. Inside she found a corroded wood-fired stove balancing on three legs in the middle of a wall. An archway gave access to a small room that had once functioned as a bedroom judging from a ripped paillasse. A hole in the ground surrounded by more bricks probably served as a toilet behind a brick partition. The layer of red earth covering the floor everywhere exposed patches of fuliginous stone. The sunlight filtering through rotting windows blanketed by a lace of cobwebs showed them covered by silver net curtains.

Straw from the filthy paillasse in the corner of the room lay scattered all over the floor. Lucy's heart sank, but she thought it a safe place until the next day. Most importantly, she had to find a hiding place for the box – too risky to keep it on her. After a glance around, she pushed it deep inside the hay, wrapped the poncho around her body, and went on to dream about the future, hoping sleep would come to ease her mounting panic.

Unknown to her, chaos now reigned in what had been her room. They overlooked nothing in their search, and the staff underwent a thorough interrogation. The same story emerged from everyone: an older man might be the only person to know something about the girl, as they had dined together. Two out of the three men vanished, but one remained in the room. These events had taken place about one hour after Lucy's disappearance. When David walked in and sat down waiting for Susy, a rough-looking, muscly man with a moustache and oily hair approached him, sitting with arrogance at his table.

'Señor, about the señorita who dined with you, do you know where she is? Her relatives want her. They're worried.'

David did not like the man. His instinct told him he was lying. Whatever this burly fellow wanted from her, it could not

The Flesh and the Spirit

be something good.

'Sorry, sir. We only ate together a couple of times. She said she was here on holiday but about to go home - wherever that is. I have no idea where she came from or when. She never talked much. I did not give her a chance!'

David tried to control his uneasiness by a forced laugh.

'But surely you can speak to her yourself? If she hasn't already gone, that is not my business.'

The man focused intensely on David, then stood up and pointed a thick sweaty finger at him.

'Señor, very important. Make sure you tell the reception if she comes again, bueno?'

'Of course! Her family must be concerned. A girl on her own... I'll say you're looking for her.'

'Don't say anything. Just tell the porter. Some people are planning a surprise.'

'I will do, sir,' he replied.

Mr Greasy, about to add something else, stared at him. Changing his mind, he strode away, vanishing from sight.

David dined alone, hoping Susy would not join him.

Where was she?

He sensed something nasty brewing for her, and he did not want the girl caught without an explanation. Before going back home the next day, he planned to take her to meet his nephew, but how to get in touch? On his way out, he asked at the desk about the young woman with the red hair, receiving a very curt answer - she had left. He could not understand her as she was adamant about going to New York with him. Was this girl in some kind of trouble?

Every little noise, every breath of the desert's wind, every mouse scurrying away caused her to jump during a sleepless night. Hunger pangs and thirst tormented her when daylight crept through, but the reek from the paillasse almost made her sick. According to her watch, three hours still separated her from the appointment with David. To venture outside now would be too dangerous. She decided to wait, but as the sun rose high in the sky, the heat inside stifled her. She would have given one of her diamonds in exchange for a glass of water, yet nothing could induce her to leave before the time. At last, with increased anxiety, she made her way to the hotel waiting for David hidden in a doorway along the street. When he appeared, she followed him, often turning to check for any sign of peril before saying,

'Don't turn around. Go where we can talk, please. I'll be keeping my distance behind you.' He did as she asked, vanishing after a few minutes into a building. On the second floor, he unlocked a door and went in. Not far from him, she remained on the landing.

'Come inside. You'll be safe here. Alex comes back much later.'

The large sitting-dining room felt fresh. Carved dark pieces of furniture complemented a bright Mexican décor.

'Sit down, sweetie. What kind of predicament are you in? A massive and greasy-looking man wanted to know your whereabouts. I do not believe he was genuine, as he mentioned relatives of yours being worried. You told me of only one.'

He sat beside her on the soft bench-like settee, waiting.

During her troubled nights, she had thought of possible explanations if asked.

'David... I was friendly with a man for a while. Our friendship ended when some thugs appeared and took him away. That's

The Flesh and the Spirit

the last time we saw each other, but they must want him, and they think I know where he is, but I don't. Those people will not believe me, that's why I'm running away. I left my room yesterday, and I spent the night in an abandoned building. I'm so afraid.'

Shivers ran down her spine. It was almost the truth.

'My poor girl. Do you need a wash? Don't worry. In the morning, we leave for New York. They will not find you there. I don't think Alex will mind a guest for one night.'

She would be safe now, soon wealthy: Susy Jones, a beautiful princess living an extraordinary life. It never occurred to her that to take the gems out of the country might prove a difficult task. She came back to earth.

'Thank you, David. I'm very grateful and moved. You'll never regret it, I promise.'

She hugged him briefly, showing an untrue emotion and experiencing considerable relief from fear.

'The bathroom is through that door, sweetie. I will have something ready to eat when you finish. Go!'

Susy bathed and slipped into a light blue dress. She wrapped the box tightly with the incredible amount of material of the discarded skirt, knotted it, and dropped it in her bag. David was waiting for her with some food.

'Beautiful again! Eat, my dear,' he said in a fatherly tone.

She devoured the cold chicken wraps and fruit, beginning to feel herself again. He observed her pleased.

'I'll tell you about tomorrow's trip. I made sure of buying two tickets. I parked my car at New York's airport, and we'll be home in half an hour. The housekeeper...'

David's voice faded into the background as she fell asleep at the table. His heart filled with tenderness as he sat watching that beautiful, angelic creature fate had thrown his way. Perhaps she would let him think of her as of the daughter he almost had, bringing sunshine to the sunset shadows of his life. For a moment, the image of his stillborn child surfaced anew in his mind.

'Have a rest, dear girl. Nobody will find you here.'

Waking up, she found two men staring at her. One was David. 'Susy, this is Alexander, my nephew.'

She murmured a sleepy 'Hello' to the deeply tanned, regular face with blue eyes looking at her. The man grinned. Lucy stood up and he shook her hand.

'You're welcome to stay the night. Uncle told me all about you and his plans. The circumstances are quite unusual, but if it makes him happy, it's fine with me.'

It was getting dark outside – she had slept at the table for hours. After a light meal, the three talked about England, Mexico, the desert, and New York.

'Tomorrow, early morning, Alex will take us to the airport. Sleep well,' said David with a hug.

He was affectionate by nature, and she did not mind in the least.

'I'll wake you both. I'm always up in good time,' said Alex. He then turned to Susy, 'the sofa is very comfortable. I'll bring you a pillow and a blanket.'

He handed them to her with a smile, saying goodnight.

Morning found Alexander standing and watching her sleep. He had seen good-looking women but never one of such perfect beauty as this delicate creature. She opened her eyes.

'Hello. Is it time? I'll be ready in minutes. Is David up?' she

The Flesh and the Spirit

asked, yawning and stretching her limbs.

'He is in the bathroom,' he answered, falling under her spell.

When everyone was ready, Alex took them to the airport with little conversation.

'Thank you, son. Come soon to visit. Keep me informed.'

David embraced him enthusiastically, and Alex hugged him back.

'Till we meet again,' he said to her with a vigorous handshake.

'Yes, Alexander,' she said with enthusiasm.

Inside the building, when it came to passport checks, David had a glimpse of her passport.

'I thought your name is Susy.'

'Officially, it's Lucy, but everyone always calls me Susy because I don't like that name.'

David went first through customs. The young man searched his suitcase and then closed it. When her turn came, he seemed more interested in Susy. She kept smiling at him enticingly. He kept his gaze on her while retrieving the skirt's large bundle from the bag, followed by two dresses, a hat, and a pair of sandals. He examined the empty bag thoroughly and then dropped everything inside it again. He handed it to her, brushing her hand with his, exhibiting a row of flashing white teeth. She smiled at him and caught up with David. The plane took off, and Lucy sat quietly going over the recent events, wondering about Rodrigo.

What happened to him? Will he ever realize that I might have the packet? Those men who are looking for me, did he tell them? Could they find me?

A terrifying thought, but about to be reborn, she had to relinquish it to the past. Her mind then hovered on Alex. She liked him, wanted to meet this gentleman with impeccable manners again, and her thoughts also skimmed over what she had left behind.

Goodbye, Rodrigo. And Sam. I hope you're both well. I'll never see you again.

She found no answers to how she would be selling her treasure without David's knowledge.

CHAPTER 16

1959

As soon as Lucy set foot in New York's Idlewild airport, she entered a wondrous world. The first impression was walking through a giant kaleidoscope of sapphire, white and red glass tiles. The sunlight filtering through the grand stained-glass window engulfed the impersonal interior with calm and soothing shades of blue and hazy purple. What an impressive sight! Her gaze lingered on that great wall with amazement. Lucy had been there already with Sam, but under the influence of drugs, she had no recollection of it.

David, amused, explained,

'You're looking at three hundred feet long and twenty-three feet high facade, the largest in the world. Beautiful, isn't it?'

'Spectacular!'

'Wait until I show you the many wonders of my city. There is so much to discover, sweetie,' he stated with pride, guiding her outside to a very long, shiny, dark blue car with cream leather seats.

She sank in its comfort, finding it difficult to believe she was in the company of a stranger. While making his way through intricate nets of freeways, David explained about some areas of the city. The skyscrapers made her feel caged in when she looked up at the strips of sky high above. Elated by the novelty, comfortable in the plushness of David's car, she watched amazed the confusion unfolding around her. Heavy traffic, crowded streets, people hastening home or going to work, a multi-racial society rushing about their business. They came across massive shopping centres, tree-lined avenues, and large properties. The electrifying uniqueness of it all left her dazed, accustomed as she was to the slow-paced life at home and the silence of the desert. They proceeded along a wide avenue shaded by mature trees until he pulled up on the driveway of a house surrounded by perfectly manicured grass and flowers.

'We're home. This district is Mount Vernon. They built this house in the 1920s. I hope you'll like it.'

The building reminded her of the centuries-old ones she had seen in England during a trip to York. It was breathtaking: on two floors, with dark V-shaped beams forming a pattern on its white walls and leaded windows reflecting sunbeams, it was breathtaking. Once inside, she stood in awe, overcome by the luxurious ambient.

How can people afford to live like this? She wondered.

'Do you like my home Susy?' he asked, grinning at her reaction.

'So wonderful!'

With a glance, she took in the lavish décor: not modern, not old-fashioned either, just exquisite. They climbed a sweeping staircase with a broad, semi-circular bannister and carved steps. She followed David upstairs, where he showed her into a sizeable and bright room with a bathroom next door to it. The simplicity of the furnishings was deceiving, and everything smelled costly.

'Gorgeous! Thank you so much.'

His eyes shone with joy as he thought his cocoon could protect this stunning butterfly for as long as she wished - hopefully, a long time.

From then on, David took it upon himself to show her around, proud of his city. He drove her happily everywhere and took her to the most famous touristic sites making a point of adding some of their histories. She fell in love with the Ammarkan Museum of Natural History, with the Empire State Building's view, with the New York Aquarium on Coney Island. From David, Susy learned about the city she now lived in, about good manners, etiquette, and the appropriate clothing for different occasions.

A new and exciting life spread in front of her. Like a cake, it waited for a final layer of perfect icing and exquisite decorations. David had excellent taste and accompanied her to purchase whatever she required. Often he also brought her to visit some of his elite friends. David still owned his law firm. A well-known lawyer, he had retired due to age and health. He told everyone he was now enjoying life with his adopted niece, daughter of a long-lost friend in England, a recently revived friendship.

For the first time since his wife's death, the man appeared interested in life again. He socialised with other human beings, satisfied and looking forward to a joyful future. Through David's affectionate gestures, she realized a man could care for her as a person and not just as an object of pleasure. She started to gain a new perspective on what living meant, and her involuntary attachment to him gradually increased. Two little people alone often surfaced from her past, and someday she would… but the here and now commanded action. Susy had to think about her next move.

She browsed through the telephone directory for something suitable, and she set about her task hoping for the right outcome. Before entering into the dingy jeweller in Brooklyn, overlooking the East River, she summoned all her courage. It was her only option, the moment of no return. Ignoring the storm in her mind, she pushed the metal door encrusted here and there with red paint. The warning bell announced her entrance when she stepped inside. A partition separated the small area at the front of the shop from the rear. A short, skinny, and bespectacled man greeted her.

'Morning, miss. What can I do for you?'

His voice sounded as unpleasant as his unkempt appearance. A cigarette hung from one corner of his mouth, whose ash fell on his stained, pale green T-shirt. He extinguished the butt in the overflowing ashtray on the dirty glass counter.

'I have something to sell belonging to me. It is precious.'

'Really? Let's see if I could be interested. You sure it's not stolen? I don't accept stuff that's trouble.'

'I inherited it.'

'Show me what you got, miss.'

Trying to control the tremor of her hands, Lucy took a little black pouch from her handbag. After dropping its contents in her palm, she flattened the small square of the velvet material on the counter and dropped the stone on it. The man showed no interest.

'Well... well... What do I have here?'

He took a magnifying glass from a basket and started to inspect it.

She doesn't have the air of a criminal. More like a fish I am about to catch, he thought. Susy held her breath, controlling her nerves and her weakened legs. Minutes seemed aeons.

'Mmmm... what do you want for this? I'll ask no questions, none of my business as long as it's above board. I had enough problems in the past.'

'What would you pay? Make me an offer.'

She tried to sound sure of herself and business-like.

'The market... the cutter... I can't tell you. First time I come across this kind of merchandise. Whatever the value, I'll take thirty percent after costs. Is it fair to you? No one would treat you better.'

She thought about it for a while.

'Very well. When will you know? If you are honest with me, I'll make you rich. I will come back to you occasionally with more. I promise no hustle. '

'Oh? How will this be?'

He pricked up his ears.

'You'll see. All I ask is my true share. I know its value. I'll trust you for now. When can I come back?'

'In a couple of days. I'll have the cash ready.'

'Fine, thank you. But if you try to-'

'No threats necessary. Two days. Goodbye.'

'It's not a threat. People you would not like meeting know about it.'

'I hear you. Your insurance, huh?'

'You bet! They're waiting for me outside. Relatives, you know.'

'I'll keep my word.'

He disappeared into the back.

His thoughts centred on this fragile woman. Was she a crook? Even worse perhaps, planted to see if he still dealt in stolen goods? No. Too small, no muscles - not an informer or a cop, but involved in something big. Could he risk it?

It's my lucky day or my worst nightmare. She seems okay, but to own this? It's worth a heap of money. Where does it come from? A dodgy history, I bet. Some looker that broad! Last time I ended up in jail, worth the risk, though.

Susy had just left when she heard the door locking behind her. He did not come across as the kind of person one could trust, but she had no choice and hoped he would believe her lies. The thought of going back there terrified her. On the point of being sick, she tried to curb her fears by viewing life from the angle of poverty, reviving her determination to succeed.

Two days later, wearing modest clothes, a hat, and sunglasses, hoping to be as inconspicuous as possible, she went back to the shop. As soon as the man eyed her, he attempted a smile showing big crooked teeth.

'Hello. Just a minute...'

He took a key from the drawer, went to lock the door, and then turned to Susy, who, by now, feared for her life.

'Stay here. I'll be right back,' he said, going into the back and returning after a few seconds with a thick cardboard box.

'Are your relatives waiting outside? '

'Yes, of course.'

'Best that way, 'tis too dangerous to carry alone.'

'It was a good deal.' he said. 'I had to bargain for the price, but I got what I wanted for us. I think you'll be happy with it. You can count it. I have already taken out my cut.'

'I'll trust you. Just tell me how much.'

She opened the box, staring at the stack of notes crammed to the top. He told her the amount. She steadied herself by holding on to the counter - one hundred thousand dollars - an absolute fortune.

'Thank you. I'll be back. We are in business. You will not

The Flesh and the Spirit

regret it.'

'Fine, miss. I'll open the door for you.'

She wrapped her treasure in a scarf and locked it inside her large bag, hurrying to make her escape, feeling a bundle of nerves. During her journey home in the taxi, she forced herself to calm down. In the safety of her bedroom, she counted the notes. The heap of money made her dizzy, and she handled it dumbfounded.

Only one diamond and not even the biggest!

She needed a bank account to realize her plans. Susy had grasped the rules of classy and wealthy women moving in high circles. They did not venture anywhere without dabbing their skin with the most expensive scents. When the women met, their first topic of conversation concerned each other's fragrance. The one among them wearing a new perfume the others liked enjoyed being vague about its name. It prompted her idea, and she thought the posh part of Manhattan would be ideal for an elite salon. An exclusive shoe shop had been her first impulse, but perfumes appealed to her much more. She informed David about her unexpected 'inheritance' from a distant relative in England.

'The money is with the executor, waiting to be transferred to me.'

'I'll help you, honey. A couple of my closest friends are on the board of the First National City Bank. It would be challenging, if not impossible, for you otherwise.'

'Thanks, David. Will you teach me about banking?'

'If you want to invest later, I'm your man. I still have a few aces up my sleeve!'

'I swear to do nothing without consulting you, Uncle.'

They both laughed.

'There's something I would like to do, though, with your help. A dream I could change into reality.'

'Really? You know I will do all I can. What is it?'

'A perfume salon. The most elegant, refined, and extravagant you've ever seen, in the plushest district of Manhattan.'

He was silent for a while, thinking.

'Nothing but the best, huh? What do you know about perfumes and the business world? You have no idea of what is involved in setting up and running something like this. You would lose all your money, my dear, and much more.'

'David, will you be the brain? Together we cannot fail. I'm determined to learn, to take a chance, but I can't do it without your help.'

She got up and went to put her arm around his shoulders, kissing him on the cheek.

This should do it, she thought, foreseeing the result of her gesture.

CHAPTER 17

Alexander finished packing his suitcase. Before visiting David, he had completed the work at hand, but David came second on his priorities list. In first place was a beautiful creature inspiring him to take care of her, hoping she would accept the love and tenderness growing inside him.

This woman had caught Alex, one of the sought-after bachelors of society, in a net from which he did not wish to free himself. He felt a teenager all over again with a crush on a girl whose life danced in her eyes, who made him behave like a different man. Although wishing to settle down, the few women on his path had revealed unimportant, uninteresting, and untruthful. Susy represented his ideal: a wife to love forever. But he had three weeks to make it happen.

Someone else was preparing to board a plane, someone hardly recognizable to people who knew him before. The thugs had ordered him to find out about the package if he wanted to live. After four months of intense research, he had found her. The penalty for failure would be his death.

He waited for her hidden behind a tree, experiencing a mixture of anxiety, shyness, mistrust, and trust - a broken man with nothing else to lose but his life. When she rushed down the street, he followed her for a while before calling,

'Lucy!'

She jolted as if hit by lightning and froze, not daring to turn round. That voice sounded so familiar. Her pounding heart joined the tension in her throat and stomach. He caught up with her from behind, grabbed her hand.

'I'm not how I used to be. Get ready. Don't be frightened,

please.'

When he moved in front of her, she stared at him, refraining a scream with her hand, and stopped breathing. Ugly scars extended from his eyes down to both cheeks. Another split his top lip on one side, giving his mouth an odd, distorted appearance.

'Rodrigo!' she mumbled, mesmerized by that sight, unable to say any more.

'You have no idea what I went through and all because I didn't know where to find the package I gave you to hide. What did you do with it, girl?'

She looked at him, still not believing her eyes.

'What happened to you?' she finally asked.

'Torture, they thought I was lying. These people have been looking for you ever since and sent me to make you talk. I'm here to ask you. Where is it? If you don't tell me, they'll kill me. They will come after you."

He was not wasting any time in niceties and held on tight to her arm. His life was at stake, no time to reminisce, she thought. His past belonged to someone else, to a handsome young man with everything to live for, but not now. After the initial shock, she said,

'Rodrigo, I buried what you gave me inside a plant pot, but when I went back to look for you, your home was in a mess. Someone had kicked the pots, and they were all smashed. They must have found the box. What was in it?'

She managed to sound sincere and convincing, but the butterflies in her stomach kept on multiplying. Yes, she was sorry, but more for herself if Rodrigo did not believe her. He watched her in silence, doubting. Was she telling the truth?

'So you don't know anything, Lucy? Or Susy? Why did you

change your name? Why did you come here? What means do you have to be able to afford this kind of life? You had nothing when I met you.'

He tightened his grip, she gave a little cry of pain and tried to wriggle out of it.

'You're hurting me!'

He eased his hold.

'I had nothing, and I owe you much, even the money you kept in the drawer. I took it when you did not come back. I lived on it until it lasted. What else could I do?'

'How can you live in this luxury then?'

'I came here to start anew, as a *companion* to an old man I met at the hotel in Mexico. He pays for everything. I'd like to help you, but believe me. I don't know where that packet is, Rodrigo.

Looking at his face made her sick.

He thought that, if true, there might be another explanation: someone else had found it saying nothing - a real possibility.

'I'm sure the gentleman will get value for money, señorita. Be happy. But if you lied to me, I'll be back, not for a visit.'

Her body shook. Her legs weakened.

'Why should I lie to you? You went through enough.'

She summoned her courage and sounded sympathetic. He stared into her eyes.

'If this is what happened, you'll never see me again. Adios!'

He turned and disappeared along a side street. Was this the end? Perhaps it was for him, but her beginning. She could let go of the anxiety in the back of her mind and believe her aspirations would soon come true. Poor Rodrigo!

After all, he stole the diamonds and should be the one to pay for it.

She wished to dismiss the ugly image of his face while

walking. Hailing a taxi to Brooklyn, she clutched her handbag where two more stones nestled in the lining.

David and Susy went to fetch Alex at the airport. He shook her hand, engulfed in mixed sensations. She was even more beautiful than the image in his mind - an exact likeness to Botticelli's *Venus*. His feelings had to remain hidden, as first, he had to win her heart. Did she even like him?

Alex came across to her as an attractive man. His unremarkable cream shirt, dark brown trousers, and polished brown shoes indexed a subdued taste. She found his air of self-assurance very appealing.

A few days after his arrival, David guessed his nephew's intentions and was pleased. Perhaps Susy might never leave. With that idea in mind, he aided the romance, making sure to keep out of the way whenever possible. He encouraged them to go out in the evening to dine and dance, to the best shows on Broadway, and to shop together. Captivated by this man with gallant and refined manners, she enjoyed the attention Alex lavished on her.

David's nephew was a learned man whose patience she admired, especially when explaining anything to her. She detected strong undercurrents in his manners and believed them to be a passionate streak, but he always refrained from advances. One evening, coming back from a show, amused by the idea, she decided to kiss him to see his reaction. At first, he just stood there, then lifted her and sat down, holding her in his arms. His kisses fell eagerly on her lips, face, neck, hands, all over her covered or uncovered body with such fury, she felt breathless.

'My beautiful woman...'

She let him kiss her, responding more and more to his increasing eagerness, fighting his restraint. She needed the union of their bodies, but when he realized this, he stopped her.

'I love you since the first time I saw you. I want you - but when is proper.'

His words washed on her like a cold shower.

'When is proper?' she asked, repressing her instincts, cooling down.

'No sex before marriage. My parents brought me up to respect women and to do what is right. Would you marry me, Susy?'

His words shocked her. That way of thinking was new to her, she ignored men like him existed, but it had been too long. She needed him. A desperate need that escalated and made her weak, wanting all of this man, his love, his passion, his experience. Most of all, apart from wealth, she wanted security.

'Alex, I can't think of my life without you and David. The answer is yes.'

'I adore you. Everyone else will.'

He took her hand, kissed each one of her fingers. She closed her eyes. His warm breath descended on her face, her ear, her neck, and desire ignited her body again.

'You're my goddess. I have you on a pedestal. I worship and respect your beauty and your womanhood. Could you love me? In time your affection will mature.'

On paper, I'm already married. Could anyone find out? So far from home, with a new name, is it possible?

He thirsted for her mouth, but her mind raced.

'I'll give you anything you wish for,' he said.

She thought about the high circles that would be within her reach. The limelight derived from their union and the benefits for a future business. Also, the prevailing feelings for him - sexual in nature - soon needed to be satisfied.

'What about your work? You don't live in New York.'

'No problem, angel. I often talked to my uncle about a studio in this city. Besides, we have contacts. I am sure it will be fine. You would not like a home in Mexico by any chance?'

'Never. I have other ideas.'

'Really? What about?'

She told him, ending with, 'I'm a very wealthy woman, with my own goal.'

His surprised expression amused her.

'If that's what you want, I'll help you as much as I can. I will do anything to make you happy.'

His words reassured her. With David and Alex on her side, how could she fail?

You're on your way, girl, to a life where every dream comes true. I will be cultured, refined, gracious, the elected queen of New York, with an old-fashioned husband. Mmmmm...

She smiled at that thought. Not once, since quitting her past, she had raked through it. Lucy did not exist. Alex could now identify her with the Botticelli's *Venus* after all —but she was a woman born from a stormy sea.

I like this new me heading to the top and one day...

That time was unknown, but the thought of her children lived inside her. She dismissed any doubts, her goals geared towards money, the glory of fame, and the pursuit of happiness.

A few days later, Alex asked,

'Where would you like our ceremony to take place, my love? Which church?'

This issue had been preying on her mind, and she said,

'There are no relatives on my side, you have only a few. I

heard that a judge could marry people in some places here. I would like that. So different. No fuss, very simple. Then a gorgeous honeymoon!'

He seemed disappointed.

'If that's what you want, honey, I understand. You don't know any of my friends, you would feel rather lost. As you ask then, we're going to-'

She didn't let him finish.

'Surprise me!'

Kissing him, she thought of the documents she would not need. Susy was getting married. Although overjoyed, David vented his disappointment.

'It should be a grand event, expensive, something to remember! My dear man, dearest girl, why like this?'

'We don't have the time just now. Susy is too busy with her scheme, and I must go back to organise for the changes to take place. When the pressure eases, the church might be an option. There's too much going on in our lives right now, true honey?'

'Of course. I'll be looking forward to planning something else.'

Not likely to happen.

Since her wedding plans only included the two of them, David had to conceal his displeasure. At the same time, Alex contacted the hotel of his choice making all the necessary arrangements.

A large diamond ring sparkled on her finger, but each time she looked at it, her lips creased in asmile. It unmatched in size and purity any of those sold.

The two of them left on a bright summer's morning. Their car journey turned out to be a long but exciting one, with a couple of stops on the way to eat and a short detour to a small and charming town. Susy's amazement was infectious, and he derived much pleasure in being the first to show her around the country. A dramatic sunset spread across the sky when they pulled in at their magnificent hotel at Niagara Falls, built to let the guests enjoy the spectacular view from each glass pane. She discovered the booking for two separate rooms.

'In the morning, you will belong to me in front of the world. Legally.'

He grinned with a twinkle in his eyes, and she smiled coyly.

Susy ate breakfast alone in her room before going to the beauty parlour. Once finished, she returned to her room where the dressmaker delivered the Pierre Cardin gown of her choice, arriving from New York. The mirror reflected a young woman in a trailing, off-the-shoulder white chiffon dress hugging her little waist and deceptively simple. Chiffon-covered hand-made stiletto shoes peeped under the hem. Susy's auburn-red hair cascaded on her back in soft waves, interwoven with tiny lilac scented flowers matching her bouquet. When she opened the door, Alex was waiting impatiently on the landing.

'You look...astonishing, my love.'

He offered his arm, and they took the lift to the foyer. Solemn and by foot, she made her way to the nearby bridge above the Falls, hand in hand with her handsome man in a pure white silk suit and lilac tie. Two male witnesses followed behind. Alex hovered on a cloud, but his vision was flesh and blood, about to belong to him from then on. The judge, in a navy and silver cape, arrived soon after holding a book. Her gaze fixed on the sprays rising like a mist below the bridge and on the people taking pictures. She pronounced the words, *Tomorrow and forever,'* felt Alex's lips on hers, and responded to his kiss. He slipped the platinum band on her finger, Susy on his. It was over. The memory of two people far from there exchanging vows ages ago almost choked her. A glance at her bespoke ring reminded her of the cheap gold band hidden away. She focused again on the scenery and the admiring glances of the crowd.

A table with a lace tablecloth, bunches of lilac flowers, and overhanging white ribbons waited for them in a snug and private dining room with spectacular views.

'Let's go upstairs,' she said, intertwining her arm to his.

'Yes, better to change before dinner.'

Alone in a bedroom for the first time, she locked the door while he drew the curtains. Susy smiled.

Nobody can see inside. What's he afraid of?

The glass panels of the window revealed flowing waters and sky alone. Her expectations intensified with each passing moment. She kicked off her shoes, slowly unzipped her dress that floated onto the blue carpet like a white cloud, and stood naked in front of him. He watched her enchanted.

'Alex...' she murmured seductively, with eyes full of promise. 'I'm here, come...' She stretched her hand to him, who did not move.

'You are the epitome of natural grace. Let my eyes feast.'

She bit her lip.

'...so magnificent, Susy!'

She brimmed with sensual magnetism and drew closer to him. Her presence enraptured him, but after taking off his trousers, he went to hang them inside the wardrobe in his underpants. Relentless, she moved sexily close to him, playing with her hair now almost down to her waist. He went to her, and the tips of his fingers lingered on her nipples. Unable to harness her cravings, she ran her nails excitedly on his chest, exploring, reaching, and leaving a red trail.

'My little Venus, I adore you but gently, let me...' he invited, kissing the tiny mole on her breast.

The eruption inside her demanded action. She expected a forceful, manly possession of her body by this man. Needing the only act that made her feel alive, she became exasperated, discovering a very slow and gentle lover. He was not rough or predatory in his lovemaking, retained total control of his body, and respected her as he did with any woman. Susy taking every initiative puzzled him.

'Not so fast, honey,' he said a few times.

Unwilling to wait or to understand his reactions, she wanted him to let go and forget his self-control. Alex allowed her to make all the moves and to satisfy every instinct as she enjoyed her power over him. He was ashamed of how she forced him to feel and found it difficult to believe his wife so unladylike.

Oh, Rodrigo! - she thought

Now that name evoked a monstrous face. Alex too had his thoughts:

Where's my little delicate Venus? This painting lacks sweetness and tenderness. She was born not from sea waves but an iceberg, a personality sprung from a volcano.

He felt utterly overwhelmed by her.

Susy resigned to the kind of bland relationship that would have to suffice for the moment as the realization of her project came first. The day he took her to a patisserie in Madison Avenue, she knew destiny had guided her steps in the right direction. Strolling along, he explained the fabulous architecture until in front of a luxurious establishment, she pointed at the small bottles inside the window and beautiful leather accessories.

'This is Rinaldo, the "honest" grandson of an influential mafia boss. He imports his goods from Italy, and they are trendy. His cousin is often in the paper but in prison at the moment,' said Alex.

'I see... his scent might be good, but mine will be better.'

'The competition will be fierce!' He laughed.

Standing outside, she studied every detail of the place before moving on. A little further, she stopped as if frozen in front of an empty shop with three large windows.

'This is it! My place! Let's make an offer, hurry!'

Her husband had never seen her so excited.

'Don't build your hopes. Properties here are rarely sold or rented, but I'll enquire if it pleases you.'

'I want this place!'

She stood there, transfixed by her visions. Walls draped with gold silk, crystal chandeliers, glass cabinets all acquired a meaning and a life of their own.

'Let's go home, Alex. Find out, now, please?'

He smiled at her passionate plea, *like a child who begs for a bag of sweets,* he thought while taking her home. She told David right away and eager to see her happy, he made some inquiries.

'Mr. Santini owns it. He relocated to Italy recently, and the place is for rental. I am familiar with that agency. He handed the number to Alex, who, anxious to please her, phoned immediately, receiving an encouraging answer.

'There are three offers on my table already. We shall accept the best one,' the agent said.

'We'll make an offer if you tell me the highest one at the

moment.'

The man fell silent for a while, thinking.

'The deadline *is* tomorrow. Yes, we will consider it. The sum must be above...'

He told his wife.

Very, very expensive, but I can do it.

'Tell him no problem.'

He forwarded the details, and they agreed to finalise the following day.

'I'll come, of course, for the legal stuff, 'said David smiling.

'All mine, Alex!'

His words interrupted her dreamy expression.

'Not yet. Something could go wrong,' but she was not listening.

Emerging from the agent's studio, Susy inhaled the air with gusto. She took David and Alex under the arm and strolled along with them towards a new life. To her request, Alex sketched the interior the way she wanted it, and her dreams did not seem too far from coming to fruition. However, being an experienced man, David expressed his wise opinion.

'In a business as delicate as the one you have chosen, the possibility of failure is much higher than success, Susy. How can you even contemplate tackling something you know nothing about without learning first-hand?'

She listened to him in silence, thinking.

'It's necessary for you to learn and gain experience from de la crème in this profession. If you aim at the best, you need to be the best, sweetie. I'll arrange it for you. When you come back from France, you'll be ready, and not before.'

'I trust your judgement. Anything you say. Thank you,

David.'

She recognized the importance of what he had said and agreed to learn all she could about the business. David organized everything to perfection.

A very excited Susy went to Paris with her husband, leaving David in charge of the work in the shop. Susy attended the well-established and prestigious Givaudan Perfumery School on the outskirts of the city. The prominent perfumer Henri Almeras ensured to show her all the skills she had to acquire. They also journeyed to the Grass region to see where the roses grew, how they harvested them, and the process of extraction and distillation of their oils.

'The most demanding instinct to develop when mixing a new scent is a marked olfactory sense. It determines the interaction of odours with each other,' said Almeras, his French accent intermingling with perfect English.

'Once you command this art, you'll be ready.'

Willing to master the subject, she concentrated all her energies on the set tasks with commendable results.

The couple had fun together. She loved that city, so different from any other place she had seen. The one-day shopping at costly and unique boutiques thrilled her. After dinner, they took a walk in Montmartre to browse or buy a painting and then strolled on the banks of the Seine. She fell in love with the people, the food, the clothes, and the streets full of character.

In the Louvre, a few artists came to life through Alex's knowledge, which she found very interesting. Susy began to appreciate the architecture of buildings. Each day she waited eagerly for her 'apprenticeship,' when she also visited the most prestigious botanists in France. These trips allowed them to travel from place to place in the lusciously green countryside, visiting botanical gardens where flowers grew just for the perfume industry. Alex sustained her every effort, encouraged and offered help if needed.

Susy acquired enough confidence after three months in France. "La Magie" - how she had decided to call it - would be a woman's wonderland. Susy planned to make her signature scents by engaging the services of whoever happened to be the best botanist of the times and anyone else who could assist in her creations. After an extensive search, she hired Mark de Kolm, a Viennese artist who also designed packages among many other artistic talents. Susy asked him to create bottles and boxes, befitting the themes of her perfumes. The idea was incredibly innovative for a decade when package design was just beginning to take shape.

Shortly after coming back from Paris, however, she started to have symptoms she knew well, beginning with the morning sickness.

I do not want a baby.

Two children's faces floated towards her again. She compared the life this newborn could have to those of Belinda and Thomas.

One day my kids will benefit from my wealth. I'll make sure.

Just now, the future loomed ahead, annihilated by this discovery, but she would not let it happen, never again. Without hesitation, she phoned her private physician.

There was no time to waste.

'I must go and sort out a delivery mistake, personally this time. I'm going to be away for two or three days. It's quite a distance, so I'll be staying at a hotel for a couple of nights.'

'Fine, my dear, if you have to go.'

   The Flesh and the Spirit

He did not dare to tell his wife what to do. She spent that time in a clinic and came back blaming her tiredness on the long journey and needing to rest. As always, he respected her wishes. Their sex life, after all, had not been right from the beginning. Susy felt relieved that he seldom made love and took it upon herself to avoid pregnancy. A minor surgery, tubes tied, and the doctors restored her peace of mind. She spared no thought for the unborn child, feeling only overwhelming relief stemming from the powerful drive to succeed in her aim. 'La Magie' was her baby now and very close to its birth.

The police knocked at the door in the early hours, and the housemaid went to wake them up. Puzzled, both hurried downstairs in their dressing gowns. The two officers stood up.

'Your store was broken into during the night. They smashed all the glass inside and the outside windows.'

Dumbfounded, they gazed at each other while Susy collapsed on the settee.

'There's an incredible mess. Any idea of who might want to do that?'

'We've no enemies. Why do this?' she answered with Alex's arm around her shoulder.

'It might be the work of vandals, even though in that area has never happened before. We'll be on the alert, but it takes time to catch these hoodlums without witnesses. Very sorry,' said the officer sympathetically and left. They dressed and rushed off to assess the damage. Susy stared at the disaster facing her through tearful eyes. Not one piece of glass had escaped the vandalism, and through the shattered windows, she heard the passers-by's indignant comments.

'I will give the men one week to fix this. I expect it done as it was, Alex.'

'I promise.'

With a hug, he hurried her out of there.

All over New York and Manhattan, billboards and newspapers advertised the imminent launch of "La Magie." Susy's excitement continued to grow: another three weeks and its doors would open to the public. She opened a box and gazed with love at the fantastic shapes of bottles made to reflect the light, thrilled at the state-of-the-art packaging.

A secret affair, that's what they represent. Women will never reveal the name of their unique scent.

Everything was nearly ready for the grand opening. At seven o'clock in the morning, the couple received another personal call from the police.

'We've bad news. They destroyed your shop last night, nothing was left intact. There must have been at least a dozen of them going in and out. Someone saw a vehicle speeding away. It's the second time it happens.'

'Yes, officer, it is, but why us? There are other shops there, why us?' She asked between sobs.

'We'll fix this, darling,' said Alex, but no words lessened her pain.

'Can you think of anyone with a grudge against you? Perhaps it's a kind of revenge. They did this on purpose, not a random act of vandalism. Was there anything valuable inside?' Alex answered.

'No, they delivered our perfumes yesterday, but we brought them here. I cannot understand what's happening. We have no enemies,'

'Obviously, somebody doesn't want you to open your business. We'll investigate, of course. Are you going to put off the opening? Let us know.'

Susy sprung up,

'We'll go ahead as planned. Please, keep an eye on it until the end of the works.'

'We shall, but if you suspect of anyone, inform us right away.'

When the policemen left, he made her sit down.

'I don't know what is going on, but it could become dangerous. Why don't we opt for somewhere else? I'll help you financially if needed.'

'Tell the fitters we must open on time. Hire more. I will pick the material for the drapes. I don't want to see that place again until it is back to how it was. Then I'll give them the last instructions.'

After that, she went upstairs and snuggled in bed.

The theme was gold. Behind the entrance's golden door awaited an airy, magical world of silk swags, crystal chandeliers, and small glass cases on glass stands. Lights reflecting on the sparkling little bottle displayed inside each case gave life to its amber, gold, or white content. People wandered around, dazed by Susy's vision of Ali Baba's cave, and everyone praised the jewels created by her imagination. Passers-by stopped to admire the spectacle through the windows and to comment on this beautiful place. Its great success filled her with pride.

The destruction of her salon before its opening had attracted even more attention. It turned out to be a blessing, and with David's help and his circle of friends, 'La Magie' soon became the iconic place for the rich and famed. Susy possessed an intuitive knack for predicting how women wanted to smell. Her scents had the allure and femininity that the elite social class enjoyed. The irresistible shapes of the bottles and their packaging added to the perfumes' desirability and fame. She set very high standards, had boundless energy, a Midas's touch, and style. The décor inside and outside the premises challenged the most classy and elegant competitors. The *avant-garde* displays attracted people to the point where many would come only to admire them. At the same time, the newspapers' exposure increased her incredible notoriety and vertiginous ascent to wealth.

My treasure is all gone. These are my gems now, and they sparkle like diamonds. Well done, Susy. You are rich, well known, and the envy of many women. Be happy. You deserve it.

After hiring a night watch, the thugs seemed to have given up, and there were no more incidents.

CHAPTER 18

1963

Since his promise to Sam, Pedro had never given up hope of finding Lucy. That particular day he was in Glide to buy a strong rope, and while in the shop by chance, he caught sight of the stack of old newspapers used to wrap the merchandise. His gaze fell on a photograph sticking out of the pile. Very agitated, he lifted a few pages of the paper and pulled it out. His attention focused on the hair: no other woman's hair equalled Lucy's, but why a different name? And together with her husband? She was married! Was it her? Pedro began to doubt, asked for the page, and hurried back.

'Tlamatini, look! Is it her?'

That was Sam's name now, 'the wise man,' since Ben's death sometime before. He had taken his place as the old man hoped: a sacred legacy to him, something for which he was ready to make any sacrifice. According to his wish, Ben had finally found a pain-free rest beside the apple tree. Deep down in the earth, his body would give life, nourish branches and fruits. The three sisters would keep dancing in the sunset with delight, grateful for the unearthly beauty of their golden apples.

'Pedro! Why the excitement?'

He handed the paper to Sam, who gazed at the woman recognising Lucy with a new husband. Why was she so deceitful? Yes, they had parted, but it did not mean their marriage never existed.

I thought you went back to the children. What did you do, my dear?

He wondered in disbelief.

I must speak to her. What she is doing is immoral and against the law.

He thought of his boy and girl. One day he would have to tell them he had done what the Lord wanted him to do. His conscience tried at times to steer him from that course, but did it mean he was wrong in his conduct? He needed strength in the pursuit of his beliefs.

'Pedro, my friend, would you go and ask her to come and discuss her unlawful actions? An aeroplane flight is too costly, but I know you like to travel on land best. Can you go to New York and ask Lucy to come and talk to me? I am sure you can find where she lives through this paper.'

'It is a very long way, Sam, and a huge place. How will I find my way when I get there?' His voice filled with anxiety.

'I will tell you what to do, don't worry. Go! Tell Lucy to come back with you to straighten out her strange life. Would you do this for me? I can't leave here. New people just arrived.'

'Anything, Tlamatini. I'll get ready, but going to that city scares me.'

'The Lord is with you, so never be afraid.'

'I find her and ask what you say.'

'God bless you. I'll be waiting for you both.'

Sam had just asked a simple man to perform a daunting task, but Pedro would never let him down. An imminent end to his long search made him happy. In particular, he wanted to accomplish what now, due to the distance, seemed impossible to achieve. Sam had pointed him in the right direction after his arrival: *go to the newspaper's building and ask to see past editions.* He had taught Pedro to read in English, and this gift had earned him his undying gratitude.

His journey took a few days by bus, sleeping in cheap motels and even under the stars. At last, one late afternoon, he arrived exhausted in New York. Wasting no time, Pedro showed the paper to the taxi driver, asking to go there. He had met people in the past talking about this city but had never wished to see it. During his ride, he felt intimidated by the sights, agog at the skyscrapers' height, the crowded streets and the noises, the roads full of cars, the bright lights, and the never-ending length of a bridge across a massive stretch of water. The cab left him in front of an impressive building with the name *New York Times* in large letters. He summoned up his courage and went through the revolving doors. Pedro headed for the reception desk, where he timidly asked for someone to help him with his quest. The man checked his dirty Mexican attire and unkempt state with curiosity. After a brief telephone conversation, from the lift emerged a young woman. She introduced herself to Pedro with a smile but withholding her hand - a reaction to his unwashed appearance.

'Miss Carpenter. What can I do for you?'

He explained about his business there.

'Follow me.'

The lift opened on the seventh floor, and they stepped out into a vast room with screens on desks, chairs, and umpteen metal cabinets along the walls.

'Will you be able to find what you're here for on your own, or would you like a helping hand?'

She suspected the answer already.

'Please, I don't know what to do,' he begged.

Sorry for him, the woman took the page with the picture and picked a roll of film from one cabinet. Pedro sat beside her. The smell of his clothes and body overcame her, but she switched on

one of the many screens. Starting to scroll older newspapers›
editions, she asked Pedro the reason for his search.

'I must find her. I was her friend once. I know her well, and
she'll be pleased to see me.' His appearance made her doubt
his words, but something in his plea moved her. When Miss
Carpenter found the article and recognised the woman in the
photo, she asked,

'I need to know why you want her.'

He did not hesitate.

'Her husband needs to talk to her. I'm here to give her the
message.'

'Did you say "husband"?'

Her ears pricked right away. As a journalist, Miss Carpenter
sniffed a story from a long distance away, and something was
in the air.

'Yes, her real husband.'

Although not allowed to hand over any kind of information,
she decided to risk it and trust her instinct. It did not take her
long to find Lucy's whereabouts. She scribbled the details on a
piece of paper and gave it to him.

'Here is the address. I am sure the lady will be as eager to
contact you as you seem to be, but do not tell anyone I gave it
to you, do you understand? Otherwise, I will be in trouble. We
can't do things like this.'

He thanked her almost in tears, and she thought for once in
her life, she had done a, hopefully, rewarding deed.

It was getting late. After a long walk, Pedro found a vacancy
in a small and cheap B&B where to spend the night. He bought
some bread, water and went back to his room. There was enough
money for his trip back, as his bus ticket was a return, and to

     The Flesh and the Spirit

pay for taxis. Exhausted by the long journey and emotional upheaval, he fell into a heavy slumber. The following day he woke early.

Almost done, Pedro, soon I'll be back to Sam with Lucy.

With this comforting thought, he became engrossed in the view from the cab's windows. When the driver pulled up at David's house, he looked around, intimidated by that beautiful home and surroundings. Pedro rang the bell, intending to honour the reason for his presence there. Eight in the morning, and nothing stirred, but he waited a while then knocked on the door. Just up, Lucy started to get ready for a tiring day. Wondering who could be at that time, she looked out of the window and froze. That figure was unmistakable.

What? When? Why?

Panic-stricken, she tried to compose herself while answering casually to the sleepy Alex.

'I'll go. A special delivery.'

She almost fell down the stairs, unable to control the agitation of her heart and mind, both in overdrive. In the hall, she stopped and took a long, deep breath before opening the door, outwardly calm and composed.

'Pedro! What are you doing here?' Her lips stretched into a smile. 'I can't talk just now. Meet me in half an hour in the corner café at the end of the road.'

Disappointed by her reaction, he said,

'Yes, as you say. I'll be there.'

She closed the door on his face. The past had just knocked at her door, and she had to find a route to safety, to the permanent, untraceable burial of Lucy, or she would lose it all.

She met him in the café, feigning a calm she did not feel but with a hopeful heart. A plan had taken shape in her mind, and its success depended on the extent of his loyalty.

'Pedro, I am sorry, but the surprise was too much after all this time. I am in a situation where nobody must know of my past, or it will be the end of me. How did you find me?'

He told her.

'Sam's waiting for us, Lucy. You must come and explain things to him. We can go today,' he added.

She was not shocked by what Sam expected her to do, as that man always banked on being right. To her, however, he was a selfish, impure mind and heart. From the moment Sam had mentioned a "spiritual communion" in place of an actual relationship, her bitterness had developed deep roots. Sam had asked her to deny their sexual urges and had discarded her like an old rug.

'I will give you anything you want, but I must be sure that you'll never tell him you found me. My life would be over.'

Taking a large envelope from her bag, she placed it on the table in front of him.

'If you want more money, just ask Pedro. Please.'

A few tears shone in her eyes. He looked at her horrified as if facing an entity from another world.

'Lucy, I can't take it. I understand what you're saying, but I promised Sam.'

'You don't know the truth. Sam rejected me as a wife, and that's the reason I left, to make a new life for myself. I did what he forced me to do, as he gave me no choice. His life will not improve if I go back with you. I would make him wretched, and my life would be over. Do you understand?'

Anguish clouded her beautiful face, panic transpired in her voice. He had heard the women talk about Lucy and Sam's non-existing relationship and had felt sorry for her.

'Perhaps you're right. I think. I swear not to tell anyone. Are you happy?'

His words startled her.

'Yes, Pedro. For the first time in my life, I have everything I dreamt of and wanted. Thank you so much. I trust you, my friend. Take this money for expenses.'

'No, don't pay for my silence. Not necessary. Adios, señorita Lucy.'

He stood up and disappeared. Doom and resignation left her, as she felt pretty sure he would not tell Samuel.

A sad Pedro went back, worrying about the lie he would tell already weighing on his conscience. Of course, Sam believed him when he said he couldn't find Lucy, but it was preying on Pedro's mind like a permanent black stain on a white cloth. Could he keep it for himself without telling Tlamatini, who still thought that one day he would find her? Which pledge was to be honoured?

'La Magie' and its perfumes became a household name among the rich and the movie stars. She also obtained permission for another salon inside the most expensive hotel in Central Park. Like the first one, it grew into a great triumph, and a franchise then followed with little exclusive shops dotted all over the best areas of New York. Sexually, her marriage had always been a disaster. She looked forward to adjustments in her life, and as soon as the possibility arose, she took it. Susy eased her grip on the business and entrusted it into David's capable hands and the handsomely paid managers. Her betrayal of Alex, although very discreet, became an addiction. She understood the kind of lover her husband wanted and satisfied him by being that person, certain to have succeeded in faking to be the 'lady' he yearned.

Alex's studio flourished due to the publicity created by his wife's astronomical climb to success. Susy learned to weave her way quietly into a new alien and glamorous world. Time had come for a house of their own, but when she mentioned it to David, he insisted they should live with him at least until after the established fortunes of the salons. The couple went along with it, as his house's size allowed the privacy each of them needed.

One evening while the two men relaxed sipping a glass of bourbon, David said,

'I'm not an interfering old man, son, but do you ever think about starting a family? I would love to hear the patter of tiny feet!'

'I thought about it too, uncle. Time to pass on my genes. I'll talk to Susy. She would make a wonderful mother, and I will enjoy being a father.'

He asked her the next day.

'Too soon, Alex, I think. First, we need a place of our own.'

Her answer let through tension and dismay.

'You're probably right. But we should start thinking about it.'

Her secret operation gave her peace of mind, ensuring there would never be a pregnancy. She asked Alex to design a house for them according to her wishes. He accepted, especially when she mentioned it would encourage her to consider having children.

She woke up feeling on top of the world. Once dressed, she admired the image of the sophisticated twenty-five-year-old woman with a glorious and thrilling life who stared back. Susy was meeting Jay for lunch, a fantastic lover and a bachelor like the others, as she chose not to have relationships with married men. At times, some areas of her past caused regrets, and a husband cheating on his wife made her uneasy. Determined to change her ways, among the men she frequented, the combination of love and sex she searched for in one man remained elusive. Alex had already left, and while brushing her hair, the maid came in.

'A man is waiting for you downstairs, miss. He said you know him very well, but he didn't give me his name.'

A boyfriend, perhaps? No one dared to visit her at home. Puzzled, she put down the brush and descended. As soon as Susy walked into the room, her heart stopped beating. She felt faint. Standing there with a ridiculous, faded poncho - one she remembered seeing what seemed centuries ago - was her nemesis.

'Sam!'

Other words died in her throat. She steadied herself by placing both hands on the back of an armchair. Blurred images echoed inside her, fuelling an internal explosion. She slumped on the sofa, and Sam addressed her tenderly.

'You're looking well. I'm here to bring your life back on track. You deceived many people. I am still your husband on paper, so you must tell the truth to the poor man who believes you're his wife. Time to cleanse your soul, Lucy. Time to go home to your children, don't you think? Leave this life behind. Begin again on the true path to the light. Will you do it? No more deceptions.'

Was he a phantom? One who made her incapable of summarizing her feelings in a few words?

Pedro! He failed me.

She stood up and faced him while he moved as if to touch her arm and she shrank away, staring at him with distaste.

'You've destroyed my life. Your fake religious ardour has led to disaster and the disintegration of all I had inside for you. I never confided in you for fear of condemnation, which has been the main reason for doing what I did, *husband*. She stressed the word going on,

'I didn't want to be condemned. I wanted you to understand, to help me cope with such a terrible stage of my life that removed my very soul. I cannot love anybody, respect no one, or feel for anyone, not even myself. I'm a phony Sam, a person who lives someone else's life, someone nobody wanted, scorned by all those who should have cared.'

'Lies destroy. You can't build on them, Lucy.'

The shrill in her voice became almost a scream.

'You talk to *me* about lying. Yes, what I live now is a lie I fabricated to survive. I was dying, and Susy was born. I'm not going to die again.'

Her defiant attitude shocked him. He watched this heartless and deceiving woman so different from the meek and needy person who was his wife in disbelief.

'Ask your husband to come home, or I'll pay him a visit.'

His words hit her like a whip, and she felt crushed by their power.

'I detest you, Sam. I will never forgive or forget what you did to me. Why can't you let me be happy? Why do you insist on believing to be such a righteous bastard? You're not a saint, only a man, as I'm only a woman. Let's live life accepting our faults and failures.'

'The consequences of your mindless actions will hurt many

The Flesh and the Spirit

people, including our children, and I can't agree with this. Call him, or I will.'

His mercilessness frightened her even more than his determination, but Alex? He loved her. She would make him understand. Perhaps it was not too late. Alex would not believe this man looking like a vagabond.

Maybe I can convince him.

Under Sam's watchful eye, she dialled his number. The urgency in her voice conveyed something wrong. Ten minutes later, he was home, only to find a man with long hair in a shabby and discoloured poncho standing there. A silent Susy was sitting down, visibly shaken and avoiding the man's gaze, while he watched her with contempt.

'Who's this?' he asked her. 'What's going on? Why are you so upset?'

Before she could utter one word, Sam answered.

'Her name is Lucy. She is my wife.'

Alex looked questioningly at her, waiting. Whatever the reason for what was about to unfold, no doubt she would have a rational explanation. Still, taken aback, many questions fought to emerge from his silence.

'Who is this madman?' he asked, frowning.

Susy went to him, took his hand in hers. He stared at her, motionless. She was unsure of what she read in his eyes but sensed the deepening of a gulf between them filled with unspoken words. Wanting to establish some sanity over the situation, she pleaded,

'Alex, it is true, but there are explanations, reasons, I can tell you...'

His incredulous gaze fixed on her as he collapsed on the edge of the couch. Recovering from the initial shock, he hesitated before speaking. After what seemed an eternity, she heard his words charged with emotion.

'Who are you, Susy? Where do you come from?'

'You have no idea what I-'

He didn't let her finish.

'Was I to be just a pawn in your game of make-believe? Did you ever love or respect me? You made me wonder at times. You were the painting hanging inside my head, The Perfect Woman. I dreamt of your hand resting in mine many years from now when the world would no longer claim your attention. My fault. Why? You were my only love.

'I love you!' she said, playing her last card.

Sam was on the point to butt in when Alex beat him to it.

'You never loved anyone but yourself, Susy, or Lucy, or whatever your name is. Besides, you lied to me about quite a few things. I've never been truly at ease and happy with you. I waited for a change, repeating to myself if I were patient enough, it would happen. Do you think I don't know about-'

He stopped there, too sore and proud to tell in front of a stranger.

'About what, Alex? I've been a fine wife to you. We enjoyed many good times!'

She sounded hysterical but kept the screams at bay inside herself.

'About what? Tell me what you mean!' she protested, ignoring Sam.

'Very well, then. I'm talking about your lovers, the baby who was never born and you faking in bed. Do you honestly think I didn't know what was taking place under my nose? I pity you. You have feelings for nobody. But I loved you just the same.'

He had spoken to her, distraught and close to tears.

'Please, let's talk in private,' she said.

Sam interrupted.

'Lucy, come back with me, now. The sooner you start to

The Flesh and the Spirit

atone-'

'Go away! I'll never come with you. I'd rather die. Go away and don't ever cross my path again, or I don't know what I'll do.'

Her voice trailed to a whisper as she tasted the salt on her lips.

'What about the children? Don't you want to know about them? See them? I cannot leave my work.'

'The children?' asked Alex flabbergasted.

'We have two. A boy and a girl,' he said.

Alex turned to Susy, reading the truth in her eyes.

'Alex! Wait,' she implored, but her words registered no emotion in him.

'I'll dissolve our ties and dismiss the plan for a home.'

Long and hurried strides took him outside the house, where he started to breathe again, hiding his agony to the strangers inside.

At the slamming of that door, her whole life reverberated within that sound.

'Lucy,' called Sam.

She moved to face him, trying to cross the abyss that a few minutes before was the floor, now opening under her feet.

'Go away. I hate you. I'll count to three, and I want you gone from here, or I'll kick you out. Go to hell and stay there.'

He turned and vanished from her sight.

Too upset to judge rationally, she locked herself in the bedroom, no longer her own. She sat on the bed and broke down. Once the sobs that shook her chest subsided, she kicked off her shoes, stepping on the plush cream carpet under her feet. Lucy went to caress the salmon-coloured marble top of the dressing table, then straightened the deep folds of the elaborate silk and lace curtains. In the mirror of her dresser, she caught the beautiful bottles of *her* perfumes, their gold stoppers shining under the lights like diamonds. This was her kingdom, her Sanctum Sanctorum, her innermost place of retreat, physical and mental, now lost to a cruel enemy. Holding her tears, she deposited her diamond ring and wedding band side by side on the dresser, unknowing and unprepared to face what that city was about to unleash on her. Uncertainties mingled with conclusions, forcing her to confront a life from which she had protected herself until now. Yet that past stared at her with the accusing eyes of two children reflected in the mirror.

It's all your fault, Sam.

To put the whole blame on him made it a little easier. Yet the life now striking her down was really of her own doing.

Where do I go from here? David! I'm sure Alex will tell him.

"Don't give up, Lucy," she heard Jean's voice.

No, she was not ready to let the circumstances that had forced her to be Susy emerge.

Better if I go now. Lucy will pack a case for Susy.

Alex did not go back home until the next day. When David learned the reason for her absence, he found it hard to digest. She suddenly came across as a scheming, unfeeling, deceitful woman. Susy had wrecked their hopes, Alex's life and his. She had betrayed the deep love of two people happy to fulfil her every desire. David plodded about like a frail man on his way to the grave, and Alex? It would take him a long time to forget her, but forgiveness, never.

A week of tearful reminiscing went by in the unfamiliar surroundings of the luxurious hotel room, empty of any warmth but full of fragrances. Sipping a potent cocktail, Lucy envisaged her next step.

Alex and David will not breathe a word about the whole business to anyone. My reputation is safe.

Divorce was common in New York. It would make the news, but that was all. Life, after all, might still show her some sparkle. She was always the 'Queen' of the elite, with an incredibly wealthy and famous kingdom.

Perhaps I should expand my empire in France, Germany, or Italy. Somewhere the weather's always right, the wine, the food.

She would ask Joey or Matt to accompany her, but she had to shelve her home plan. A little pad near the Park would be ample, but she had only peeped at the developing outcome. The past of such a well-known woman could not be hidden - and various rumours sprang up. The chatter grew, altering by word of mouth from a rivulet into a fast-flowing river where Miss Carpenter of The New York Times went fishing for a scandal.

Sam. That bastard never gives up. He is always ready to do anything to appease his ego. Now I stand alone against the widespread opinion. What can I possibly do or say to repair it? It will blow over. People will overlook it. In the end, 'La Magie' is me, my magic! Women love me. I will wait.

Not long after these events, she received a letter. Alex was divorcing her on the charge of polyandry. Hiring one of the best lawyers in the city helped her get away with a huge fine and a very stern warning. The following day, she decided to go and have lunch at the Women's Club, where her various friends gossiped and made mincemeat of their respective husbands. After one day in Court, Susy wanted a sympathetic ear and her closest friend's wisdom.

Today, Tuesday, Vera would be there. She stepped lightly in the posh club's tearoom and smiling waved at the girl, who turned her head in the opposite direction without even acknowledging her presence. She knew well the other two women, but they ignored her too. Surprise and unbelief took over.

So! They are going to avoid me now, I guess. How quickly the news spread. Those damned reporters!

She saw other people there gazing at her, whispering to each other. She stormed out of the room, going to drown her sorrows in a couple of cocktails - or perhaps three - she was not counting. Once back to the hotel, the reporters assaulted her, wanting an interview. She escaped them and locked herself in her room. Without undressing or removing the makeup, Lucy laid on the bed caressing her mink coat. Breathing in the scent of her perfume, she slept until woken by the world around her.

When the papers started digging into her life, it did not take long for her identity and background to become public. Susy received no more invitations to parties, and nobody answered her phone calls or letters. New York's unforgiving Hi Society had buried her under whispers and newspaper articles. She needed to start anew on the strange planet she now inhabited.

I'll not let them destroy me. Susy will find a way to climb up again, and I'll show them all. At least, no amount of digging has revealed my affair with Rodrigo, she thought, needing to hold on to the few dreams left.

Still, for 'La Magie,' the end drew near. The sales in her shops dropped dramatically. While trying to face this inevitable downfall, she had to accept her financial advisors' counsel and resign to the closure of a few salons.

To save any of her collapsing businesses became impossible and one by one, she disposed of them all. Only her accountants and lawyer seemed to befriend her while rejection and loneliness were her daily bread. Even though her empire's crash cost plenty, it found her still in a stable financial position. Yet, a new venture anywhere became an unrealistic dream. Men still flocked at her door, offering all sorts of help, but she did not want anyone. Her only need was time to think and decide which route to take next. The lawyer advised her to move to another city with her money, but Susy did not take his advice.

Alone and rejected as Lucy had once been, she still considered New York her home, her lifeline, and was not ready to give up.

Lies: the destruction of Lucy, the making of Susy and her undoing. My castle, built on lies, has fallen at the first breath of wind. I could have invented some stories for Alex, but I chose not to. I wonder why.

The constant flow of her life's events flooded Lucy's mind. Rodrigo, David, her lovers, Alex, the diamonds, and Sam – the root of all her troubles. She should have despised him. Contempt and pity prevailed, but forgiveness was out of the question. Susy's recent past was glorious, rich, even satisfying. It was possible to rebuild upon the ruins if she planned carefully, without hurry. She deserved a worry-free time for a while, perhaps with one of her boyfriends. Her reflected image came back satisfactory. She attempted a smile and kept brushing her hair, counting the strokes. One, two, three... one hundred. The future? Another time, not now.

From the hotel, she moved into a small rented apartment in Manhattan. Knowing she would not be welcome to David's house, she asked her maid to pack and send her belongings. While choosing the clothes to wear for a holiday, she tried to be enthusiastic. Mick, the man of the moment - a middle-aged rancher with more money than sense, stayed her friend, hoping for something more. From Alex or David, she anticipated only silence. Then she received a letter. The handwriting was familiar. She threw it in the wastebasket, but something made her pick it up again.

What does he still want from me? Has he not done enough damage?

"Lucy,
Shortly before your grandfather's death, Annie sent the children to an orphanage. She visited them now and then, but she says that she could not manage any longer because she was very sick. You must go to them. After all, we gave them life, and the thought of them having to suffer for lack of care and love does not give me any tranquillity. Can you sleep well knowing this? Can we ignore the damage we are now doing by not trying to atone for our misdeeds? I cannot leave even for one minute, new people arrived, but you can. Just think about them, and God will wash away your sins. Please go.
Sam."

She read the letter a few times, anxious for a hint of a change in his viewpoint, but his words only conveyed the wrong meaning. She thought long and hard, imagining the two strangers she would face. She had never asked herself what lies Annie and Mark had told the children. Perhaps that their parents were dead? They might as well have been, she thought with remorse.

The Flesh and the Spirit

Lucy ignored, of course, the discussion between Annie and the six-year-old Belinda. It had taken place in the kitchen while the girl sat watching her 'mum' peeling potatoes.

Annie always eluded Belinda's questions, but the girl insisted so long that she had found it difficult not to answer.

'My friends at school say that dad looks like a Granddad because he has lines on his face and white hair. And they say that you're old, too, because your hair is white.'

It took her aback.

'When they say that again, just tell them that you were adopted.'

'What does it mean?' she asked, puzzled.

'It means that when you were born, we were older than your friend's mums and dads. When your parents died, we adopted you.'

'What's adopted?'

'We became your new mum and dad.'

That explanation seemed to satisfy the child. Annie was aware people had known for a long time the children did not belong to them.

'Go clean your hands. Tea's ready.'

The girl had obeyed, and she had examined herself in the mirror, studying the grey-haired woman with furrows on her face, embroidered there by a miserable life. She had followed with her finger the hard lines around her mouth. Was it too late? Was there still a little happiness waiting for her?

How old were they now? Lucy asked herself. Seven and nine. *Would they recognise their Auntie?* Very unlikely. Then all came back to life: the drugs, the confession of a man now dead, Annie's endless anger, the loss of a good friend, Sam's rejection. She needed to be strong enough to bear stepping back in the past, as the kids were more important than Lucy, the woman she had just resurrected for their sake. Perhaps she could even attempt to find out about her mother. Shelving any other plan without asking herself for how long, she did not dare to look at the debris towering high behind her in that city.

Tomorrow might be different.

When Mark's illness had worsened, the result of his feeble protests about the wife's treatment of the kids had altered his point of view. If anything happened to him, he was sure they would be better off away from her, and therefore he had agreed to send them to the orphanage. Annie had welcomed with open arms the chance to remove two people she had never wanted and arranged it right away. Accompanied by a stranger carrying one suitcase, they left their home never to go back. She was free at last, in control of her own life, of whispers and curious glances endured for years. Shortly after Mark's death, she started a typing course.

Lucy found herself again on a plane bound for England. From high up in the sky, Bradford was a small village compared to New York. Would her flat still be there? First, she had to visit grandma, even though she did not relish the thought. The airport's formalities over, she took a cab to her destination. Nothing had changed in the terrace and a glance to Jean's house next door brought back many good memories. She left them into the beyond and pressed the bell. Her grandmother came to the door. At her sight, she tried to shut it in her face, but Lucy pushed it open quickly before she had the time to do so. The strength of one could not compare with the other, and Annie had to relent.

'Go back. There's nothing here for you anymore. I'll give you the kids' address, but go away.'

'Before I go, you old bat, tell me why you sent them to that place. You don't look ill to me.'

Annie closed the gap between them enough to fasten the safety chain to the doorpost and spoke through that opening.

'I don't want you. You are the thorn in my flesh. I lost a husband because of you, the chance of a proper job or a career because of kids I didn't want. Just before his death, I finally got rid of them. It's your turn. I couldn't care less, and I can't pay for their keep. Wait,' she came back in a few minutes with an address on a piece of paper, handing it to her, and then shut the door.

A vicious wave surged inside Lucy. She screamed her rage through the heavy door, making sure Annie understood every word.

'You don't know anything! You were both hypocrites! Do you know why my mother pushed me away? I am your husband's and your daughter's child! His guilt made him take anything that came along, and I'm glad he's dead. I wish you'd die too for making everyone's life miserable. I loathe you as much as you detest me. My mother, your daughter, perhaps is still alive, do you know that?'

Silence ensued.

'Are you listening? Ask Him up there to forgive you because I never will. Do you hear me, witch? I'm going now, and I don't want to hear from you ever again.'

With a kick to the door, Lucy disappeared.

Leaning against the doorpost, Annie slowly slipped onto the floor. Now everything was clear - an ugly secret, an inconceivable reality she had lived through blindfolded. One man, her husband, a lifetime shared with a monster, a sinner now probably getting in hell what he deserved. He had made love to her, his wife, and then… She felt as if her heart wanted to explode as the pain in her chest intensified. With great effort and pressing her hand on it, she made her way to the bedroom. Annie lacked the strength to open the drawer and destroy what she intended. She dropped on the carpet and remained still.

CHAPTER 19

In her letter to Mrs. Paterson, the woman in charge of the orphanage, Lucy informed her of Annie's death. She also pointed out she was their mother, although they knew her as Aunt, and wanted them back. Enclosing their birth certificates, her own and Sam's as proof of their identities, she arranged a visit with a phone call.

The old stone building stood on Bradford's outskirts, surrounded by a brick wall with a metal gate that gave access to unkempt grounds. Lucy rang the bell, and a man came to open the heavy wooden door, which had seen better times. The high vaults of the ceiling expanded the noise of the door locking behind her. She breathed in the pungent odour of bleach that impregnated the air. The sporadic and tired-looking furniture in the vast hallway and in the room he let her in, signalled a cold severity. She waited for her children with mounting anxiety. Would they acknowledge who she was? Did anyone ever tell them about their Aunt, or would they be reluctant to go near her? What should she do if that was the case? Was this a mistake? Better to leave things alone. A short woman arrived and introduced herself,

'Mrs. Paterson.' she said, briskly shaking hands with her. 'Please come to my office. We need to talk.'

Lucy followed her to a small room with a desk, two chairs, and a filing cabinet.

'Before any release, I must have proof of your financial position. Will you be able to support the children? Do you work?'

Surprised by this question, she took a minute before answering.

'I'm just back from the USA. I can keep us going for

some time, and I own my home. I will look for employment, something that will not interfere with their free school time. I want to be there for the two of them.'

'Very well. You can keep the children for a while, but without an income, we must review this. It's for their own sake, you understand. We've to keep an eye on them.'

'I'm their mother! Not a permanent decision? I can assure you they will never be short of anything. Now, bring them here before I go and find them myself!'

The woman answered Lucy's calm but cutting tones of voice by saying,

'Wait in the room you were in,' and left.

Through the open door of that room, Lucy made out a long corridor with white walls and grey floor tiles. The word endless was appropriate regarding the place, the waiting, and her agitation. Then a spindly woman showed up at the far end of the passage holding by the hand a blond girl, the spitting image of Sam and a ginger-haired boy, her double. As they approached, she felt everyone's gaze on her.

'Children, this is your Aunt Lucy.'

Two pairs of eyes scrutinised her silently, embodying a whole world of indifference. Belinda said timidly,

'Hello. Where are we going?'

'Is it far away?' asked Thomas.

'We're going to my house. There are lots of toys waiting for you.'

'Do you have a teddy bear?' he asked.

'Yes, a big one. Do you like bears?

'I've a small one mum gave me. Where is she? Are we going to see her? She never comes to see us.'

'I told them she hadn't been well,' the woman said.

'I want to see her,' said the boy sadly.

'She went away for a while, so I'll be looking after you. We are going to enjoy ourselves, I promise.'

These kids were cute, sad but sweet. She intended to bring a smile to their lips

'You'll let me know when they'll be back, of course. The children are polite. I think they will be fine with you. Just watch Thomas, as lately his breathing has been erratic, but nothing worrying. Probably the effect of a nasty cold. Are you sure you don't want a bag with their clothes?'

'No, thank you, I'm going to buy a new wardrobe for them.'

'Well then, did you hear that you two? Go now.'

She let them all out of the front door and fastened the heavy bolts behind them.

For three days, she had worked hard, making the flat welcoming and suitable for two young children, but she was unsure whether they would like their new home. She wanted to talk to them in the taxi, but found them incredibly shy, which she expected under the circumstances.

They are still young, seven and nine, and there's plenty of time for them to get used to you.

Both children shouted excitedly when the cab passed what had been their home.

'There lives our Mum! Our house! Are we going in?'

'No, I live very near it. You've been to my home before, don't you remember?'

Belinda shook her head in denial,

'Only your hair,' she said.

Something tugged at Lucy's heartstrings. They appeared disoriented at her home, but she welcomed them with hot chocolate and biscuits before showing them their room. On a twin bed, Teddy stood upright, waiting for two little arms to hold him. The girl smiled, running to squeeze him tight. Thomas lifted Bunny and then knelt beside the train set in the corner of the room while his sister cuddled a doll in a pink tutu along with the bear. Their transformed faces stirred something inside her, something unknown. Whatever it was, compelled her to kiss them tenderly, receiving a hug in return.

'Thank you, Auntie,' said Belinda, while her brother concentrated entirely on the rails. Lucy noticed his ashen skin.

He needs sunshine, this boy.

Throughout the following days, their time together meant fun times, new clothes, shoes, games, playing in the park, meals in restaurants, but Lucy preferred nighttime.

'Tell us a story, please. We like stories!'

Her imagination began to draw from her time in the desert: beetles, snakes, goats, cacti, flowers, all of them a good source. They would then slumber peacefully, but she remained longer, worrying about Thomas, watching and listening to his irregular chest. She remembered the words of that woman, *"The trailing of a bad cold, nothing to worry about."* Through love and care, she might be able to improve his health.

Those two adorable, gentle kids were *her* children, but they retained the gloom she looked forward to removing. Their happiness and laughter mattered to her above all else, and her conscience demanded any sacrifice in this pursuit. Every time she bathed or helped Thomas dress, she was also aware of his permanently cold hands and feet. He never complained, but she ensured he would slip into a warm bed every night. As the bond between them grew, she decided that the best thing

The Flesh and the Spirit

for everyone would be to go back to the USA. Lucy could give them so much more over there: selected schools, friendly people to mix with, perhaps even get in touch with Uncle Sam. Even the right man might come along - someone suitable for her children. It seemed the path to follow, but first, she had to sort out a funeral.

A thick mist started to settle on the fresh grave where Annie lay beside her husband. Lucy and the children shivered in the freezing air, waiting for the interment to be over fast. Her dark musings revolved around the man buried there. He seemed to come back to life for a few minutes, and she heard his last words again. The hate for him survived intact, but Annie had been a victim, too. A poor woman who never knew the evil under her roof. Could she judge her grandmother less harshly?

Nobody shed tears on her grave. Lucy had dealt with the children's pain at home, taking the time to explain death from a child's perspective. Was she to blame for Annie's heart attack? She had only told her the truth. The police had found her because Annie did not answer the phone to one of her friends, who became suspicious and called them. That was all.

The children did not have a "mother" any longer, but she was going to give them what they had never had from her: love. Lucy envisaged her kids' bewilderment at the scale of New York's amusement parks, theatres, cinemas, and museums. Still, before all else, she had to perform one duty she did not relish since there was no other to do it. The letting company had asked her to remove all personal belongings from Annie's home, ready for the new tenants to move in.

With the children at school, she let herself into the house.

Don't think about the past. Don't let it get to you. Just hurry and do what you must.

In a cupboard, she found some brown paper bags and a couple of cases. The bedroom contained the majority of the items to clear, and she tackled it first. Lucy tipped in the first drawer's contents in the open suitcase on the floor: nightdresses, stockings, and underwear. Another held brassieres, pants, and handkerchiefs that joined the heap. About to tackle the last one, she spotted a yellow card among the jumpers. She turned it over and froze: the woman who stared at her could only be... *mother! That man! That...*

The train of her thoughts came to a halt when tears blurred her eyesight falling on the black and white snapshot. Shocked by the discovery, she dried it, held it, and saved it in her handbag. She dropped all the clothes in the case, but she searched the house for other clues before going home with a fruitless result.

At home, her thoughts revolved around the best way to trace her mother. Unable to detach her eyes from that image, she wondered if she was still of this world. The idea seemed far-fetched, as the war had taken many lives, but where to begin? In her hand, she held the only clue as, on the back of it, very faint handwriting in pencil read 'The mill, 1937'. In the background behind her mother figured an old building. Was it important?

I need someone who can find out.

Before heading for the police station, Lucy took the children to school. Once she arrived at her destination, she found the information desk in the foyer.

'Can I speak to someone about a missing person, please?'

'Sure, Miss. Your name and address, if you don't mind.'

The young policeman eyed this elegant and good-looking

The Flesh and the Spirit

woman with admiration. She gave him her details.

'Just a minute. I won't be long,'

He disappeared through the door behind him, returning shortly after.

'You can go inside, Miss,' and let her in closing the door.

A man sat at a desk with one hand on a stack of papers, holding a cup with the other.

'Thank you for seeing me, sir. I am at a loss on what to do. I need your help.'

She intended to get straight to the point. The face of the grey-haired officer lit up, and his lips parted in an involuntary grin.

'Sit down, miss. What can I do for you?'

'It's about my mother. I want to find her. She disappeared before the war, and I don't know what happened to her. All I have is this, ' she said, handing him the snapshot.

He turned it in his hands.

'Very like you, isn't she? Unfortunately, we can't deal with this kind of inquiry. Very sorry, miss.' He handed it back to her.

Mr. Dempsey, (she read the small name tag on his desk) I'm willing to pay. Can you suggest anything at all?'

'Well… maybe George. He's private, you understand. One of our detectives but retired now through an injury to his leg. Our George still does some work for us, but mainly privately. He's the best at his job.'

'Could I get in touch with him? The sooner, the better, please.'

He scribbled something down and gave it to her.

'Says here that I sent you, and he's to help you in any way he can. His name is George Wilkins, and that's his phone number. He doesn't give his home address to anyone.'

'Thank you so much.'

She stood up and shook his hand.

'A pleasure, Miss.'

He got up, going to open the door for her. Her perfume lingered in his room above the aroma of black coffee long after she had left.

A few days later, while deciding between her return to America or to look for her mother, an envelope arrived. The note inside said,

"Dear Lucy,
The enclosed, addressed to you, arrived at the house of a man called David. He traced me and sent it.
Give me news of the children, please.
Sam."

Very curious now, she read the letter inside the envelope.

"Lucy,
When your life became public, and the papers said you were a very wealthy woman even before your marriage, I understood. It was too late for me, but the people after you saw it as well. They traced you to your first salon. Mr. Santini, the nephew of a mafia boss, afraid you would ruin his business, told his uncle, who tried to prevent you from opening the shop near him. They are determined to take back all you owe. Make sure no one knows where you are, or you will be in danger.
For old times' sake. Goodbye.
Rodrigo."

This revelation shook her to the core. To go back was not an option, and England might be a safe place for them all. She had to transfer her money right away, forget about her possessions and warn Sam. It was a matter of life or death - her own to be exact, and because of her children, she cared about living more than ever.

I cannot make mistakes. I cannot overlook one single detail.

The whirlwind in her mind prevented her from sleeping that night. Memories of New York and her fantastic success now seemed unreal. So many had envied and admired her! She relived her adventure with the jeweller in Brooklyn, her marriage to Alex, then David's kindness, and what she had left behind. Still, here was her chance to gain something she thought vanished forever: her children's love.

All I had, it never really belonged to me. It was a loan to repay, one way or another, but the manner of the final reckoning was not up to me. Susy lost it all, but Lucy will gain something she was never going to experience.

She stepped into the kids' room and sat on the armchair listening to Thomas's breathing until overtaken by tiredness, she nodded off.

Next day she wrote,

"Sam,

I cannot stress enough the importance of what I am saying. Tell nobody where I am, or you will endanger us all. Remember, NOT TO ANYONE. Believe me and do as I ask."

She let him know that the children would be well cared for from then on and included their photo. To sort out three lives and find her mother now turned out to be her priority and duty.

Enjoying the kids and developing into a mother gave her hope for the future. Yes, she blamed herself for past mistakes impossible to amend, but she had learned caution, perhaps preventing new ones. For the first time, Lucy did her best in guessing how her mother had felt.

I wonder if she ever thought about me. I hardly thought of my children.

One day, she might know the whole story from her lips. One day, she would also have to let her son and daughter into her secrets. Would they understand and make allowances like she strove to do for her mother?

CHAPTER 20

'Mr. Wilkins, I need to see you. Can we meet?'

She explained who gave her his number.

'At the train station. The first ticket sales you see. What colour's your hair?'

'Red and long. You can't miss me.'

'Is the morning good for you? Ten o'clock?'

'Perfect, Mr. Wilkins. Thank you. Till tomorrow then.'

The following day, while waiting for him, someone tapped her on the shoulder. She turned towards a tall man with a grey coat and hat leaning on a walking stick.

'Mr. Wilkins?'

'Yes, let's go where we can talk. Across the road, there's a coffee shop.'

The limp did not appear to hinder him in any way, as he moved faster than Lucy expected. She found his manner quite abrupt and off-putting, but she followed him.

'Tea?' he asked, sitting at a table.

She nodded.

'Well then, what's your problem?'

His dark eyes surveyed her face. Finding it unsettling, she opened her handbag and withdrew her mother's photograph, handing it to him.

'I want to know what happened to her and if she is still alive. Can you do it?'

'I think I can, but it will cost you a great deal of money. There might be travelling involved, hotels to pay for, and extra expenses.'

'Whatever you need, but find her please, Mr. Wilkins.'

'Call me George. I will get to work right away, and I will keep you informed by post. Two hundred pounds will do just now.'

'Wait here. I'll go to the bank across the road.'

She came back ten minutes later and handed him an envelope.

'It's all there. Let me know as soon as you find anything out, please. And call me Lucy.'

'Very well. As I said, I'll do my utmost. Bye for now.'

He shook her hand.

'Goodbye, George. Thank you.'

She watched his speedy departure.

Sam received her letter with the photograph of his healthy and grown-up children. It freed his mind from any doubts, knowing of the loving life their mother was now providing. At the same time, that photo haunted him. Every time he set eyes on it, the guilty feelings to the bottom of his heart awoke, became a little more intense and disquieting. During those times, he questioned himself about the right and wrong of past actions. The answers evaded him. They seemed to belong to another man's life, not to a priest. No matter how much he wanted to believe to be still entitled to that name, in reality, he was a married man with children. The 'children' of 'his' church needed him, the two in that picture even more.

Have I been wrong? I did it all for His love. Lucy was only my chimaera.

His doubts became fodder for ambiguity. What had enriched his life slowly began to fade, leaving a trail of depression and dissatisfaction. Only in the garden, his preferred place, he found some inner serenity. Sam often sat near the apple tree, talking to the man he missed above any other human being.

Ben, help me. Tell me what to do. I'm losing sight of myself. Perhaps, I'm the worst sinner of all. Have I deceived myself? And also, have I deceived God? You would have told me, would you not?

His torment became apparent, took its toll on his mind. The gradual change affected his judgement. Tlamatini - the wise man - lost his wisdom and grew indifferent to everyone and everything. He spent more and more time as a recluse in his room, absorbed in thought. People worried, especially Pedro, but nobody could do or say anything to drag Sam out of the obscure place he inhabited.

CHAPTER 21

'Where is it sore?

'Here,' he said, trembling and pointing at his chest, wretching again.

The boy's colouring alarmed her.

'I'm here, darling. We'll go and see a nice doctor. He'll soon make it better.'

Not knowing what else to do, she dressed them and took Belinda to school before hurrying to the emergency department. Thomas' pains had almost gone. After a long waiting time, the young consultant appeared very confused.

'I'm not too sure about it. I need some more analyses. I'll take a blood sample just now, and you can go home. Is he always this pale?'

'Yes, he was sick often lately, and now these problems with the chest. I'm worried.'

'We'll find out, and you will be informed right away.'

Sometime later, the physician called her.

'We need him here for a while, for more tests. Can you bring him?'

Days passed, going from one doctor to another, various specialists coming and going, until the results.

'I am unfamiliar with the findings, and I'm not certain. I'm inclined to think of a blood disorder, but we need a definitive opinion from an expert in this field. The only man who could confirm it and possibly help him through some new techniques is Professor Morgan Rathwell, who practices in New York. We can alleviate the symptoms, not cure its root.' The hurt of this revelation wounded her deeply, leaving only one thought:

He needs to go as soon as possible, not stay here without

The Flesh and the Spirit

hope.

'Doctor, I will take Thomas to this man. He must get well.'

'Don't build your hopes too high. If what I think is right...'

'Can I take him home? What can I do, meanwhile?'

'Nothing, I'm afraid. The boy's health will deteriorate. This medicine might help the sickness. I'm so very sorry.'

She took Thomas home, her mind racing towards the best feasible solution.

'Auntie Lucy, do I have to go back? I don't like it.'

Her little boy's sadness upset her.

'No, my darling. Sleep now. I'm here, and all will be well because I love you.'

'Me too,' he said, exchanging the embrace.

The emotion was suffocating. Belinda, present to this scene, sat on her brother's bed, kissed him and then whispered,

'I love you too, auntie.'

Lucy's eyes welled up. They were both safe in her arms, and she determined not to let anything or anybody stop her from ensuring their well-being. With her daughter settled and cosy under the blankets, she held Thomas's fragile frame. She caressed his white face, and the love radiating from Lucy created an aura of bliss around him. Hoping her body heat would warm his cold skin, she slipped into bed, holding him close, listening to the beat of his heart and his chest. Sleepless, a horrible thought took hold of her. She recalled her pregnancy and the cocktails of drugs she had taken without worrying about the unborn child.

I am to blame.

The overwhelming guilt gave her no peace, and salty drops fell on the boy's pyjamas. For the first time in her life, Lucy confessed to the Almighty all her wrongdoings.

Help him to be well. Punish me, but don't take my son.

She sat half of the night in the kitchen, thinking, going back to the past, unsure what seemed to her the only means of solving the problem. Finally, she made up her mind, took a pen and a paper, and wrote.

'Dear Sam,

Thomas is very ill. He suffers from a rare condition of the blood they find difficult to diagnose. The only person able to identify with certainty and treat this disease is in New York. As I told you, I cannot go back under any circumstances. You must come over to fetch him. If you don't, our son will probably die. Do you understand? Only because his father thought a church more important than he is. You told me once that I needed God's forgiveness. If you don't do this for him, God will never forgive you. I still have money, and I can afford it.'

She did not sign it and included some money.

Sam's state of mind was deteriorating until the letter came with the effect of an electric shock, and he started to climb out of his darkness into the light. Immediate action was required. Any delay and the consequences might be disastrous. He called Pedro, explained the reason for his departure, and left him in charge.

'I might be away longer than I think. Will you pack a small bag with peyote and the herbs on this list? I'll take it with me.'

The faithful man obeyed right away.

Lucy opened the door, and there stood Sam. Very surprised, she let him in without a word.

'I just arrived. I'll do anything you ask. We shall save our son.'

He was skinny, emaciated, in very low spirits, but her heart remained encased in stone as far as he was concerned.

'Have you eaten?' she asked.

'Two days ago, but don't bother. Where is Thomas?'

'Asleep. I didn't expect you so soon, without warning.'

'The urgency in your writing, how could I ignore it? They *are* my children.'

That's an improvement. He remembers it, after all.

'You can go and see the kids while I make something to eat. They're both sleeping.'

He hesitated outside their door. Strong emotions stirred inside him, about to step into a past he had tried so hard to disregard. Was he ready for it? As he approached the twin beds in the soft pink light of the room, he entered a dream where two little angels slept soundly, clutching bunny and a dolly. He sat on the boy's bed, aware of the irregularity in his chest, and brushed his forehead lightly with his lips. Sam took his little daughter's hand and held it softly in his before closing the door again, shaken to the core.

'He is like you. His hair is the exact colour of yours.'

She attempted a smile.

'And Belinda's your double. Same unruly hair too!'

'His skin is so white. What's going to happen? What can I do?'

While eating the omelette she had prepared, he waited for answers, noticing the difference in the flat from the way he remembered it. Everything was new and fresh. Such a long time,.. so many things had happened since leaving with her. The people who had returned were not the ones who had left.

'Thomas was in and out of wards for some time, said Lucy, Something's wrong with his blood, a life-threatening illness. The specialist who can help him is in New York. He has been successful in curing another two people with the same symptoms.

They can do nothing more here. It's urgent.'

'I'm ready. It will cost a huge amount of money. Can you pay for all this?'

'Yes, even for an operation, if needed, and other expenses. You will have to stay until they say Thomas is fit enough to come home. Just keep me updated every day.'

'Count on it. I'll be his shadow. He will miss you, though.'

'Yes, but I think he will trust Uncle Sam. He is going to be well and fly. He loves aeroplanes. I wish I could come.'

'Why can't you? What kind of trouble are you in to put your life at risk?'

'Don't ask. Tomorrow I will organize everything. Will the settee do for you?' she asked, changing the subject.

Sam did not dare to insist. She made up his bed on the sofa with blankets and a pillow. Although following her every move, he did not wish to bring back memories.

'Till tomorrow then. A couple of days will be enough to sort everything. I am going to be busy, and you can spend more time with the kids. I'll talk to them. Goodnight,' she said.

'Goodnight. Thomas will be fine.'

She glanced at him with curiosity about saying something, changed her mind, and disappeared into her room. Lucy had noticed a slight change in him. The stern tone in his voice had gone, and the seriousness in his eyes mellowed.

He's humbled at last and maybe acknowledges for the first time that I exist, that I'm a human being, imperfect but with feeling and that he is a real" father" of real children.

Does he have any feelings for anyone apart from God? She wondered.

CHAPTER 22

Sam and Thomas boarded the aeroplane and when it lifted off, the boy's euphoria made him smile. Sitting by the window, he kept asking uncle to look. There was a big sea, mountains, clouds, and the excitement coloured the boy's cheeks. Nevertheless, from then on, Sam had to carry him everywhere. Thomas was weak, and his body feather-light.

Upon arrival, they went to stay at a boarding house close to the private clinic. Lucy had arranged everything via phone calls. During the next three days, the boy underwent all the necessary analyses and examinations. On the fourth day, professor Rathwell asked to see him in his consulting room. Sitting at his desk, a middle-aged and sympathetic man with hair of pure silver and highly tanned skin welcomed him while tapping with his pen on a file in front of him. He spoke with a strange accent and a soothing voice.

'Our findings are clear. Thomas' bone marrow does not make enough new blood cells. The symptoms are irregular heartbeat, shortness of breath, chest pains and sickness. The name is Aplastic Anaemia, the reason for his permanently cold hands and feet along with the paleness of his skin. We can treat it with transfusions and new remedies since it has not progressed very far. If we do not achieve the right result, there are other methods of treatment to try. I am quite confident,' he said. 'In a similar case, the girl recuperated fully. We just go slow, day by day.'

His words relieved Sam's anxiety, and Sam immediately phoned Lucy as he did every day.

'Thomas and I slept in our hotel room until now. From today, the clinic will be our home for a while. He takes it stoically, very excited by the new environment.'

'When will they tell you what the next step is going to be?'

'Not long, I think. I'll phone you.'

Sam tried to reassure his son when answering his questions.

'When are they going to give me new blood, Uncle? Will it hurt?'

'No, Thomas. They will tell you everything. As soon as you're well, we go and buy the biggest ice cream you can eat.'

'Like the one we saw in that tall glass? With lots of chocolates on top. I can eat it after, can I? Now I just get sick.'

'Afterwards, you can have anything you like son. I promise.'

'Can I tell Auntie on the phone?

'Yes, Thomas.'

He still found it impossible to believe that this pale, courageous and precious little man was his son.

On the day of the procedure, Sam reassured Thomas. He held his little hand and kissed his forehead. He wanted desperately to be with him but had to wait and leave it in the Lord's hands. Time became a source of anxiety until the doctor appeared with a reassuring half-smile on his lips.

'Everything went well. Let us hope he will be strong enough to get over the initial trauma. The procedure and the strong drugs are much for a small sick boy. I believe you want to remain beside him. I will arrange it. We will find out within forty-eight hours. Be positive, try to relax a little.'

Sam phoned Lucy.

One month later, father and son boarded the flight back to England, with a bag containing a cocktail of various pills for the boy to swallow daily. His now rosy cheeks heralded what seemed to be a recovery to total health. For the first time in a long time, Lucy allowed her emotions to overflow publicly. Sam was radiant, and Belinda hugged her brother with no intention of letting him go.

Thomas's return to health did not last. A week later, he fell ill again. Knowing the history, they advised them to keep him in bed, as he needed his strength to fight this battle. Sam never left his side. Lucy only to look after Belinda and to perform the normal every day's tasks.

Unknown to her, Sam started treating Thomas his way. He made tea with the peyote and other herbs - a potion learned from Ben - as he had witnessed the power of these mixtures umpteen times. Unknown to anyone, each day, Sam gave his son some of the 'medicine,' and when Thomas dozed, he knelt in prayer beside the bed. Inside him, two different beliefs fought for supremacy: his unshakeable faith in the mixture he made and his total trust in God. Sam aimed at uniting the two. Now aware of how priceless that boy's life was, he started to question his choices. His devotions included a plea for absolution.

The boy's condition worsened, and he slept most of the time. An ashen colour took over the semblance of health, but doctors were helpless. Then one morning, Lucy called Sam from the children's room, where Thomas was standing up.

'Uncle, I'm well now. Auntie is going to make chocolate!'

They gazed at each other, overjoyed and emotional. Sam wondered who or what had performed that miracle. Was it the prayers? The peyote? The medication? A combination of all three? He squeezed Lucy's hand, transmitting his happiness to her, but she pulled hers back as if touching hot coal.

The ordeal had ended, and Lucy did not wait long to ask him the question to which she guessed the answer. He made her uncomfortable, yet he was only a guest, a person who at night occupied her settee.

Do I feel anything for this man? Yes - Indignation, contempt, and indifference. He is a stranger who once owned my heart and threw it away. His presence unsettles me, and I hate it.

Sam enjoyed being with the children, but she knew what the church meant to him and - relieved - was ready to accept his return to the desert.

'Have you decided when you're going? Tell me so that I can prepare the kids. They're rather attached to you and will miss you.'

'I must go back. It's tough to leave but I must do what's right. I am leaving in the morning. The sooner, the better. There will be plenty to sort out. New arrivals need help, and Pedro can only do so much. I'm sorry. I wish I could stay longer. My heart remains with the kids, but I will come back soon, if possible.'

Her sigh was one of respite.

'Fine. I'll send pictures and tell you what's happening. Poor Ben, I'm sure you all miss him. Take care.'

'You too. The children are lucky to have you as a mother. Tell me how they're doing at school and remind them of Uncle Sam.' Tempted to hug her, he busied himself packing his bag instead.

While he was in New York with Thomas, Lucy had received

written communication from George.

'I went to the mill where your mother was employed before the war. It is still functioning, and some of the people have been there a long time. I met a woman who worked alongside your mother. Her name is Betty, and she told me everything she knew. I wrote it all down for you. That was the easy part. From now on, it will slow down. Don't expect a report for a while, but I'll be working on it.'

She waited anxiously to hear from him again.

Four days later, a brown envelope dropped through the letterbox, which she opened a little anxious. Step by step, her mother would come closer, hoping the truth would not be as ugly as she had imagined after that man's revelation.

For Lucy: report - was typewritten on the first page and underneath it, she read:

'After talking to Betty Douglas, your mother's friend and co-worker, this is what transpired:

<u>**REPORT ONE**</u>

1938 - According to Betty, Rose - your mother, had changed abruptly, more so when she discovered her pregnancy. From a carefree girl, she had become very depressed, withdrawn, and quiet. She never said it, but everyone guessed the baby's father was John Ramsden, a handsome young man who worked there, too, and worshipped her. It appears your mother wanted nothing to do with the baby girl. Her conduct surprised people, who thought of her as a heartless woman when she left the child with her grandparents to bring up. Even Betty detached herself from her. Rose went to stay with John, and they kept working in the mill. The women shunned her, and the men ignored him. After less than one year, John died because of an accident at work. Betty was the one to give Rose the bad news, and she thought that Rose had lost her mind. John and Rose were going to marry, but he died on his birthday before then. After his death, she refused to talk to anyone and withdrew within herself. Betty is sure her wages alone did not cover the rent. A month later, Rose disappeared. No one at her work expected it, and the gossip lasted a while. My trail stops here. I will keep you informed if I find out more.

George.'

She sat there with the report in her hands, ebbing thoughts and speculations. Her mother's suffering crept among those words, became real, added to what she already knew. One act of unspeakable evil had taken away her will to live, making her insensitive to all. A terrible secret had forced her to deny and reject its constant reminder: Lucy. *He* had coerced her to submit, and another man had taken the blame.

That man, John, must have loved her so very much. Mother, oh, mother.

Lucy's pain, now sown in the soil of understanding, let seeds of love germinate. She needed to find out whether her mother was still alive.

The Flesh and the Spirit

CHAPTER 23

Lucy's busy life as a mother transformed her way of thinking. She relished every minute of the day with the children. Thomas' health progressed from mediocre to excellent, a normal boy who could play football and run with his friends.

One evening she approached the subject closest to her heart.

'How would you two like to call me mum? I feel like your mum!'

Thomas answered first.

'Can we? Really? Can we tell everyone that you're our mum, Auntie Lucy? I mean, mum.'

'Of course, my darlings,' she said, smiling.

'Mum wouldn't mind from Heaven, would she?' asked Belinda.

She took the blow.

'Of course not. She'll be happy to see that I love you so much and want to be your mum.'

'She never kissed us,' he said.

'She never hugged us as you do. She never made us buns as you do!' said Belinda.

'You like my buns, huh? And the hugs, the kisses, and... the... tickling!' she said, while all ended in a giggling heap.

Happiness had a name: *mother.*

Still no news from George. What was he doing? Why did he not write to her sharing his progress? Too much time had passed without hearing from him. When the brown envelope fell from the letterbox onto the floor that morning, her heart missed a beat.

Dear Lucy,

This report is to inform you of the stage I am at in tracing your mother. As I said, if I do not write, do not worry. I will write when I have something to communicate to you. It takes time.

George

<u>REPORT TWO</u>

I spoke to your mother's landlady. John and Rose were renting the attic room as brother and sister. A short time after John's death, unknown to the property owner, Rose left some money for the rent without a word of explanation, no reason of why she was going. The woman, therefore, ignored Rose's whereabouts -- as she had gone without forwarding an address. Mrs. Hirst also said that after John's demise, the girl was consistently distant and depressed. Only by chance, when opening her window that day, she had caught Rose loading a bag on a gipsy caravan that drove away. Along with a man in the next building, she remembered it heading south.

To follow their tracks is becoming more complex. I go through towns and villages asking questions. Someone might remember seeing them, but don't forget it was a quarter of a century ago. Until next communication.

George.

After Thomas' recovery, Sam travelled back to Wirikuta, resuming life as if nothing happened. Many sought his help, but a slice of his past started threatening the future. He stared at the children's photographs, a constant reminder of people who needed him more than those in the church. Defenceless young beings were growing up in a world of good and evil, right and wrong. It was the parents' duty to protect, guide, and above all, love their children.

While attending to his tasks now, guilt eroded Sam's convictions about his importance in the church. The years beyond him reached out to show his ineptitude, the weak attempts to become a husband and father that lacked practice and dignity. He could teach Pedro to do what he was doing, but it would take years: the peyote rituals, the plant's secret recipes, the knowledge inherited from Ben. Could he ever bring himself to leave Wirikuta and hand over all the excellent learning? This place was his Eden, the cure for his sick soul. It enslaved him with sunrises and sunsets, with nights when the cosmos, almost within reach, transported him nearer to Him. Could he forsake the magic spell of the apple tree, the man always in his mind still delivering nourishment in death, feeding roots as he had fed *his* roots? And the desert - his place of worship, his temptress, his refuge from himself. New reflections, like minted dreams, possessed him. He needed time.

In her anxious wait for a letter from George, Lucy counted the days, then the weeks, five to be exact, since she had last heard from him. While reading his reports over again, she tried to imagine her mother's life. This time the postman rang the doorbell, handing her the bulky envelope. With the children at school, her time was her own, and she put on hold the daily tasks still to do.

'Dear Lucy,

Here, you will find a very detailed account of my work - every movement, every difficulty, and every progress, hence the reason for its length. You might want to skip some of it. Please do. But this is the way I proceed with my investigations. The years in the Force have everything to do with it. I am down south now, following a promising trail. Till later,

George

<u>**REPORT THREE**</u>

'...and everywhere I went (a detailed record of locations and people he had interviewed followed) they gazed at Rose's photo and I asked about the caravan. I was beginning to despair, for it seemed that the time elapsed made the task of finding out anything an impossible one. I went into a small cafe to eat, passing the photo around. An old man had a vague recollection of two people passing through their little town just before the war. The man, a gipsy, played the violin well, usually in the town's square. The thin girl dressed in black appeared ill, miserable, and never said a word – he thinks she was dumb. She went around with a hat to collect the offerings, with eyes permanently fixed to the ground. He felt sorry for her and remembered tossing his last few pennies in the hat. They left the next day. Soon after that, they declared war.

My first decent lead. I trusted my intuition. I visited...'

George went on listing a few towns and villages where he had been and those where he intended to go next, ending as usual with,

'I'll write as soon as I have more.

George.

Why was my mother ill and with a gipsy? Why would she stay with that man?

Questions without answers yet, and as the story became increasingly weird, she speculated and waited. A letter from Sam surprised her. He never kept the communication going, and she was the one who occasionally sent him a picture and told him about the kids. What could he want from her?

"Dear Lucy,

I never wrote before, but lately, it is a need

The Flesh and the Spirit

getting stronger. I keep on thinking about our kids, and I watch them get older in a few snapshots. I am missing so much! I do not believe that you forgave me for the way I mistreated you, and I understand you can only hate me when you think back. It is my fault. If it were possible, I would act differently about many things I did. Time can only mellow deeds, not rub them out. I can tell you that, since spending short periods with the children, I cannot find again the peace that once gave me serenity and a path ahead. I am struggling, Lucy, and at times, the need to amend what's gone pushes me to start anew in the world I left behind, that world where you live with them. Should I find a resolution to this inner conflict and reach the decision of coming back, would you mind terribly? I will not interfere with your routines. All I ask is to be with them whenever convenient for you. I would find accommodation, of course. What do you think? Whatever you decide, I will understand.

Sam"

She reacted with anger and impatience to this surprising, meek, and confusing turn of events. It was her moment, and she strove to dismiss this man and his problems from her mind. Unintentionally, perhaps, Lucy was repaying this man with the same coins. In her list of priorities, the children's well-being came first, then finding her mother, learning to cope with her doubts about the future. Last was Sam, along with a question mark: *Was he really on a different course about the way he thought of God? Would he relapse again in the old ways?* She had no intention to risk her kid's mental confusion.

I must do something first.

'Dear Sam,

You alone can deal with your issues. I am about to move into a bigger home, as we need more space. I am also busy with something producing positive results. I will not tell you what until done. Just now, I am only interested in the kids, my enterprise, and moving house, all of which will take time and effort, but I am excited about these changes. Sorry, Sam. I might not be able to write to you for a while, don't take it badly. We'll discuss your return in the future once we settle in our new home. I wish you well,

Lucy'

She acted quickly and rented a four-bedroom flat in a well-to-do area of Bradford, letting out their property, which helped to pay for the new one. Now each of them had a room. With her funds almost gone, she worried about the days ahead. Without a second thought, she sold her jewels, everything except a thin, cheap wedding band.

To begin with, I need a part-time job during school hours.

George had her new address, and she waited impatiently again.

REPORT 4

Dear Lucy,

'…and from Fareham, I traced Rose to Portsmouth. Afterward, it all went blank. I made inquiries in the office where they keep the documentation of War Casualties, but there was no trace. They also let me go through their files dating back to wartime, but I came up with nothing so far. I will carry on with this line of inquiry, the only one left.

George

At last, a flickering flame in the dark. *Mother, where are you?* She carried on unpacking with a lighter heart.

Reading meanings between the lines, Sam understood Lucy's unwillingness to take him back in their lives and wondered if she would ever be ready.

We both need more time. Lucy has to forgive, and he resigned himself to an uncertain future.

George had worked on the case for three months, turning every stone over, chasing every clue, but still nothing. How could a woman disappear? Dead or not, he should have found out by now. Today, he was visiting another institution to examine more dusty archives.

He asked for information to a charming and chatty woman. She seemed to enjoy being helpful and lead the way to the basement, pointing at the tightly stored files.

'From 1939 to 1956, top-shelf. From 1956 to now, second right. Enjoy!'

Smiling at him, she disappeared.

George sat down and started the laborious task of going over names and dates. His search lasted a long time, but he found nothing and went back upstairs. The 'smiler' asked him,

'Any luck? What are you looking for exactly?'

He explained.

'Did you consider the psychiatric folders? They keep them separate from the rest, just an idea. Try the first shelf.'

He thanked her and went back. His leg bothered him after hours of sitting on a chair, and he rubbed his eyes. Needing a break, he stood up, but something attracted his attention. The entry read:

'September 1939 - A nameless woman was admitted with bad shrapnel injuries to her chest and hip. She displayed a total loss of memory, and she had nothing to reveal her identity.'

<u>REPORT 5</u>

'...I asked what happened to people in those circumstances. They told me about a particular unit in another building that handled cases dealing with various conditions. A couple of patients had never recovered their mental faculties, and I obtained permission to see them, just in case. Do not build your hopes. It's a wild guess, my last one.

George.'

After a lengthy explanation from George, the doctor let him go alone to see a woman they called Jane. He also warned him to tread lightly when talking to her if she turned out to be the person he was looking for.

'Don't be too quick in informing her about a past life. A sudden knowledge could be too upsetting with her memory loss.'

George walked into the room, where a woman sat knitting near the window.

'Good afternoon, Jane. My name's George. Can we talk for a while?'

She stopped knitting, turned around, and lifted her eyes to him with an empty stare. He went closer and shook her hand. The years had physically ravaged her, and the short hair had turned silver, but the resemblance and his gut feeling told him this woman was Rose. She seemed lost.

'Jane, your real name is Rose. They gave you another name

The Flesh and the Spirit

because you didn't remember.'

'I am...Rose, you say?'

'Yes, Rose Jones,' George repeated softly,' born in Bradford.'

'Where is Bradford? How do you know all this?'

'Bradford is in England, not too far from here.'

He found her calm and detached composure unnatural and unnerving. However, in her eyes, he seemed to detect a glimpse of curiosity, so he went on.

'You have a daughter, Lucy, who hired me to find you.'

Expecting some kind of reaction to his words, he was disappointed, as Rose remained indifferent. She stared at him for a while, as if at a shadow in the room before answering.

'I am Rose, and I have a daughter, you say? And I am from Bradford.'

'Yes. Your daughter will come soon. Would you like that?'

'My daughter? I don't remember her. I don't remember anything.'

She was confused. Due to the evident distress on her face, George decided not to proceed further. Lucy had to take over from there.

'I'm going, Rose. It is the end of my search but the start of yours. Goodbye, love.'

He left deeply saddened and satisfied with a job well - and sometimes, luckily - done.

She received another envelope and sat down to read it. Her hand shook when she tore it open.

<u>REPORT 6</u>

Dear Lucy,

I went to the psychiatric unit about which I wrote to you.

Are you ready? Good and bad. I think I found your mother. However, it is not too reassuring. I spoke to the doctor in charge. He mentioned that your mother has suffered from total amnesia for twenty-five years, according to her dossier. They moved her to various institutions before ending up in that ward. There never was any improvement, and she relied on the people in the hospitals. Her illness occurs when a person blocks out information about a stressful or traumatic nature. It could be associated with the war, abuse, or a disaster she witnessed or experienced. The memories still exist but deep inside the mind and cannot be recalled. There is a chance they might resurface - either on their own or when triggered by something in her surroundings. She was almost dead when they found her with shrapnel wounds - one buried in her chest and one in her hip. This event leads me to deduce that a bomb probably exploded not far from where she was. She is lucky to have survived. Your mother suffers from depression, anxiety, confusion, and they treat her with anti-depressants. She has never been able to retrieve one single episode, and the doctor thinks she never will. I am genuinely sorry, Lucy. Your mother is living, but she is not aware of it.'

To prevent her emotions from taking over her reason, she strode through the house, thinking of this woman incapable of recalling a time lost to her for so long. She was someone who survived each day in a world to her unknown and indifferent. She glanced at that line again, "... the result of traumatic events... the war... abuse..."

Abuse, abuse, abuse, words that entered her mind like a storm. Abuse, explosion...

My mother doesn't want to remember.

This revelation annihilated all her previous suppositions.

    The Flesh and the Spirit

Now she knew.

I'll make it up to her and love her. I'm coming to take you home, mother.

When she contacted George, Lucy had made her plans, but somebody else had already made his own.

His dark, highly tanned looks seemed out of place on that rainy and cold day. He climbed the two flights of stairs before knocking. Lucy opened the door, about to ask who he was looking for when the stocky man pushed her in and shut the door with one hand gripping her arm with the other. She screamed and wriggled to free herself without success, thinking he might be a burglar.

'Who are you? What do you want? I have no money.'

He was hurting her now, twisting her limb into a spasm.

'Never mind who I am. How much? What's left from their sale? We want every penny back.'

Terrified by his presence, she attempted to recover from the shock.

'You better tell me and quick. Did you think we wouldn't find you? No, your boyfriend didn't talk. Corpses don't talk. You want to join him?'

Lucy screamed again, hoping someone might hear her.

'Nobody else is at home, bitch. No one can help you.'

He tightened his grip and put one hand on her mouth to suffocate her scream.

'If you dare... I'll cripple you. Where are they?'

Lucy had no options.

'I'll not lie! Let go of my arm, please.'

He pushed her on a chair so violently she hurt her back and lacked breath.

'I'm all ears.'

Massaging her sore spots, she started to tell the whole story. He plunked himself on a seat in front of her and just listened. In the end, she said,

'Because of what happened, it's all gone. I'm looking for work now to survive.'

He knew she was not lying about having any money - his boss had already checked, and no diamonds either. They had already dealt with the shop owner where she had sold them but still hoped there might be cash somewhere.

'Where did you stash the remainder of the money? And the stones?'

He twisted her arm again, so hard the excruciating pain caused her to scream again with tears running down her face. He moved his finger from side to side.

'No screaming, or I'll break both your arms. And don't lie to me.'

His distorted face showed a ferocious mask that spoke of mortal danger. Even though with crazed butterflies in her stomach, the idea came to Lucy like a bolt of lightning.

'All I have left is my life. Take it if you must.'

He stood up, knife in hand. Notwithstanding what she felt inside and the sweat betraying her, she managed to seem unafraid.

'I'm not lying. You would find out.'

If he went back empty-handed, his boss would not like it. He put the knife to her throat, staring into her eyes. Her terrified expression pleased him. Should he kill her? He was deciding what to do. A glance at the décor's low standard told him she might be telling the truth: she was not rolling in money. Revenge? Too late. He would tell his boss that he was sure she

The Flesh and the Spirit

had told the truth after a few cuts here and there.

'Let's say I believe you, but I don't know if my boss will. For your sake, I hope you've been straight with me, or next visit I'll kill you - after long torture, of course.'

He got up and was gone. Lucy's shakes subsided as she locked the door. She resumed breathing normally. Still trembling took a couple of aspirins for the terrible pain in the arm and back, preventing her from wearing a coat. On the way to fetch the children from school, her tears mixed with the drops of rain.

Rodrigo, I'm so sorry.

Lucy phoned the hospital to find out about the release of her mother into her care.

'Doctor and psychiatrist will perform a joint assessment, but no such thing is necessary in Rose's case. It will be a formality. She has been a long-stay patient well-known to them. Mr. Wilkins informed us about you. We saw the snapshot, and she might be your mother. In line with the rules, as the closest relative, it's in your power to discharge her. You understand, of course, that you must tell your doctor and arrange regular check-ups for her. A nurse often will come to check, and you'll be able to ask her any question until you have learned what to do. We are confident you can supervise her. Everything will be ready for you, and we can prepare her.'

The outcome pleased her. Brenda, the middle-aged widow next door to Lucy, was happy to earn extra money by looking after the children. Their enthusiasm for the news of a grandmother overcame the disappointment of her sudden departure.

Throughout the six hours' journey to Portsmouth, Lucy

concentrated on the best way to cope with the situation that awaited her.

I'll talk to the doctors and keep to their advice. She might improve, recall parts of her past, but I must not try to make her confront events for her non-existent. Accept your mother as she is. Give her love, some quality of life, make it worth living.

When finally the train pulled into the station, the clock's dirty face indicated four o'clock. Lucy jumped in a taxi and tried to curb her agitation.

The pungent smell of disinfectant wrapped itself around chairs, tables, and posters affixed to the white walls. After enquiring at the desk, the receptionist directed her to an office where a doctor appeared a few minutes later. She introduced herself, proved her identity, and presented him with Rose's photo. Next, they sat down, and he talked about her mother's mental state.

'Tell me what to do doctor. What's best?'

'Do nothing. All you need is patience. Give her the medication as prescribed and make her feel at home. Who knows, the love you will provide could aid her recollections. She'll miss this place, though.'

He then told her what to expect at their meeting and the difficulties she might encounter at home.

'I told her you were coming and of your intention to take her away from here. Do you want to go to her now?'

'Yes, but we travel tomorrow. It's quite a long way back.'

She followed him to a small lounge painted grey with blue chairs lined along one wall. Rose sat near the window, knitting an endless red scarf, which she placed on the table when they entered. Lucy tried hard to control her emotions. This woman

   The Flesh and the Spirit

was her mother, the one she had believed dead for so long. The motionless, emotionless person who fixed on her an empty stare, who stood up and kept watching her with curiosity, was her mother. In a soft voice, holding her hand, she said,

'I'm your daughter, Lucy. You don't remember me, and for many years I thought you were dead. I wanted to find out whether you still lived. I am a stranger to you, but I will love you very much and look after you for the rest of your life. In the morning, I'll come to take you home.'

She obeyed the urge inside her and embraced her mother, who remained rigid, saying,

'This is my home. I don't know you, Lucy.'

'You will,' she said, intense and emotional. 'You will.'

CHAPTER 24

On the train back, Lucy tried to communicate with Rose by telling her about Thomas and Belinda. Listless, her attention focused on the countryside.

I must not forget I am taking her away from the tranquil shores of her existence into the unknown. Her behaviour might alter to less detached and more talkative and participate in our everyday life with time. It is all I want. The rest will probably never happen.

When Rose walked into Lucy's home, she asked,
'Is this where I lived?'
'No, I just moved in.'
She did not volunteer any other information, waiting for her mother to ask first. The children came in.
'Mum! We missed you so much!'
They hurried to kiss her before inspecting Rose with curiosity.
'Are you our granny?' Thomas asked.
'I... don't know, I...'
Lucy came to her rescue.
'Grandmother is very tired. Let her sit down and keep her company while I make some food and fix her room. She'll be living with us from now on.'
'I'll be quick,' she said to her mother, who sat with hands crossed on her lap, looking around in dismay.

Rose tried her best to adjust to an alien environment, to life, to the idea of grandchildren. Lucy to cope with her depressed moods and the aloofness that, even if decreasing, often hurt her.

The Flesh and the Spirit

'Mother, are you happy here?'

'Happy? I think so.'

Lucy's heart sank.

'I love you so much,' she said, hugging her, but her mother's cold unresponsiveness wounded her.

Just give your love, don't ask for anything back.

Unaware, she had blossomed into a woman who put herself last.

While watching her daughter making breakfast Rose said,

'I saw something last night, a man, a name, John, a room. He was your father, I think. That image is so alive, like yesterday.'

'Mother! That's terrific! You're not a useless vegetable, as you always say. You're a woman imprisoned by many years of darkness. I'm sure you›ll get better.'

'Do you think so? I hope you're right and one day I'll feel normal again. Thank you, my dear, for all your warmth and love.'

For the first time in her life, Lucy felt her mother's arms around her. Time stood still within a moment of such intensity and grandeur that remained sealed in Lucy's heart until the end of her days. Now she could tell Sam about her mother. He would then understand the reason for not writing sooner to inform him of her new address. After all, he was the kids' father. She explained briefly about the events leading to Rose's discovery, about his home and hers, the children, and her mother.

'I hope all is well with you,' she wrote.

The setting sun's tongues of fire streaked the horizon when Sam plodded into the garden to wait beside the tree. Nature's smells wafted in the breeze, and he inhaled deeply, contemplating the view always cherished. The stars were still hiding from the light in the sky, and the dramatic nightfall engulfed his world in red and gold colours. Wirikuta had taught him to delve deep inside himself, to hear the desert's silence and its whispers, to which he had been deaf for some time.

Overwhelmed by the magic around him, he watched the apples again transform into sublime spheres of light, and he waited for the three sisters - Aegle, Hesperie and Aerica, to appear. They invited him to join in their magical dance of life and death - not only to honour the ending of the day - but also an old man resting among the roots of their tree. Once more, he saw them floating in the dying sunlight with their golden robes and long red hair streaming in the zephyr, blending with the shadows beginning to fall. Strange how their locks resembled Lucy's. He had a vision of a beautiful girl who once loved him and who came to him with the joy of youth. That young woman had made him happy, had satisfied his every need, and had given him two children. She had achieved success in her life and found peace and fulfilment at last. That woman had succeeded in all at which he had failed. He never knew what a fortunate man he had been to have such a girl in his life or what love truly meant until now.

At that exact moment, something extraordinary happened. One apple fell to the ground. Sam gazed dumbfounded at the fruit. He bent to pick it up and held it in the palm of one hand, touching at the same time one of the tree's spreading roots. Ben's answer to his question upon his arrival echoed in his ears: *"...they leave when their search is over."*

I understand, Ben. You're right, as always. Goodbye, my friend.

For the last time, his eyes captured the twilight that, day after day, had woven for him bewitching temptations. Then he went to his room to write down all that Pedro needed to carry on

Ben's work.

On the point of going to bed, the bell rang. Wondering who could be at that late hour, she put the safety chain in place, then opened the door and emitted a little cry.

'Sam! What are you doing here? Did you get my letter? We're all well.'

'Sorry to drop on you like this, but I miss those two too much. I am here to stay.'

She looked at him, astonished.

'Come in. You don't seem to be well.'

'I have been sick for too long. Where are they?'

'They're asleep.'

'Can I see them?'

She showed him a door, and he stood with his hand on the knob before going inside. Irradiated by the soft pink light in the room, his daughter slept with a doll beside her. Sam gazed at this angelic being for a while, kissed her forehead, and walked out, his eyes questioning Lucy.

'Here. Next to Belinda's room.'

She opened the door, and he went in. His son, too, was sleeping peacefully, clutching his bunny, his rosy cheeks sign of restored health. Sam sat on his bed, held his son's hand, kissed him lightly on the cheek, leaving with an aching heart for the power of those moments.

'Come on. I'll cook you something and a cup of tea. Why didn't you tell me about your arrival? The sofa would be ready for you.'

'It doesn't matter. I will go and find somewhere to stay tonight. Then I'll hunt for accommodation.'

'Sit down. I'll be quick.'

'I don't want to interfere with anything. How's your mother?'

'Tiny steps forward. She only knows that you live abroad.'

His drawn face, thin body, worn trousers and shirt far too big for him, filled her with pity.

'The path I am following is real, but it leads me to a place I cannot recognize. It will take time, Lucy.'

'I understand. There's no need to talk about it yet. I'll make you a hot drink,' and she left him alone.

A heavenly silence reigned inside the room. Watching the coal fire, physically and mentally shattered, Sam fell into a heavy sleep on the armchair. Before retiring to her room, she covered him with a blanket. How long would he stay?

He will not last away from Wirikuta.

The happy cries of the children woke him up.

'Uncle Sam! You're here!'

They jumped on him, exchanging hugs. Lucy walked in.

'Time to get ready for school. Get dressed, you two!'

They hopped happily away while Rose appeared and glanced at him, puzzled.

'Mum, my husband, Samuel. He has come back to stay in this country.'

The word 'husband' had an odd ring to it, but what else could she have called him? Her mother said hello, then left, going into the kitchen.

'Sorry for last night, I was overtired. I'll go now. I need to find a place to stay.'

'Do you have any money?'

'Enough, I think.'

'Just a minute.'

She took some notes from her handbag and closed his fist on

them.

'A loan, till you get settled.'

'No, I can't-'

'No more said, Sam. Do you have our phone number?'

'Yes, thank you. And the children?'

'I'll tell them you'll be back soon.'

He left, but his presence unnerved her as it always did.

Rose's remembrance of the past seemed to focus on a single event. She spoke about it umpteen times but often adding one more small and vivid particular: a large loft room, John, his violin, the music, a tablecloth with a red flower embroidered in the middle. During the recall, her face altered and came to life. She lived her memory, as she belonged to it.

'Your father, he played the violin. So beautiful! I can hear it.'

Her daughter watched her with adoration, happy for the little nuggets of remembrance but also afraid for them both. If her mother regressed too far back, the consequences could be disastrous for a fragile mind.

We'll cross that bridge together if and when we come to it, Mum.

As she knew, Sam had no financial means after giving her most of his money, and she felt obliged to exchange that generosity. Since Sam's return a week before, he had lodged at a cheap B&B while looking to earn a wage. When he phoned her to say he had found a job as a taxi driver, she smiled.

'You can go and live in your flat. I was renting it out. '

'Why are you so kind to me? I don›t deserve it,› he said,

'It's the sensible thing to do. One more week and the flat will be accessible, still furnished. I'm glad you have a job.

'I want to help you financially.'

His contribution would help, she thought, amazed at the determination in his voice.

Lucy never mentioned she was broke. A few hours of work in a grocery store near home stood between her family and starvation when the children were at school and Brenda kept company to her mother.

'Phone me when you want to see the children.'

'How's your mother?'

'A little better, I think. Her depression has lifted, and she is not on medication.'

'I'm happy for you both. I'll talk to you later. Bye for now.'

His thoughts of Wirikuta were growing dimmer, allowing him to reach for a brand new future.

I need to find a proper job, she thought. *Mum will be with Brenda. She likes her, and the kids will be with them for a couple of hours when back from school. I must look for something I can do. Perfumes were her best option.*

In a navy suit, white blouse, and high heels, after a dab of perfume to her wrists - the only treasured memento from the past - she was ready. Her splendid hair, pinned with a mother-of-pearl comb on either side, streamed behind her. In the city centre, she asked in beauty shops hoping for vacancies, then in large stores, until her feet felt sore in the stilettos. She did not imagine finding work would be pretty challenging, but she was not ready to lose heart.

I will try until I collapse.

Money ran out. Sam contributed a little, but she required a more substantial income to keep them all. At home, she still smiled at everyone, cooked dinner, spent time with the children before bedtime, and conversed with Rose. Sleepless nights brought no counsel, but her worries transformed into a panic when she received a letter from the orphanage. They required proof of income, or they would remove the children from her care. Lucy collapsed on a chair, deep in thought, then got dressed, took the kids to school, and began her daily trek determined to find a job anywhere, of any kind.

After hours of trudging about the town with high heels, throbbing feet, and low morale, she sat on a bench to take off her shoes and dry a few tears. Her children: she stood up, wrapped the blister on her toes with her handkerchief, and was ready. Near closing time, she spotted a shop on the side street.

I might as well try there too

After a glance at the perfumes and cosmetics displayed in the two windows, she went in.

'I see you sell top brands. That bottle over there - traces of sandalwood and jasmine, plus a hint of oriental spices - an intense one, and that one - subdued violets, musk; that one...' she went on describing others.

'Have you learned the composition of them all?' said the woman, amazed.

Before she could answer, a tall and impeccably clothed man emerged from the back shop.

'I'm very impressed. Can we help you? Are you looking for something special?'

He asked in perfect English with a slight intonation she believed to be foreign.

'I am after a job. Do you have any?' He was surprised.

'I'm the owner, Maximilian Aubert, Max for short. And you are?'

'Lucy. Nice place,' she said, shaking hands with him.

'As it happens, an employee had to go last week, and I intended to advertise. Let me think about it. Come back, and we'll talk.'

She thanked him and left under the watchful eye of the attendant who prepared to close. She got home in pain, with blisters on her feet. Fares for buses or taxis were out of the question. She had already borrowed some money from Brenda and had to pay the rent.

'Thank you for coming back. I feel you are well qualified for this position. We need to talk about it, of course, what about a little aperitif? I have a few questions before I can offer you a job as manageress.'

She refrained from hugging him, kissing him, telling him how he was about to save the lives of four people and when her eyes glazed over, he understood.

'There's a nice place just along the road, shall we walk?'

She nodded, hoping her feet would not let her down.

'Yes, fine. Thank you.'

Maximilian's thick lips parted in a wide grin.

In the dim lighting, relaxed atmosphere, and sipping a glass of delicious wine, she was totally at ease. Soon her eyes sparkled, and a radiant glow spread on her face.

'Are you French?' she asked.

'On my father's side, my mother comes from Bradford. They met on one of his trips to England to buy some materials and fell in love. She ran away from home, going to Paris to marry him. My mother came back here during her pregnancy because she wished her baby to see the light in her country. My father travelled to be with her, leaving his business. Not long after my birth, we went back to France, but my mother and I often returned to Bradford because of her family and relatives. I spent my life between here and Paris. A romantic story, is it not? Now that my life is an open book, tell me of yours.'

The Flesh and the Spirit

She admired his aristocratic manners, and his penetrating brown eyes unsettled her. A strong jaw, a Roman nose, the lights playing with the silver streaks through his dark hair, caused something to stir inside her - an undeniable sensation of excitement, probably due to the drink.

'My story is not as charming. I was in New York for a while, where I learned about perfumes. They are magic.'

She smiled at the word before continuing,

'I managed a salon for a few years.'

It was not a lie, only a short version of the truth.

'The job's yours if you want it. I'm happy such a knowledgeable person came to my shop.'

The rest of the conversation established her wages, timetable, and time off.

'Thank you, Mr. Aubert.'

'Start tomorrow, at nine o'clock?'

'I'll be here. I need to go now. Thank you again.'

'Where do you live? Can I give you a lift? My car's parked outside.'

'You're very kind.'

If he only knew how her feet felt!

He had given her the job but not only out of kindness. She saw it in his eyes and the angle of his arm as he opened the car door for her. Lucy stepped out of his red Ferrari light-headed, floating on the pleasurable time spent with him and blaming the drink.

Rose's memories still extended to John and the room, although often adding snippets but without any significant progress. Her daughter and the children understood her inner loneliness. Lucy asked her if she was willing to help with

Brenda when they came back from school.

'I need to work, mum.'

A smile creased the woman's lips for the first time.

'I can be trusted then, my dear? I'll love to do it with Brenda.'

Her mother was at her happiest with Thomas and Belinda around, and they doted on Grandmother. Rose now arranged her grey hair nicely in a knot on the back of her head, kept neat and tidy, and the apprehension of a lost child had disappeared. What more could Lucy ask?

The Flesh and the Spirit

CHAPTER 25

What Sam had left behind did not seem to weigh on his mind. He viewed with new eyes, gaining different perspectives every day. He visited the children as often as his job allowed, but always when Lucy was at home. Knowing where she worked, one day he decided to wait for her and bring her home in his taxi. He parked beside a red Ferrari, wondering what kind of person could afford that car when she came out with a man. He opened the Ferrari's door, let her in. With a roar, the car vanished around the corner. A volcano erupted inside Sam. He forced himself to sit and cool down. It did not occur to him his wife could see another man, as she had blossomed into a different woman.

I must let Lucy understand who I am becoming.

He invited her to dine out on his day off as a thank you gesture, he said. No harm in it, she thought, accepting.

The reflection of the man in the mirror that evening was not Samuel. His blond hair had acquired lustre after the haircut. A new suit replaced worn-out and discoloured clothes. Fashionable shoes peeped from under his trousers, and a bunch of red roses waited on the table. Satisfied with himself, he stepped outside and stopped a cab. When Lucy opened the door, the surprise on her face pleased him.

'Sam...'

She finally recovered and inspected him from head to toe.

'You are not the same person!'

'Are you ready to go out with this one? These are for you.'

Her amazement amused him.

'Thank you. Lovely roses! Let's go.'

The elegant dark green, soft woollen dress hugged her in the right places. It outlined a twenty-seven-year-old body that, although mellowed by age and motherhood, was still beautiful and desirable.

A bottle of wine accompanied an excellent meal in a French restaurant. Entertaining conversation from Sam - who recounted many funny episodes from his life as a taxi driver - and plenty of laughter made their time a most enjoyable one.

'We can be friends, don't you think?' he said.

'Yes, we can.'

He's a handsome man, a different man.

She gazed with tenderness at the unruly lock of hair on his forehead as he swept it back with his long fingers. The times she tried to keep it in place using her face cream brought a smile to her lips, and he asked,

'What are you smiling at?'

'Your hair. I'm remembering.'

'You were determined to stick it back! All your efforts, but it never worked,' and he laughed.

She's so beautiful and a different woman.

As if meeting for the first time, they found out about each other and their goals. The magnetic attraction Sam had once for Lucy was still there, unchanged. He wanted to make love to her for as long as their bodies would allow. A flame burned inside his heart, but the ominous shadow of another man hovered on his fantasies.

'Max, I feel like you do.'

'Then quench my thirst Lucy, be mine.'

He took her in his arms, staring into her eyes.

'We've waited too long. Here is the key to my flat. Come

The Flesh and the Spirit

tonight, mon cher, will you?'

'Yes, I will!'

She kissed him, pushing her body against him and feeling his hand searching under her blouse. Shivers darted down her spine.

Not now, Lucy. Someone might come in.

She forced herself to part from him, aware of his heavy breathing.

'Tonight Max. Our first time.'

'You're right, mon cher. I'm going home. I'll be waiting.'

He left hurriedly, blowing her a kiss.

Sam went to fetch the children on Saturday morning to take them out for the day.

'I might bring them back late this evening. We're going to eat lunch first and then we'll go to the park. After tea, we're off to the cinema.'

'No problem. Brenda will be here to babysit.'

He refrained from asking her where she was going.

'Perhaps next week we could go out again? I got a wage rise.'

'I'm happy for you. I do like you, Sam, but I feel uncomfortable. I would rather keep our friendship as it is.'

'As you wish, Lucy. Have fun tonight.'

Is she going out with him?

With that thought gnawing at him all day he made his plans.

I will follow her after work, but if she doesn't go straight home? What could I do? I might lose her forever.

Did she care about him, even a little? He realized how much he loved her, and that love had a tight hold of him. He knew that the only drug capable of quenching his longing was the possession of Lucy. Inside him, desires he tried to contain flowed like a river, and he thought of a plan sure to lure her.

'My beautiful woman, some champagne?'
Max handed her the glass. Sitting next to each other on the large sofa, breathing air overflowing with anticipation and desire, they lingered. He knelt on the carpet, removed one of her shoes, and stroked her foot lightly before taking off the other. The touch of his hand on her naked skin sent goose pimples to every part of her. She rose. Lucy's feet touched the soft, deep pile. The longing worked its spell on their bodies, and inhaling her scent, he took off her dress in slow motion. She undid the buttons of his shirt, touched his chest, his belly.

Unhurriedly, one item at the time, he got rid of her underwear until she stood naked in front of him. His tongue touched her ear as he whispered,

'Close your eyes.'
With shivers over her entire body, she obeyed, ready, and saw Sam's face. It broke the spell.

'I can't. As much as I want to, I can't.'
Max let go of her breasts.

'Lucy, I want to be with you. I must be with you...'
She disengaged herself from him, hurried to put her dress on and picked up the rest of her things saying,

'I think I love someone else, Max. I need to understand,' and she left him.

He filled his glass, and when the bottle of champagne was empty, he fell asleep with his frustration.

At home, she found the note right away.

The children are sleeping at my house tonight because I am concerned about Thomas.

The Flesh and the Spirit

Lucy furiously changed into a skirt and blouse, panic creeping into her mind like a dangerous beast, and arrived at Sam's breathless with worry.

'What's wrong with him? Is he hurt? Where is he? Where are they?'

'Calm down; they're both fine. I'm sorry, I needed to speak to you.'

'Are you crazy? Couldn't you wait until tomorrow? What's come over you?'

His eyes warned her of the danger.

'You're still my wife. I'm your husband. *This man* has always loved you. He just didn't understand anything then. Could you, could you care for me? '

It was all there, in his eyes.

Go, Lucy, go, but her legs refused to obey.

He took her in his arms, held her with force, and she breathed him in, gazing into his pleading eyes.

'Don't scream, or you'll wake the kids,' he whispered in her ear.

He pulled her head back by the hair, his hot lips sliding down her neck, his hands tightening on her breasts. He laid her down on the carpet, and his thighs made her prisoner.

'Oh, Lucy! How much I love you!'

'Is it love?' she questioned.

He did not answer, as he was going to make her *feel* his love. His soul reached out to her who, warm and tender, abandoned herself to him, aware of something sublime flowing between them she could not hinder.

Time to let go, Lucy, and her kisses fell all over his body like heavenly dew.

No more living among shadows, sunbeams of love ignited

new lives, and when their eyes met, both recognised the message.

'Sam, I forgive you.'

She belonged nowhere else but in his strong embrace. It was impossible to compare the flame of a candle to that of a fire. What had been there once still bound them together, a survivor of time's and life's erosion.

'You're mine, and I'll be yours forever if you want me.'

'Yes, Sam.' In her words and in her eyes, he sensed a lifetime.

The largest of all diamonds, their had been concealed in a mine of human passions. Once buried deep, now exhumed had to be polished to sparkle again. They smiled at each other, conscious of the miracle just shared. Lucy spotted his little bible on a shelf among various books.

You'll gather dust, she thought with a sense of triumph while still in his arms.

Max returned to France to open a boutique, but before going entrusted her with his business running.

'Sometime in the future, you might want to buy me out? I'll offer it to you at a good price.'

'You're a gentleman.'

'And you're a rarity, mon cher.'

He left, blowing her a kiss.

Sam moved in with Lucy, with the children's full approval, and they all began the journey of a lifetime. They rented the little flat again, and Rose seemed to thrive on the love and care bestowed on her. Now and then, she remembered a few more details about her room and the tunes that Lucy's 'father' had played. Sam's boss liked him. He also understood this well-educated man deserved a better job. He asked his son in the local council, which employed him as a librarian. With his background, Sam learned quickly.

'Lucy?' They looked at each other, knowingly.

'We have so much to be grateful for, my darling! But in our past, there's a great deal to comprehend and to forgive.'

Nothing stirred in the house except their emotions. Unasked questions weighed heavily on both of them, asking for the truth before banishing them beyond reach.

'We experienced much within a short time, darling,' she began, 'our faults shaped the kind of people we're now. When we broke the mould and started all over, we learned some lessons, but there's a life of learning ahead. One day, when the children are older, we must tell them everything. I don't want them to live a lie like I had to do.'

'What lies? Is there something you did not tell me, darling? Please trust me.'

I need to tell him. There must be no secrets between us, and maybe, at last, he will understand.

'I'm going to tell you everything, and then we can bury it forever.'

While she recounted to him all that had taken place in the past, her turmoil reached high peaks of distress. The more he heard, the more he loved and admired this woman who had gone through hell, as he had done. What a fool he had been! A blind, deaf, insensitive, selfish jerk. *Could she ever forgive me?* He listened without interrupting. When she finished, his eyes moistened.

'My love, I'll spend the rest of my life making amends for what I did to you. I'm finally facing the whole truth about myself. How can you still care for me?'

'My feelings for you survived somewhere. They were sleeping, waiting for a new kiss of life. What we have now Sam, is real, it's love.' They sat silently for a while, holding on to one another: it prevented them from drowning in the deep sea of their feelings.

'My darling,' he said, 'the children might suffer by knowing, but we'll make them understand that life is never perfect because people are not. We start here and now. How do you do, Miss? My name is Samuel,' he said, standing up to shake her hand.

She stood up as well, grinning.

'I am Lucy. Happy to meet you. Will you come to bed?'

'Mmmmm, so soon? We just met!'

'Time is precious sir,' she joked, and pulling him by the sleeve, dragged him to the bedroom, closing the door.

For the first time, people who belonged together were under the same roof as a family.

Lucy's expertise in the field of perfumes, combined with her appearance and manners, transformed an everyday business into something special. Her advice to clients on the scent to wear according to their skin's qualities was in demand, and soon she could buy the shop. Sam helped her any way he could. Belinda and Thomas loved to call him dad. Their secure and loving family life had changed them from shy people into warm, self-assured human beings of whom to be proud. Rose had learned to live for the day, her greatest happiness her adoring grandchildren. Since moving in with her daughter, she had spent her time hoping that somehow, her memory would return. She analysed every tiny shred of her images, adding them to those already in her mind, attempting to solve her life's puzzle. Sam and Lucy always listened to her patiently, often with an understanding look into one another's eyes that spoke of all the tenderness and love they felt for her. Alarm bells had never sounded until one day when Rose appeared very thoughtful.

'How did you find me?'

The question caught Lucy by surprise. Her mother had never asked before now.

'I hired a private investigator.'

'Yes, but how did he find me? Who told him where I was?'

The dilemma she had been afraid of was presenting itself, needing a solution.

To tell or not to tell.

She refused to lie to anyone, ever again. She would answer her mother's question, but without volunteering any information.

'My grandparents never talked about you. I think they thought you were dead. When my Grandmother died, I had to go and clear the house of her belongings. I found a photograph of you in a drawer. We looked very much alike, and I determined to find out what had happened to you, so I hired that man.'

'But how could he find me without an address?'

She had to tell her, at the risk of endangering the make-believe niche of 'normal life' her mother had found. Lucy wanted to protect her, even though only Rose could resuscitate her past. The doctor had been clear.

'There was a date on the back of the photo. George started there.'

'What date? What place was it?'

'It was the mill where you worked.'

'Did I work in a mill?'

'Yes, Mother.'

'And what did this man do?'

'He went there and found a woman you were friendly with still working in the same place.'

Rose sat for a while, thinking.

'A friend, you say? If we got in touch with her, I might remember more. Lucy, would you take me to this woman? What's her name?'

'Betty. And yes, of course, mum. I'll arrange it if she's willing and if you want me to.'

'Please. As soon as possible?'

'I'll do everything I can. I promise.'

'Can I come too? Perhaps in that place...'

'Better if I speak to her alone, she'll be at work. I will go during lunchtime.'

'Thank you. I'm very excited now.'

'Something might come of it, but don't build your hopes too high,'

As promised, she went to the mill the next day asking for Betty.

'Please, tell her Lucy wishes to talk.'

A few minutes later, a plump woman with a red face and grey hair dashed in, inspecting her with a critical eye.

'I'm Lucy. Rose's daughter.'

'My friend Rose? Who worked next to me? So long ago!' she said, astounded. 'You're beautiful. You are a lot like her.'

'Rose is alive, Betty.'

'Where is she? What happened to her? Sweet Jesus! So many years, but I never forgot. One day she just disappeared. A man was here to ask me about her. Is he a friend of yours?'

'That man found her.'

'How wonderful to chat with her again! When can we do

this?'

'It would be good for her, I think, but you must understand that she has no recollection at all of her past life. Something caused her condition, and she's been trying to remember for twenty-five years. We hope that, by visiting old places and people, her memory will improve.'

'Poor Rose. I'll do all I can.'

'Why don't you come to our house? We can talk in peace.'

'I'll come for sure. Does the evening suit you? Where do you live?'

Lucy wrote her address and phone number.

'Thank you so much, I'll tell her. See you soon.'

The next day would be a happy one - or one to forget.

When Betty saw her friend, she rushed to embrace her.

'My dear! So many years!'

Rose stared at her for a while, but the hope of placing that face somewhere vanished.

'Your daughter said you don't remember, but don't worry love, talking about the past may help you.'

'Thank you. I'm grateful.'

'You still look the same. Older but as pretty as ever. Me, even plumper, unfortunately!' Her laughter filled the room with a warm glow.

'Where do we start? 'She asked.

'A room... a man's face... Can you tell me about it?' said Rose.

Betty talked about their work together, about John and their romance leading to Lucy's birth, then giving her away to the grandparents to raise, and everyone's unfavourable comments. Being her friend, she did not understand it either, and their relationship had grown cold. Then she told her about John's death, Rose's response, and her disappearance. Mother and daughter did not interrupt Betty's account. Rose sat in silence, a statue unaffected by time and place, while Lucy tried to control her emotions.

'Do you remember now? Does it help?' Betty asked Rose.

'I know that John was Lucy's father, that we lived in that room and a few other things.'

'I'll take you for a visit to the mill, it will be good for you. That room you had... I'll ask the owner of the house if she's still there. We can meet regularly. We can go for a coffee and a slice of heavenly cake. Would you like that? Percy, my husband, he'll not mind, the gentle soul.'

'Yes, I'd like that very much. I can't thank you enough.'

They arranged to see each other once a week in the bakery near Lucy's home, perhaps even go for a walk. Rose liked the happy woman with a twinkle in her eyes, and said to her daughter,

'How could I do what I did, giving you to others? Why did your father agree to it? Were we such bad people? I can only condemn a mother for doing this. I am a heartless person.'

Deep sadness took hold of her, and she sat, staring into space. Lucy had to bring her back somehow.

'Mum, you were so young, unprepared for a baby, even financially. We all have our valid reasons for doing what is unforgivable. Wrong choices seem right at a particular time, but we live long enough to repair our mistakes if we want to. Don't be hard on yourself. You suffered so much, and you still are.'

'Thank you, my dear. So, I disappeared because I was broken-hearted about your father's death. But where did I go?

What did I do? How did I live? There are so many questions still needing answers! I'm sure Betty will help. She's such a nice woman.'

'Yes, she is. Let's go to bed for now. I love you.'

'How can you after what I did to you?'

For the first time in over twenty-five years, Rose's eyes filled with tears, while Lucy succeeded in controlling her own.

'You're only human, like the rest of us. We've all done what we regret bitterly, but life goes on. Let's go to sleep. Tomorrow is full of hope.'

When Rose switched off the light in the room, she was desperate for a different kind to come on in her brain.

Sam was glad Rose had a friend.

'It'll be something for her to do darling, a little independence, too.'

Christmas was approaching. The engraving on the back of the watch she bought for her husband said,

'Lucy to Samuel, love forever and one day.'

She set the table with a white tablecloth, red candles, napkins, and a surprise packet at each seating place they would open before the meal. Sam was first to unwrap his present. Everyone's eyes fixed on him as he freed the box from its golden paper and opened it. He removed the watch from the box, reading the inscription aloud.

'Thank you, darling. I love it!'

Rose stood up, shaking.

'The watch - your father, Lucy...'

She collapsed on the chair, the colour draining from her face.

'Mother, what's wrong?'

Worrying, they all went to her. Rose managed to say,

'I remember now. Your father's watch, his birthday, the engraving on the back. I put it on his wrist, but he was dead.' Panic-stricken, regardless of everyone's efforts, they could not ease her angst.

After that day, nothing was the same. Rose grew depressed and had to go back on medication. However, Betty's visits brightened her up, but she was so desperate to retrace her past steps that her friend took her to the mill one day. Rose began to recollect some fragments: the window in the loft room, the furniture, the bed, and a white piece of material painted with roses and stuck on the dark wooden panelling. Roses, roses, her mind rejected the image. She feared those roses as if alive, threatening, haunting her. She wanted to hide from those roses. Their importance grew and prevented all that needed to emerge from her mind. The roses, the roses, they were taking her over, possessing her.

'Sam, I worry about her. What she remembers is doing her harm.'

'We can't help her, Lucy.'

'How can I just let it happen? I'm watching her withdraw into a terrible pain she cannot bear. She is afraid of a painting of roses she remembered.'

'Did you speak to the doctor in Portsmouth?'

'Yes. He said it must follow its course, but if what she suppressed from her memory is deeply traumatic, the outcome is uncertain.'

'She still sees Betty, doesn't she?' he asked.

'Just now, it's all she cares about.'

'We can only hope and pray.'

Rose was ready to go out and meet her friend.

'Shall I come with you, mum? Do you want to go?'

'Yes, I want to go. I'll be fine. I am not a child, dearest.'

Lucy surrendered.

The chilly spring breeze caressed her hair when she stepped outside. With her mind empty of thoughts and the tepid sun on her face, she was about to pass the flower shop when she froze: the roses. All of a sudden, she had a vision of painted roses on a headboard. They stared at her through watery eyes and with screaming mouths until their stems became legs chasing her on the pavement - the roses; threatening, evil. While trying to get away from them, she ran with her heart pounding, blindly escaping her persecutors.

On the road, a screech of tyres, a loud crashing noise, then silence, before voices rose to a scream.

'The woman is dead,' someone said.

The broken-up car had crashed into a street light. The driver was bleeding from his head.

When her mother did not come back when she should have, a worried Lucy went to the coffee shop to find out.

'The woman you're talking about, the one who comes here to meet her friend, she didn't come today. The one waiting left. There was a terrible accident down the road. Did you hear about it?' she asked. 'My customers went out to look. A little dear died, she ran on the road, and the man driving the car was badly wounded.'

Lucy froze, and then panicked. She rushed to the nearby police station. The description matched, and seeing her distraught reaction the officer telephoned Sam. When he arrived, his wife was in a state of shock. Quiet tears had soaked the collar of her blouse and kept flowing without her being aware. The officer explained. Sam guided her to the car, shaken to the core by the news, and drove home.

Rose's passing inflicted an unbelievable blow on the whole family, a nightmare from which none of them woke.

'My fault. I shouldn't have let mum go.'

'Lucy, nobody's to blame. Just destiny my darling.'

'Why didn't she go to the cafe to see Betty? Why run on the road? Where was she going, Sam?'

'Who knows the thoughts invading her mind? Let it be. We have no answers. There are no answers.'

The hearse made its way to the cemetery, followed by two cars: Sam's with the family and Betty with her husband. The priest's words echoed in the silence, and a bird's song high on a tree interrupted the stillness of the place.

Just a little bird like you, mum, but he cut your wings, and you could not fly ever again. The mystery will linger, but someday... Now you're finally at peace. I love you.

Through tearful eyes and with her heart about to burst, Lucy said goodbye to her mother.

Time passed, life resumed. Belinda studied to be a psychiatric nurse and Thomas to be a doctor.

'Sam, the time has come, to tell the truth to our son and daughter. I'm afraid. I don't want to lose them.'

He sat beside her.

'My love, they're caring people. They understand others' pain. Physical or mental. Our boy has never forgotten his illness, and Rose's difficulties have influenced Belinda's choice. They are entitled to our total honesty.'

After the evening meal, Belinda helped to clear the table, and then all sat down. Sam spoke first.

'We have something to say concerning our past. You are entitled to the truth about your grandmother and us. You're of an age when you can understand and hopefully forgive.' Brother and sister exchanged puzzled glances.

'Dad? Why forgiveness? Even though you are not our real parents, you gave us so much more than they ever did,' said Belinda.

'We *are* your true father and mother,' said Lucy.

Silence fell. Son and daughter looked at each other.

'Mum? Dad? That's wonderful! Isn't it, Thomas?'

'Best news ever, but I don't understand why did you not tell us before?'

Their response reassured Lucy.

'Your father and I have much to say. We'll be here for quite a while.'

The couple's past, their experiences and mistakes floated slowly towards two people astonished by the incredible tales delivered by the voice of one or the other. Lucy only omitted particulars of her relationship with Rodrigo and Alex. Some doors had to stay shut. Sam ended saying,

'This is our past. Mum will tell you about your grandmother another time. Right, darling?'

'Yes,' she said, watching her children, waiting for the effect of their confession.

'Your stories are incredible! So much lived in such a short time! What an experience! Dad, would you ever go and revisit Wirikuta? If you do, I'll come with you,' said Belinda.

'Me too,' said Thomas. 'I wonder if they need a doctor.'

Sam and Lucy glanced at each other, knowing what the other was thinking.

'So you forgive us for leaving you?' asked their mother.

'The drugs... they transform people, I learned it through my work,' said Thomas.

'And you both came back for us, left it all behind,' added Belinda.

Emotions sealed the room, passed from one to the other, and caused a few tears.

'Time to retire, our dear son and daughter,' said Samuel.

Stories, stories of long ago to accept, learn from, understand, and love. All revolved around the suffering of people they loved. Moving on, living, loving, forgiving, that's what they had learned from their parents. Brother and sister were now ready for the future. Thomas went to work in a hospital in Africa. Belinda remained in Bradford as a dedicated psychiatric nurse, married, and gave them a grandchild.

'Yes. Life is wonderful, my love,' Lucy heard Sam say as he bounced little Ben on his knees.

The Flesh and the Spirit

Forty years later

'I'm tired my love. I'm going to rest awhile.'

'Go, old man. Shout if you need company.'

'Old man? Where is he? Are you betraying me?'

He smiled at her lovingly, coughing.

'I wouldn't tell you if I was, jealous as you are. Weak heart, a cantankerous old fool!' she remarked with an adoring gaze.

'Go! Rest!' Lucy ordered, carrying on with her knitting.

He stood there looking at her hair gathered in a bun at the back of her head. He pulled out the combs and watched it cascade on her shoulders. His bony fingers intertwined softly with the silky mass of silver, his heart brimming with the love of that very first time so long ago.

'I love you,' he whispered in her ear.

'I know it,' she answered tenderly, turning her head to face him, letting her eyes speak to him.

When he bent to kiss her gently on the mouth, she closed her eyes, accepting with delight, tasting the kiss of his vanished youth revived on her lips.

'Go, my love. Rest. I'll make cocoa when you wake up.'

Sam slowly headed to the bedroom, took the bible from the drawer of his bedside table and read:

James 2:26

"For as the body apart from the spirit is dead, so also faith apart from works is dead."

He smiled and closed the little book with care putting it back and taking out the small package covered in brown paper. Samuel held it with shaking hands and arthritic fingers, unwrapped the wooden box, and stretched on the bed. He stroked it fondly, lifted the lid, and dropped the dried-up apple into his hand, staring at it.

Oh, Ben! so much time. I'm old now. The memories are not as clear, they shrunk like this apple, but I've never forgotten you. Soon I'll see you again.

He closed his eyes… and the apple fell from his hand.

END

www.ingramcontent.com/pod-product-compliance
Lightning Source LLC
Chambersburg PA
CBHW071724190726
48292CB00003B/603